CATHERINE RETURNED TO WHERE THE SLIDING GLASS DOOR HAD BEEN SMASHED.

She'd already noted the absence of blood; now she looked for other indicators.

"They would have headed for an exit," she muttered to herself. "Fork in the corridor—right or left?"

She went left, shining her flashlight at the floor, sweeping it from side to side in slow arcs. When she'd traveled twenty feet, she stopped, returned to the fork and went the other way.

Ten feet down it, a tiny piece of broken glass glinted on the floor.

She followed the corridor all the way to the nearest fire exit, then pushed it open. The ground outside was soft, and held the impression of two sets of running shoes; one large, one small.

They headed into the desert, and quickly disappeared on rocky, sun-hardened soil.

Dawn's not far off, she thought. *Hyperthermia will work for them for a while, keep them from noticing how cold it is. Once that sun is up, though . . .*

She wondered how quickly she could get a tracking dog out there. If Theria Kostopolis and John Bannister collapsed out in the desert, the heat would kill both of them even quicker than it normally would.

Original novels in the CSI series:

CSI: Crime Scene Investigation
Double Dealer
Sin City
Cold Burn
Body of Evidence
Grave Matters
Binding Ties
Killing Game
Snake Eyes
In Extremis
Nevada Rose
Headhunter
Brass in Pocket
The Killing Jar
Blood Quantum
Dark Sundays
Serial (graphic novel)

CSI: Miami
Florida Getaway
Heat Wave
Cult Following
Riptide
Harm for the Holidays: Misgivings
Harm for the Holidays: Heart Attack
Cut & Run
Right to Die

CSI: NY
Dead of Winter
Blood on the Sun
Deluge
Four Walls

CSI:

CRIME SCENE INVESTIGATION™

DARK SUNDAYS

a novel

Donn Cortez

Based on the hit CBS series "CSI: Crime Scene
Investigation" produced by CBS PRODUCTIONS,
a business unit of CBS Broadcasting Inc.

Executive Producers: Jerry Bruckheimer,
Carol Mendelsohn, Anthony E. Zuiker,
Ann Donahue, Naren Shankar, Cynthia Chvatal,
William Petersen, Jonathan Littman

Series created by: Anthony E. Zuiker

POCKET **STAR** BOOKS
New York   London   Toronto   Sydney

Pocket Star Books
A Division of Simon & Schuster, Inc.
1230 Avenue of the Americas
New York, NY 10020

This book is a work of fiction. Names, characters, places, and incidents either are products of the author's imagination or are used fictitiously. Any resemblance to actual events or locales or persons, living or dead, is entirely coincidental.

First Pocket Star Books paperback edition June 2010

POCKET STAR BOOKS and colophon are registered trademarks of Simon & Schuster, Inc.

For information about special discounts for bulk purchases, please contact Simon & Schuster Special Sales at 1-866-506-1949 or business@simonandschuster.com.

The Simon & Schuster Speakers Bureau can bring authors to your live event. For more information or to book an event contact the Simon & Schuster Speakers Bureau at 1-866-248-3049 or visit our website at www.simonspeakers.com.

Cover design by David Stevenson

Manufactured in the United States of America

10 9 8 7 6 5 4 3 2 1

ISBN 978-1-5011-0274-5
ISBN 978-1-4391-6930-8 (ebook)

For my son Dez,
who did his best to arrive at the same time
the final galleys for this book did.

1

THE VIEW FROM the Panhandle Casino's penthouse suite was impressive, but to truly appreciate it you had to use the rooftop pool; one wall was clear glass, letting the swimmer enjoy the glittering lights of Vegas twenty floors below while floating weightless in heated water. The suite's owner, Andolph Dell, provided swimming goggles for his guests for this precise reason, and during one of his parties there was always at least one person contemplating the vista while holding their breath.

But not at this party—because on this particular Sunday night, there was a zeppelin.

A more accurate description was *dirigible*, for it was only twenty or so feet long and less than a third that in diameter. It was black, cigar-shaped, and piloted by a grinning clown wearing black coveralls.

No one was sure which direction the dirigible had come from, if it had risen from the ground or descended from the skies. It had simply appeared, circus music blaring tinnily from tiny speakers, floating at the penthouse level and circling slowly like a bird looking for a spot to land.

The clown wasn't so much piloting the craft as riding it; a large propellor at the rear provided thrust, powered by the clown's furiously pedaling legs. He gripped the handlebars tightly, leaning back in his seat, never pausing to wave at the crowd on the roof who were cheering him on, or even to glance at them—despite his wide, maniacal grin, he seemed to be a clown who took his zeppelin flying very seriously.

And then the zeppelin burst into flames.

The theme of the Panhandle Casino was the Gold Rush. There were plenty of pickaxes and gold pans on the walls, while women dressed as dancehall girls dealt blackjack and spun roulette wheels. But Andolph Dell had decided old mining equipment and a few corsets weren't a big enough draw; these days, in order to compete, a place needed something unique.

Dell had gone with bears.

Specifically, he'd built a large, glass-walled environment in the middle of the casino floor. Sensitive to modern attitudes toward animal exploitation, he'd ensured that the environment was completely soundproofed and that the bears spent only a few hours a day on display, in a daily rotation shared among sixteen animals. The rest of the time they lived on a ranch outside the city, where they were cared for by an experienced professional staff. The animals themselves were all rescued specimens, obtained largely from zoos or circuses that could no longer take care of them; they lived a pampered life on the ranch, punctuated with brief interludes riding in the back of a specially designed tractor-trailer, followed by a few hours staring at hordes of goggle-eyed tourists while snarfing back treats.

A flaming dirigible crashing to earth in the parking lot was not on their usual agenda—and the event occurred at the worst possible time, during the bears' transfer from truck to casino.

Jordan Tanner worked the midnight-to-eight-A.M. shift at the Panhandle as senior security officer. He had overseen hundreds of bear transfers and probably as many parties, and the bears had always provided much less trouble than the partiers . . . until now.

There were two other officers in the monitoring room with him, watching the sequence of events unfold. Kyra Bourne was to his left, Kevin Priest to his right. None of them could quite believe what they were seeing on the bank of screens in front of them.

"Oh my God," Kyra said. She was a twenty-two-year-old from Alabama working her way through a criminal-law degree. "It just hit the ground. It's still burning. No way he could have survived that."

"Fire department's on its way," said Kevin. "What is this? Is this a terrorist attack?"

Tanner shook his head. "A guy in a clown outfit? That doesn't—"

"The bears!" said Kevin. "The bears are loose in the casino!"

Security monitors showed two bears lumbering between slot machines as panicked tourists screamed and ran.

"How many?" Tanner demanded. "Where's the third one—"

"There!" said Kyra. "It's moving a lot faster than the other two—"

The third bear wasn't lumbering. It was running. And someone was trying to outrun it.

"It's chasing a guard!" said Tanner. "Who is that?"

"I don't know, I can't see his face—"

"Is it Hernandez? I think it's Hernandez—"

A high-pitched bell started to ring. Someone had triggered the fire alarm, adding to the panic as guests scrambled for the exits. All of the elevators headed for the ground floor, where they shut down after disgorging their passengers. The penthouse had its own private elevator—but when the car arrived, it was empty.

"Oh, no," said Tanner. "The alcove for the penthouse elevator. It's got him cornered."

"Tell him to shoot the damn thing!"

"I can't raise him—wait, that's not him—"

"He's trying to open the elevator—why isn't it opening?"

"It's locked down and he's too rattled to remember the security code," said Tanner. He leaned forward and started tapping keys. "I'm opening it remotely—if he can get inside I can shut them and he'll be safe—"

"No!" Kyra shouted. "It's rushing him! It's in the—"

Bright arterial blood sprayed the lens of the elevator's camera. All they could see was red.

"What a mess," said Nick Stokes, surveying the smoking wreckage. "Took out an SUV, a pickup, and two subcompacts."

"If Grissom were here," said Greg Sanders, "he'd probably say something like 'Oh, the zoo-manity.' "

"Probably. But his would be better."

Greg shrugged. "Hey, you try working in a pun involving a flaming zeppelin and three rampaging bears." He paused. "Maybe I should have gone with the Goldilocks thing . . ."

"I'd prefer if you didn't," said Sara Sidle. "Blondes have to deal with enough jokes as it is." She glanced from the parking lot to the entrance. "How are we doing this?"

"The bear's handlers have recaptured the three escapees," said Nick. "Two came right back, while they had to use a tranquilizer dart on the third. Crime scene's been cleared, but it's gonna be messy—I'd like both of you on it. I'll take the *Hindenburg* out here."

"Let's do it," said Greg.

He and Sara headed into the casino. It was deserted now, the entire building ringed with yellow crime-scene tape.

"Weird to see the place empty," said Greg. "Kinda postapocalyptic."

"Post-ursine-alyptic, you mean. Nothing clears a room like a four-hundred-pound carnivore times three."

A large, frowning man with a shaved head and

muscular arms crossed against a massive chest was waiting for them at the private elevator alcove.

"Jordan Tanner," he said. "I'm in charge of security at this time of night."

"CSIs Greg Sanders and Sara Sidle," said Greg. "So this is where the attack took place?"

Tanner nodded. "It's where it started, yeah. The guard was trapped against the doors, so I opened them remotely. The bear rushed him."

Sara glanced at the keypad beside the elevator doors. "So the body's inside?"

"I'm not sure."

Greg frowned. "What do you mean, you're not sure?"

"The elevator camera was . . . splashed. We can't see what's inside. It's not on this floor, anyway—the car went down after the doors closed. He must have hit a button before . . ."

"So the elevator's in the basement?" asked Sara. "Why aren't we?"

"Regular staff elevator is still in lockdown. And as for the stairs—well, I'll show you."

Tanner led them around a corner to the fire stairs. The door there was propped open, while four firemen struggled to get a makeshift stretcher of chain-link fence through the doorway. Sprawled across the mesh was an unmoving mass of black fur, its long pink tongue lolling out of the side of its bloodstained muzzle.

A man with a short gray beard and a baseball cap that read "Bruin Rescue Ranch" was supervising. "Careful!" he snapped. "Don't drop him! Keep his head supported!"

"That's his handler," said Tanner. "He's the one who tranqued him. Nobody else has been down there since the staff bolted."

"What's down there?" asked Sara.

"Offices, mostly. When the bear came out of the elevator, it started wandering around. Staff elevator was frozen, so everybody ran for the fire exit and got out."

The firemen finally succeeded in negotiating the unconscious animal out of the stairwell. They lugged it toward the exit, the handler barking orders every step of the way.

"Let's see what we've got," said Sara.

"There's no body," Doc Robbins said. He stood beside Nick, leaning on his arm crutch and gesturing with his other hand. "Either this guy walked away from the crash, or the fire vaporized him completely—which is impossible."

"Not completely," said Nick. He used a stick to lift a partially melted rubber clown mask. "See? Part of his face survived."

"That's great. Call me when you have something that isn't made out of rubber—I'm going to examine the victim of the bear attack." He headed toward the casino entrance.

The damage to the vehicles had mostly been done by fire; the dirigible hadn't weighed enough to do serious harm through impact alone, and its twenty-story plummet had been slowed by the physics of the craft itself.

Nick got to work documenting the wreckage, dropping markers and taking pictures. He found no footprints—clown or otherwise—leading away from the crash, no blood trail or spatter. He did find bits of electronics, fragments of framework made mostly of balsawood, and a small electric motor. He bagged and tagged everything, then took samples of the ashes that remained.

Doc Robbins had joined Greg and Sara at the open elevator car on the basement level, where there was an abundance of blood—but no corpse.

"There's no body?" Doc Robbins said. "Again? What happened to this one—did the bear eat him?"

"I'm no expert, but I don't think bears do that," said Sara. "I mean, there's nothing here at all—no clothing, no shoes, not even a bone fragment. These bears are well fed, right? Even a starving grizzly in the wild wouldn't lick his plate *this* clean."

"Well, there's no drag trail," said Greg. "It didn't haul him off somewhere to snack on later."

"So where is he?" said Robbins.

Tanner walked up. "That's not the only question. I don't know *who* he is, either—none of my people are missing."

Greg pointed at the floor, where bloody bear pawprints led from the foyer toward the offices. "We might not know where the guard is, but we know where the bear went."

They followed the tracks away from the elevator. The bear had gone down the hallway to the very end, where it had apparently stopped in front of a large metal door.

"What's in here?" asked Sara.

"It's where they keep the alternate casino chips," said Tanner. "State law says the casino has to have them on hand in case the ones in use are compromised."

Greg tried the door. "It's still locked, but we're going to have to take a look inside."

"I have the access code," said Tanner. "Step back, please." He blocked the keypad with his body and entered the code, opening the door.

Greg stepped in and looked around. Wheeled shelving units lined the walls, filled with clear plexiglass cases full of casino chips. "I don't see any tracks."

"Bears," said Sara, "tend to be more interested in fish than chips."

Greg grinned. "I see married life is already changing you."

Sara gave him a look. She paced the room, studying each rack of chips. "It doesn't look as if anything's been disturbed, but the casino should do an inventory of these chips, see if anything's missing."

"I'll make sure of it," said Tanner. "But I don't know why anyone would even want to steal these. They're the new kind, with a radio-frequency ID chip embedded in each one. Until they've been activated, they're about as valuable as a Starbucks gift card with no money on it."

"Worthless money and a nonexistent guard," said Sara. "What's next?"

Greg shrugged. "Porridge that's too hot or too cold?"

The bear tracks doubled back down the hall,

where they entered the first office on the left. "The tracks go around the perimeter," noted Sara. "Nobody else was attacked?"

"Not that I know of," said Tanner.

Greg surveyed the room, which held half a dozen cubicles. "So it charges in here, runs around the outside of the room—giving everyone not only a good look at it but enough time to escape—then heads back out the door."

Sara was already on to the next room. "Where it does exactly the same thing," she said. "It's like the bear was *herding* them."

"Maybe it was raised by sheepdogs?" Greg suggested.

It was the same in every office. The bear's wandering was methodical, ending just outside the door to the fire stairs where it had been shot with a tranquilizer dart.

"And still no guard," said Sara.

Greg stood in the blood-splashed elevator, peering at the wall. "Lot of spatter in here, but look at this." He pointed to the railing at waist height that ran around the periphery. "Is that a footprint?"

"Could be," said Sara. She looked up. "People trying to escape bears sometimes climb trees—maybe the guard went up instead of out?"

"Exit hatch is closed," said Greg. "Could be he used it, then put the cover back in place."

Tanner nodded. "There should be a stepladder in the supply closet. I'll be right back."

One mile past the Vegas city limits, a man and a woman shamble out of the desert. The moon above them is a giant eye, staring at them with cold, unblinking hostility.

The woman's throat has been cut, but the wound has long since stopped bleeding. It hasn't healed; it's run dry. Her eyes are empty and lifeless, her skin as white as hospital linen under the lunar glare.

The man is lean and muscular, his hair a black military bristle over a skull etched with scars. His right hand is bound in a kind of sling, the wrist lashed to the forearm with strips of torn cloth. The arm bears only a cursory resemblance to a human limb; it is covered with thick, overlapping scales of a deep orange, and it ends in a hand tipped with long, curving black claws. The hand twitches grotesquely as the man walks, flopping against his chest and waggling its long fingers like a spider on its back.

The many-hued lights of the city rise before them: flame-flickering reds, lurid alien greens, blues and whites arcing like lightning.

"Tired, Bannister," the woman says. Her voice is a harsh croak. "So tired."

"Soon, Theria," he promises. "We're almost there. You'll be able to rest then."

"Rest. Yes. Rest forever . . ."

They continue on, their footsteps slow but resolute. They don't pause when they reach the sign at the outskirts; they already know exactly where they are and where they're going.

They're in hell.

2

SARA PUSHED OPEN the hatch in the elevator's roof cautiously, then poked her head inside. She shone a flashlight around.

"No guard," she called down. "But I think I've got some transfer on the edge of the hatch."

Greg handed her up a pair of tweezers and an evidence bag. She collected the sample carefully and handed it back down.

Greg studied the sample. "I think there's some blood on it, too."

"There's more blood on the edge. I think our guard must have been here."

"But he's not now? Maybe he climbed up to the next floor."

"I doubt it," said Tanner. "We were right outside that door a few minutes ago. I didn't see any blood or signs that it had been forced open from the other side."

Greg put the evidence bag aside. "Maybe he climbed up to another floor?"

Tanner shook his head. "He'd have a long way to go. This is the owner's private elevator, and it only stops at three places: here, the main floor, and the penthouse suite. Ain't nothing in between but a twenty-story concrete tunnel running straight up and down."

Sara clambered all the way through the hatch and stood up on the roof of the car. Her flashlight's beam found the steel rungs of a ladder set into one wall and a crimson smear of blood on two of them. "I've got blood on the ladder." She shone her light straight up. "Can't see anything above me—if he's stuck somewhere up there, he must be near the top . . . Hello! Is there anyone up there?"

Her voice boomed and echoed up the shaft, but there was no reply.

"I'm not climbing twenty stories without safety gear," said Sara. "Let's use the regular elevators and try this from the top."

Sara grabbed a more powerful searchlight from her vehicle, then ran into Nick as she headed for the lobby. "We're going to the roof," she said. Greg was waiting at the elevator and gave Nick a quick run-down of what they'd found.

"Two missing bodies, huh?" said Nick as they rode up together. "No idea what happened to yours, but I've got an idea about mine."

"Does it involve a really, *really* hungry bear?" asked Greg.

"Nope. But I need to talk to someone who saw the dirigible before it went down."

The elevator let them out one floor below the

penthouse, and they all followed Tanner to the fire stairs. "There was a big party going on here until all the excitement started," Tanner said. "Once the alarms went off and the elevators locked down, everyone had to use the stairs. Of course, we tried to keep everyone out of the casino—last thing we wanted was more people on the floor while the bears were roaming around."

They went up the stairs and Tanner unlocked the door at the penthouse level. "Party's over now, but some staff are still here."

The fire door led to a small foyer that also held the private elevator. A gigantic display of tropical flowers in a cut-glass vase adorned the opposite wall, beside a wide, arched doorway.

A broad-shouldered, short-haired security guard in a black tuxedo stood in front of the doorway, his arms crossed, a transparent cord coiling from one ear into his collar.

"This is Ian Stackwell," said Tanner.

Stackwell nodded. Greg went straight to the elevator door and began to examine it. "Have you heard any strange noises from behind here?" he asked. "Banging, scratching, maybe moaning?"

Stackwell frowned. "No, sir. But it was pretty noisy in here until a little while ago. I could have missed something like that."

Sara nodded. "I think we should go all the way up— the elevator machine room should be right above this."

"You two go ahead," said Nick. "I'm going to stay here and talk to a few people."

They returned to the stairwell and went up another flight. Tanner punched in the code that opened the door, and they stepped out onto the roof. The elevator machine room was a blocky structure only a few feet away.

Their footsteps crunched on the tar and gravel roof. The beam of Greg's flashlight fell on the door to the machine room—it was ajar. "This door looks like it was forced open," said Greg. "Hello? Anybody up here?"

No answer. They pushed the door to the machine room open. Inside, the motor that moved the elevator stood silently, thick cables leading from twin spools down through an opening in the floor. A hatch that led into the shaft itself stood open beside it.

Sara switched the spotlight on and shone it into the shaft. "Hello? Is there anyone there?"

Still no reply. "Greg, I'm not seeing anything. The shaft is empty, all the way to the bottom. If our guard was here, he's not anymore."

"Oh, he was here. Look." Greg shone his flashlight at one corner of the room. A pile of bloody clothes lay in an untidy heap.

Greg knelt and studied them. "Pants and shirt. So now we have a missing, unidentified, injured guard in his underwear. This case keeps getting better and better." He glanced over at Tanner. "Uh, and by better, I mean weirder." He took out an evidence bag and stuffed the clothes into it.

Sara stood and walked back to the door. "Greg, take a look at this. See these scratch marks on the frame? This door was broken into from the *outside*."

"So . . . the guard, bleeding profusely, manages to climb twenty stories, then gets naked while someone else breaks in?"

"Blood loss can affect critical thinking—he might have been delusional. Or maybe he didn't undress himself—whoever broke in could have."

Greg nodded. "Maybe someone from the party was out here. They hear someone in distress, bust down the door, get him out of his clothes to see how badly he's injured."

"And then what?" said Tanner. "Nobody at the party reported any kind of medical emergency."

"Maybe he didn't survive," said Sara. "The guest panicked, went back to the party, and didn't say anything."

"In which case," said Greg, "there's only two places he can be. Up here . . ."

Sara walked over to the roof's edge. ". . . or down there," she said.

Nick started with Stackwell, the doorman. "What time did the party start?" Nick asked.

"Ten o'clock."

"You have a guest list?"

"Yes, sir." Stackwell pulled a small notepad from his breast pocket. "All these people were preapproved by Mr. Dell. I was told that they were also allowed to bring dates or friends."

Nick took the notebook and studied it. "High rollers, huh? I recognize a bunch of these names."

"Mr. Dell's parties are always popular."

"I'll bet. I don't suppose you saw the flaming zeppelin?"

"No, sir. I stayed at my post all night. I did hear other people talking about it, though."

"How about other staff? Bartenders, servers?"

"One of the servers, Linda, brought me out a club soda afterward. She says she saw the whole thing."

"She still here?"

"She's inside, cleaning up."

Nick thanked him and went inside. The penthouse suite was large and sprawling, the pool clearly visible through a wall made of glass. Comfortable couches of teal and caramel were arranged artfully throughout the space, and empty wine glasses and plates of half-eaten food were clustered on low-slung tables of polished teak. A woman in her twenties dressed in a short black skirt and blue silk blouse was busy filling a plastic bus pan with glasses but stopped when Nick walked in.

"Hi," said Nick. "Are you Linda?"

"Yes. Can I help you?"

"I'm Nick Stokes, Las Vegas Crime Lab." He showed her his ID. "I understand you saw the whole flaming-dirigible incident?"

She leaned the bus pan against one hip. "The blimp that caught on fire? Yeah, I saw it. Second-craziest thing I've ever seen in Vegas—I mean, the thing was being driven by a guy in a clown suit."

"So I hear. Can you show me where you were when it happened?"

"Sure." She put the bus pan down on the table, then led him to the other side of the room. A large sliding glass door led to a deck area with seating and patio tables.

Outside, Linda stopped next to the waist-high railing that led around the deck. "I was right about here, I guess. Didn't see him at first—I don't know where he came from. He was suddenly just there, pedaling away like crazy, about twenty feet from the edge."

"Uh-huh. Did he wave at anyone?"

"Ummm . . . not that I saw."

"How about *look* at anyone? Did he turn his head at all?"

She thought about it. "I don't think so. He seemed really focused, you know? I think he just stared straight ahead the whole time."

"And how did he react when the craft caught on fire?"

"That was the weirdest thing of all. He didn't. I mean, he just kept pedaling away, like nothing was wrong. And that creepy circus music kept playing, all the way down . . ." She shuddered.

Nick nodded. "If it's any consolation," he said, "I'm pretty sure he didn't suffer."

Greg stepped back from the roof's edge and lowered his radio. "If our guy did a half-gainer off the roof, either he never reached the bottom or he got up and walked away. Uniforms did a sweep of the perimeter and didn't find a thing."

"Well, I don't think he dropped in on the party." Sara was over by the ten-foot-high wall that separated the elevator machine room and ventilator ducts from the rest of the roof, presumably so people relaxing poolside wouldn't have to stare at industrial fixtures. "Topped with razor wire, no less," she noted. "Guess Mr. Dell is serious about his privacy."

"And if you did get over it," said Greg, "there's

a security camera." He pointed. "Even if someone scaled it, they'd be spotted—either by the camera or by someone at the party."

"Unless everyone was busy watching a burning blimp," said Sara.

Tanner shook his head. "I was on duty. There was a lot of commotion right around then, but nobody came over that wall. You can check the footage yourself."

"We will," said Sara. "Nick said he was going to do interviews with the partygoers. I'll get him to ask about any possible wall vaulters, too."

They spread out, looking for anything else on the roof out of the ordinary.

Greg knelt beside a pipe and said, "I've got something odd here."

Sara joined him. "It's bent."

"Yeah, and there are fresh tool marks on it, too. Pretty deep scratches." Greg snapped a few quick photos. "Whatever did this must have exerted a lot of force."

"Like the kind of force exerted by a tethered dirigible?"

Greg considered that. "You think our flying clown and bleeding guard are connected?"

"I don't know. That guard had to have gotten off the roof somehow."

"Yeah, but the dirigible crashed before the guard was attacked. That puts him up here while the *Hindenburger* barbecues down in the parking lot."

"Which leaves the other side of this wall," said Sara. "Guess we should see how Nick's doing."

*   *   *

Andolph Dell was a tall, broad-shouldered man, with a spreading paunch he hid with expensive, hand-tailored suits. His hair was short, brown, and well groomed, his face just a little pudgy. He stalked out of one of the penthouse's back bedrooms with a glower on his face, plainly upset by the evening's events.

"You!" he barked at Nick. "Can you tell me what the hell's going on?"

Nick gave him a professional smile—he'd dealt with rich people before.

"Not yet," he said. "I'm Nick Stokes, Las Vegas Crime Lab. You're Mr. Dell, correct?"

"That's right. Are we under attack by time-traveling Nazis or something?" His tone was more incredulous than angry. "I mean, a *blimp*? I didn't think those things even *could* catch on fire anymore."

"Mr. Dell, do you have any idea what this might be all about?"

"How the hell should I know? Bears running wild in my casino and flaming clowns on zeppelins—I mean, what the *hell*?"

"Well, you *were* having a party."

Dell frowned, then smiled. "Oh. I see. Okay, I may throw some pretty memorable shindigs, but this was *not* part of the entertainment. Any idea who that poor guard was yet?"

"We're working on it." Nick glanced over and noticed Sara and Greg walking through the door. "In fact, I have to confer with two of my colleagues right now. Excuse me."

Nick joined his fellow CSIs as they headed toward the pool. "What have you got?"

Greg crossed his arms. "A bloody guard's uniform, a machine-room door that was broken into from the outside, and a stressed-out pipe with some heavy-duty tool marks."

"No guard?"

Sara shook her head. "No guard. Nothing at the base of the building, either. We think he must have come this way."

"Blood trail?"

Greg and Sara glanced at each other. "No," said Greg.

"I've got something similar," said Nick. "The clown piloting the dirigible never took his hands off the handlebars, never turned his head, never spoke. Want to guess what I found in the wreckage?"

"A small electric motor?" said Greg.

"Bingo. The clown was a dummy—paper suit and rubber mask over an inflatable body is my guess. The motor drives the pedals and makes it look as if the clown is riding the thing."

"So who was really in control?" asked Sara.

"My money's on someone at the party," said Nick. "Someone with a clear view and a remote control."

"Not to mention a burning hatred of clowns," said Greg.

Bannister and Theria stand outside the building and watch zombie tourists in loud shirts stumble in and out of the entrance, maggots squirming in sockets behind designer sunglasses. The corpses grip skulls with their rotting hands, sucking fluid through straws jutting from the eye sockets. "Hard Risk Café" is painted on the white bone. Rock music blares from loudspeakers shaped like coffins, dead pop stars singing about loneliness and heartache.

They enter.

Inside, the theme of the place becomes clear. Buddy Holly screams as he burns in the wreckage of a plane; the wings have been turned into roulette tables. There's a fountain in the middle of the room built around a white bathtub—in it, a bloated Jim Morrison sinks beneath the surface while a giant hypodermic needle sprays neon red into the air.

No one takes any notice of Bannister or Theria as they stagger through the crowds. They are only two more victims, after all, in a torrent of suffering.

Skeletons bounce dice made of bone off craps tables covered in human skin, the croupier raking in piles of pills and syringes from the losing bets.

Theria stops, leaning against a column upholstered in rotting blue suede. "Leave me here, Bannister."

He looks around. "Here? Why?"

"It's as good a place as any."

"Does this place mean something to you? Does it remind you of something, of a happier time—"

"No. Music is for the living. I hear nothing but noise."

"Then how can you rest?"

She has no reply to that, but after a moment, she repeats her demand: "Go on without me."

"I won't do that. Not to you."

"Bannister." Her voice is weary and completely devoid of hope. "I'm not even real, Bannister. Don't you know that?"

"You're real to me, Theria. And you deserve better than this."

She neither agrees nor denies this. After a moment, she pushes herself away from the column, and they continue on their way.

3

RAY LANGSTON HAD BEEN many things in his life: a university professor, an MD, an author, and now a crime-scene investigator. But regardless of his current title, he always defined himself by one simple aim: he was trying to leave the world a little better than he found it. He had done that through medicine, through teaching and writing, and now through the pursuit of justice.

But no matter what his current title, he never forgot his previous incarnations or their responsibilities. A part of him would always be an academic, trying to find the best way to communicate what he had learned; part of him would always be a doctor, looking for the best way to fulfill the Hippocratic Oath.

Even after being forced to take a suspect's life in self-defense. That shooting had shaken him personally, but his core beliefs still held. He had not killed the man out of anger or fear; it had been a matter of survival, with no other choice available.

Still, the words "First, do no harm" rose in his mind more often since the shooting, a reminder of his obligation to uphold life. Doing so by putting criminals behind bars might not be as direct as doing so by saving a patient's life, but it ultimately accomplished the same goal. The intellectual satisfaction thus derived was, in some ways, more fulfilling than the emotional.

But then, his specialty was forensic pathology. He had usually been at least one step removed from the process of saving lives . . . and had always been oddly comfortable with that.

Maybe that was why he didn't mind his office's proximity to the morgue.

Then again, it might just be Doc Robbins's company. He and Robbins had found common ground in a number of areas—rare blues music among them—and took turns in supplying the soundtrack to whatever autopsy was currently being performed. "If the bodies that pass through our hands wind up crossing the River Styx," Ray had told Robbins one evening, "there's no reason they can't enjoy the sounds of the Mississippi Delta first."

Ray was currently listening to a little Muddy Waters on the sound system of a crime lab Denali as he drove through the desert night. He was on his way to meet Catherine Willows, supervisor of the lab's night shift and Gil Grissom's replacement, at a facility a few miles outside Vegas city limits. They had a somewhat unusual crime scene to process, and Catherine had told Ray his background might come in handy.

He pulled into the parking lot of a long, low-slung building with two separate wings. The Nevada Neurological Studies Institute didn't look much like a medical facility—let alone one that did cutting-edge research—but Ray's experienced eyes spotted the dark outline of an incinerator's smokestack, used to dispose of medical waste.

He parked, took out his customary oversize CSI kit on its rolling luggage stand, and wheeled his way to the front entrance. He noted that Catherine was already there, parked right out front.

There was no receptionist on duty at this time of night, but a security guard met him at the front door and directed him to one of the wings. The hallway was long and dimly lit, reminding Ray of night shifts when he was an intern; he'd always enjoyed that sensation of stillness, of being one of the few people awake and alert deep in the A.M. There was a certain serenity to it.

He heard voices up ahead, one of them Catherine's. He turned a bend in the corridor and saw broken glass scattered at his feet, the remains of a shattered sliding door that sealed off the ward. The sign above the entrance read "Secure Area."

Catherine Willows, dressed in a blue CSI windbreaker and ball cap, was talking to a balding, bearded man in a white coat.

"—didn't think he was violent," the man said. His attention shifted to Ray as he walked up. "Hello. I'm Dr. Hiram Wincroft."

"I'm Ray Langston from the crime lab. Hello, Catherine."

"Hi, Ray. Ray here is being too modest; he's an

MD, too. Hopefully that'll be an asset for our investigation."

"What, exactly, are we investigating?" Ray asked.

"Two of our patients have escaped," said Wincroft. "Two of our more . . . *unusual* patients. One of them used an office chair to smash through this door— The other is much more passive."

"How about security?"

"The guard was making his rounds at the time. He came running when he heard the crash, but they were already gone."

"What can you tell us about the patients?"

Dr. Wincroft paused, then loosened his tie. "Damn air conditioning must be on the fritz again. Hot enough to fry an egg in here. All right, the one who busted the glass is John Bannister. Formerly Sergeant John Bannister, now discharged. Served in Iraq and wound up in a coma for a week after a bomb he was defusing went off. He began to present some very unusual symptoms at the VA hospital where he was getting poststress counseling. They were having trouble diagnosing him, so they sent him here. We eventually figured out he was suffering from corticobasal degeneration syndrome."

"How old is he?"

"Only forty-two. We still don't know what causes CBDS, but it rarely shows up in men his age. But he started displaying limb rigidity and gait disorder—he walks very stiffly." Wincroft paused. "Sometimes it almost looks as if one of his goddamn feet is nailed to the floor. Doesn't so much walk as *lurch*, like a goddamn *zombie*."

Wincroft abruptly shrugged out of his lab coat,

tossing it aside. "Lord, it's hot in here. You ever see a zombie movie? Dead people rising from the grave, trying to eat people's brains . . ." He laughed. "Not that most people use them, anyhow. Most people don't have the sense to come in out of the rain!"

A look passed between Catherine and Ray.

"Doctor," said Catherine, "are you feeling all right?"

"Fine, absolutely fine. Must be that chicken I had for lunch, making me a little scattered. Chickens have extremely small brains, so you have to be careful about . . . uh, catalytic metabolism refraction." He began to unbutton his shirt.

Ray stepped forward and peered into Wincroft's eyes. "Doctor, have you taken any medication recently?"

"What? No, I haven't."

"Your pupils are fully dilated. Your skin is flushed and you seem to be overheating, but you're not sweating."

"Really?" Wincroft frowned, clearly trying to concentrate. "Yes, of course. That explains why my thinking is so . . . what were we just discussing?"

"I'll see if I can find a nurse," said Catherine.

Ray had Wincroft sit in a chair, then conducted a few basic tests. He found that Wincroft's heart rate was elevated, his mouth dry, his vision slightly blurred. He displayed both muscle weakness and a heightened stretch reflex.

Catherine returned, a nurse in tow. "Ray, I think we have a problem."

The nurse, a leggy blonde in her thirties, had stripped down to her underwear, white stockings, and orthopedic shoes. She looked at them blankly, then giggled.

The doctor and the nurse weren't the only ones affected. It soon became apparent that everyone on the ward was experiencing the same symptoms—the CSIs were forced to move them all to a different part of the building and isolate the entire wing.

Fortunately, the total affected was less than a dozen people. The Institute was primarily a research facility, with few patients staying there full-time. Both CSIs changed into hazmat suits before returning.

"What do you think, Professor?" Catherine asked as they surveyed the broken glass through the transparent plastic of their face plates. "Epidemic or mass poisoning?"

"Chemical exposure is my guess. The onset of symptoms is too sudden and uniform for anything bacterial or viral—people don't all get sick at exactly the same time and in exactly the same way."

They made their way down the hall. "I've got a break room over here," she said. "Coffee urn, some pastries. I'll take samples for a tox screen."

He nodded. "I'm going to check Bannister's room."

Ray continued down the hall until he came to an unlocked room marked 2C. He pushed it open.

The room was spare and simple, with a hospital bed, a dresser, and a small table with two chairs. There was a window with reinforced safety glass but no bars. Ray turned on the small lamp over the neatly made bed, then searched through the dresser drawers. He found only some clothes and a few toiletry articles.

He looked around the room, trying to see things not through the eyes of a doctor but as a CSI. He looked under the bed, behind the drawers, beneath and behind the dresser itself. Nothing.

Then he looked up and noticed the air vent near the ceiling.

He stood on the bed and examined the vent. There were scratches on and around the heads of the two screws that held it in place. He took a multitool—he'd learned quickly how essential it was always to have one on hand—undid the screws, and pulled the grille off.

He peered inside. He could see something round and metal, pushed far back into the duct. He reached in, grabbed it, and carefully pulled it out.

It was a small, green metal canister, with a U.S. Army insignia stenciled on one side and "BZ-4598" on the other. The end was capped with an aerosol nozzle, jammed open with a safety pin. He heard no hissing noise—the canister appeared to be empty.

Catherine hefted the canister in her hand. "Feels empty. Whatever BZ-4598 is, it's not in here anymore."

"No," said Ray. "It's all around us. The ventilation for this building probably branches out to each wing from a central location; it only spread in one direction, from the point of release outward."

"Canister says it's from the army. Nerve gas?"

"As a matter of fact, yes. BZ is the common term for three-quinuclidinyl benzilate. It's an incapacitating agent developed by the U.S. military. The good news is it's nonlethal; it was designed to disorient enemy troops, not kill them."

"And the bad news?"

"It has a host of neurological side effects and a long duration—up to ninety-six hours."

Her eyebrows went up. "Four days? That's one hell of a trip."

"And not necessarily a pleasant one. In its later stages, BZ produces extremely lifelike illusions, three-dimensional hallucinations that seem absolutely real to the person experiencing them. None of the staff has demonstrated that particular symptom yet, so I'd say they're still in the early stages— they were probably exposed less than four hours ago."

"What's the next stage?"

Ray shook his head. "Stupor and loss of consciousness, I believe. I'll have to do some reading up on it—it's not exactly a common condition, so I can't recall all of the particulars at the moment."

Catherine smiled. "Hey, don't beat yourself up— nobody can memorize every esoteric scientific detail in existence, no matter how big an expert they are. I'm just glad we have your expertise on tap."

"All I need is Internet access. I can log on to a medical database and get the information quickly."

"There's a workstation at the nurse's desk."

Catherine walked up to the nurse's station, where Ray sat staring at a computer screen. "I sent the canister to the lab and did a search of the other rooms just to be safe. Didn't find any other canisters. About the only unusual thing I discovered was a torn sheet in one of the rooms."

"Maybe used to bind a wound? We didn't find

any blood drops, but one of them could have cut themselves on the broken glass."

"Maybe."

Ray nodded and leaned back. "All right, here's a brief overview of the effects of BZ and an approximate timeline. It's a glycolate anticholinergic, developed after World War Two. It's odorless, stable in most solvents, and extremely persistent—it will stay on some surfaces for up to three weeks. However, its efficiency rapidly diminishes once it's no longer aerosolized." He took off his hood. "The air should be safe, and don't worry about coming into contact with objects that have been exposed—any accumulation will be too small to have an effect."

"Good to know." She took off her hood, too.

"BZ works by competing for acetylcholine at receptor sites for exocrine glands, cardiac and smooth muscles, and neurons. This produces dry mouth, inhibits sweating, and causes an initial rise in heart rate. Body temperature rises, making the skin flush.

"But these are all secondary. BZ's primary effects are to the central nervous system and may be delayed as long as four hours after the initial exposure. Stupor, lack of muscle coordination, and hyperthermia are the next phase, which lasts to around the twenty-hour mark.

"Phase three is where the party really starts. Confabulation, delusions, hallucinations that seem utterly real. The subject will frequently deny that anything is wrong. Attention span is shortened, and mood can swing from quiet contemplation of imaginary objects to sudden bursts of aggression."

"Dr. Wincroft seemed fairly cooperative."

"He's still in the first stage. But he was already demonstrating some of the more pronounced CNS effects—inappropriate profanity, use of clichés in language, disrobing."

"So this chemical turns people into frat boys?"

"There's also slurred speech, overuse of colloquialisms, deterioration in handwriting . . . so, yes." He paused. "But there's another symptom that's even more troubling. *Folie a deux.*"

"A . . . folly of two?"

"A *madness* shared by two. It's a rare syndrome, also known as shared psychotic disorder, where two or more people have the same set of delusions. Under the influence of BZ, this extends to shared hallucinations."

"Wait. Are you telling me two people exposed to this chemical can both see the same thing . . . that isn't there?"

"Precisely. I know it sounds surreal, but subjects dosed with BZ have been observed doing such things as playing an imaginary game of tennis. Both players saw—and reacted to—a ball that existed only in their minds."

"Must have made calling line shots hard."

"If both of our escapees have been exposed—and I think we have to assume that they have—then whatever illusions they're experiencing . . . they might be experiencing together."

"Meaning any irrational or aggressive behavior could be amplified?"

"It's possible. Each will validate the other's experience, providing reinforcement for the entire scenario. For whatever world they're living in . . ."

4

"Ms. Fynell," said Nick, motioning for the woman to take a seat on the other side of the interview table. "Thanks for coming in. I know it's late, but—"

Emma Fynell batted away his apology with a casual wave of one elegant hand. Her nails were a glossy black, encrusted with tiny spirals of rhinestones that glittered in the artificial light of the interview room. She wore a long black coat, high-heeled stilettos, and sheer black stockings. If she had anything else on under the coat, Nick couldn't tell. Her hair was long and dark with streaks of violet, and she wore just enough makeup to emphasize the fact that she really didn't need to wear any. "Not at all. I was still up, and just a little bored. Now I have something to do."

Nick smiled. "Yes, ma'am. I was hoping you could tell me about the party you attended tonight."

"Which one?"

"The one in the penthouse suite of the Panhandle."

"Oh, the *interesting* one. Flaming aircraft and rogue grizzlies."

"That would be the one, yes."

"What would you like to know?"

"Where were you during the aircraft incident?"

She thought about it, idly scratching her wrist with one shiny black talon. "At the far right of the railing. Next to this sweaty little man with a cigar."

"Did you notice which direction the aircraft came from?"

"From the north, I think. Someone shouted—a woman—and everyone turned around and stared."

"Did you see anyone with any kind of mechanical device in their hand?"

"Like a cell phone? Practically everyone. Snapping pictures, mostly—even me. Would you like to see?" She dug into the small purse she'd tossed on the table when she first arrived and pulled out a tiny, slim phone. "Here. It's a bit blurry, but then, so was I at the time."

She handed it to him. "Can you send these pictures to me?" he asked. "I'm going to be collecting as many as possible."

"Absolutely." She smiled and took back the phone, her nails brushing his hand as she did so. "Just give me your number . . ."

"Did I see someone with a remote control? No," said the short, swarthy man on the other side of the interview table. He smelled strongly of cigar smoke and appeared to be still a little drunk. "But how the hell would I know? I was busy watching other things, you know?" He gave Nick a leer that suggested those things had little to do with burning zeppelins.

"Sure. Mr. Carvonas, did you happen to notice anything or anyone else at the party that seemed out of place?"

"Hey, I'm not one to judge. But as far as weird goes, the mummy in the wheelchair was kinda odd."

"Excuse me?"

"Big guy, too—musta been three-fifty, easy. All wrapped up in bandages like he just escaped from King Tut's tomb. Or maybe a Weight Watchers meetin' in Cairo. Heh."

"Let me get this straight. You saw a three-hundred-and-fifty-pound man in a wheelchair, completely wrapped in bandages?"

"Yeah! And he had his own private nurse with him, too—cute little thing in a white outfit. Strong, though—she was pushing that wheelchair all by herself. Didn't see 'em for long, though. They disappeared pretty quick."

"Did you notice them talking to anyone else?"

"Nah. I mean, I wasn't really payin' attention. And then that joker zips by in the Goodyear blimp—well, maybe the Goodweek blimp, it wasn't that big—and *kablooey*." Carvonas paused. "Come to think of it, I never noticed that mummy guy afterward, either. We all had to leave by the fire stairs—wonder how he got down?"

"That's a very good question," said Nick.

"All right, got it." Greg snapped his cell phone shut. "Nick says nobody on the roof saw someone climb over the wall, though most of the guests were on the other side of the party watching the zeppelin. Nobody saw anything like a remote control being used, either."

Sara stared down at the pool. Underwater spots threw rippling blue light across her face. "Maybe the controller was concealed. Do any of the penthouse rooms have windows that face that way?"

"We can check that side of the building. But that's not all Nick had to say . . ." He told her about the large, bandaged man in the wheelchair and his nurse. "Someone saw them heading for one of the bedrooms. Worth checking out."

"In a second . . . do you see that?" She pointed at the bottom of the pool.

"Where?"

"In the far corner. I thought it was just a shadow at first, but now . . ."

She stopped and looked around, until she spotted the long-handled pool strainer mounted on one wall. She grabbed it and used it to scoop up the underwater object.

Greg plucked it out of the net when she brought it to the surface; it was a small black plastic case with a single button on it. "Looks like a garage-door opener," he said. "Seems awfully simple for something that's supposed to control an aircraft."

"It does—but do you see any garage doors up here?"

"Yeah, you've got a point. Maybe it does something else. Or did—I doubt if it still works after being dunked."

"We should keep looking, in any case."

There were three guest bedrooms along the south side of the building; the north side was taken up by the master suite, the door locked. "Security guard told me Dell doesn't allow people in here during parties," said Greg. "But the guest bedrooms are open-access."

They checked out the first one. "Nice digs," said Sara. "King-size bed, fifty-two-inch flat screen, wet bar, minifridge, en-suite bathroom."

"And a window with a clear view of the fly-by— if the drapes weren't closed."

Sara slipped on her UV glasses and shone an ALS over the rumpled bedspread. "I think I know why, too. That damp spot isn't a spilled drink."

"Well, it *was* a party . . . funny they closed the drapes, though. Who did they think would see them?" He paused. "Okay, in this particular case they'd have reason to worry, but how often does a bedroom window get buzzed by a guy in a personal zeppelin?"

"Who—being an inflatable dummy—wasn't able to see anything anyway."

"But they had no problem having sex a few feet away from a packed room full of party guests."

"There's a lock on the door." She shrugged. "Wouldn't bother me."

Greg started to say something, then thought better of it.

They found the wheelchair in the third bedroom, collapsed and shoved under the bed. Greg snapped a photo before Sara hauled it out.

"So Mr. Mummy didn't roll out of here," said Greg.

Sara studied the wheelchair, then unfolded it. "There's a storage compartment under the seat, made of vinyl. From the way it's bulging, it's not empty, either." She tugged the zipper open. It was full of wadded-up gauze bandages. "Looks like he didn't leave as a mummy, either," said Sara.

"This bedroom is the closest one to the wall dividing the roof," said Greg. "And unlike some hotel rooms, the window opens." He peered at the sill. "I've got tools marks on the sill. Looks like a match to the others we found."

Sara finished searching through the collapsible compartment. "Nothing but gauze—maybe we can get some DNA off it."

"I've got something else, too." Greg pulled out a pair of tweezers and pulled a tiny fiber from the edge of the window frame.

"More gauze?"

He held it up and squinted. "I don't think so. It's too coarse."

Nick returned to the Panhandle, where he tracked down the doorman, Ian Stackwell, in the staff cafeteria.

"Yes, sir, I remember them," said Stackwell. "Really big guy, with his own nurse. They weren't on the guest list, but another guest gave me the okay to let them up."

"You remember their names?"

Stackwell frowned. "Something Russian, I think.

Olegchenkov, something long like that. I wrote it down in the log."

Nick pulled out the notebook the man had given him earlier and flipped through it quickly. "Olegchenkov, you're right. You've got a good memory."

Stackwell smiled. "Part of the job, right?"

"You didn't write down the name of the nurse, though."

Now Stackwell looked embarrassed. "I didn't? I guess I—sorry. My mistake."

"How about the guest who vouched for them?"

Stackwell shook his head. "All I remember is that he'd just come from the pool. He was wearing one of the guest robes, and he was toweling off his hair. Mid-thirties, average height, clean-shaven."

"Okay. You've got a security camera outside that elevator, right?"

"Only on the main floor, plus the one inside the elevator itself. Nothing on Mr. Dell's floor."

"I'm going to need copies of all the security footage from tonight, for both of them—and for the camera on the other side of that dividing wall, too."

Nick took the security logs back to the lab and went through them minute by minute, starting with the feed from the main-floor camera that showed the party guests arriving. He captured a screen shot of every guest and stacked them up in a separate file labeled "Guests."

Nick studied the screen closely when the large man in the wheelchair arrived. He wore a loose-fitting robe draped over his frame, but beneath it, every inch of skin seemed to be wrapped in gauze.

Archie Johnson, the lab's resident AV expert, walked up and peered over his shoulder. "Wow," he said. "Who's the king-size Tut?"

"The name he gave is Olegchenkov," said Nick. "And he's more like a ghost than a mummy. People saw him arrive at a party, but no one saw him leave."

"So he's still there?"

"No. Sara and Greg searched the place, and I had the owner let me into his private quarters to look around—nobody there. They did find the wheelchair and bandages, though, so I figure he must have just slipped out with the other guests."

"How about the nurse?"

"Don't have a name for her. She probably left with him, but there are no cameras in the fire stairwells, so I don't know for sure. All I can really say at this point is they definitely didn't use the elevator, because no one did."

"Fire-alarm lockdown?"

"Not so much fire as Smokey. Bears loose in the Panhandle."

"That'll make their insurance rates go up. You have footage?"

"I do. There was only one actual attack, a guard who got trapped in an elevator—but there's something weird going on. We haven't been able to find his body. And don't even get me started on the inflatable flying clown."

"I won't. Frankly, it sounds like a dangerous path to go down."

"Anyway, I'm glad you're here. Something I need your help with." He switched tapes, then hit play. "This is the bear attack itself, from outside the elevator."

Archie watched intently. "Guy looks terrified—can't blame him."

"It gets worse. The doors open, the guy dives inside, and the bear charges after him before the doors can shut." He stopped and switched tapes again. "This is the footage from inside the elevator."

Archie's head jerked back. "Oh, man. That's—messy."

"And therein lies my problem. The blood got all over the lens of the camera, and from that point on, pretty much all you can see is red. I was wondering if you could clean it up for me, maybe pull a few images out."

Archie shrugged. "Blood work isn't usually my thing, but I'll see what I can do."

"Thanks, Arch."

Ian Stackwell studied the face on the laptop open on the interview table. "No, that's not him, either."

Nick sighed. The picture Stackwell was looking at was the last of the series of shots he'd pulled from the elevator footage; it looked as if the man who'd vouched for the nurse and her patient hadn't arrived in the elevator.

He tried something else. "How about this guy?" he asked, tapping a key and calling up a shot of the guard who'd been mauled.

Stackwell peered at him. "No, definitely not. Not even close."

Nick thanked him and said he could go. After he'd left, he sat and thought.

Footage from the camera aimed at the dividing wall had shown nothing—nobody had climbed over or even come within the camera's range, including the mysterious missing guard. Bodies were disappearing left and right, whether alive, dead, or artificial—and so far, the only crime he had was arson. No murder, no robbery, no suspects.

Time to take a closer look at the physical evidence.

5

"THE SECOND PATIENT'S NAME is Theria Kostapolis," Catherine told Ray. "That's about all I've been able to learn from the staff. Wincroft's really out of it. Think you can find both patients' files if you look around?"

"Yes, of course," Ray said.

"Good. You do that, and I'll process the rest of the scene. Between the two of us, maybe we can figure out which way they headed."

Catherine returned to where the sliding glass door had been smashed. She'd already noted the absence of blood; now she looked for other indicators.

"They would have headed for an exit," she muttered to herself. "Fork in the corridor—right or left?"

She went left, shining her flashlight at the floor, sweeping it from side to side in slow arcs. When she'd traveled twenty feet, she stopped, returned to the fork, and went the other way.

Ten feet down it, a tiny piece of broken glass glinted on the floor.

She followed the corridor all the way to the nearest fire exit, then pushed it open. The ground outside was soft and held the impression of two sets of running shoes, one large, one small.

They headed into the desert and quickly disappeared on rocky, sun-hardened soil.

Dawn's not far off, she thought. *Hyperthermia will work for them for a while, keep them from noticing how cold it is. Once that sun is up, though . . .*

She wondered how quickly she could get a tracking dog out there. If Theria Kostapolis and John Bannister collapsed out in the desert, the heat would kill both of them even quicker than it normally would.

Ray located the medical files of both John Bannister and Theria Kostapolis in Dr. Wincroft's office, in an unlocked file cabinet. He hesitated before looking at them, unsure of the legality of what he was about to do—but this was a crime scene, and the information could prove vital to saving two lives.

Besides, he was also a doctor. This could simply be viewed as consulting on another physician's case—he didn't think Dr. Wincroft would object.

He sat down at Wincroft's desk, opened Bannister's folder, and began reading.

Bannister's corticobasal degeneration had initially presented with symptoms of depression, irritability, and difficulties in walking. An MRI had showed posterior parietal and frontal cortical atrophy, as well as atrophy in his corpus callosum. Shortly afterward, he had begun to display indications of dementia: confusion, reduced alertness, and visual disturbances. The disturbances included double vision, hallucinations, and misinterpretation of what he was viewing; in one instance, Bannister had insisted that the coat rack in the doctor's office was in fact a skeleton.

The initial diagnosis was DLB, dementia with Lewy bodies. Hallucinations were common in DLB, presenting in three-quarters of all cases. While many patients with DLB saw people or animals, Bannister frequently demonstrated a condition known as reduplicative paramnesia, the conviction that a location has been duplicated or moved from one place to another. During an interview with a doctor at the VA hospital, he was convinced that the entire building was located on the slope of Mount Everest, even going so far as to request a bottle of oxygen because he was worried about the thinness of the air.

But that wasn't the only odd manifestation of Bannister's CBDS. He was also suffering from anarchic hand.

"I'm Hieronymus Grupper," the dog handler said, shaking Catherine's hand. "And this is Nicky Carter the Second—the best damn tracker since the original."

Catherine eyed the panting dog where it had flopped down on the clinic's tiled floor. "The original?"

Hieronymus was a short man with a big head and froggy eyes, dressed in baggy tan shorts, a plaid shirt, hiking boots, and a beat-up straw hat. "Sure. Nick Carter was a Kentucky bloodhound around the turn of the nineteenth century—tracked down six hundred and fifty men in his career. Named after a famous dime-store novel detective, though nobody today seems to remember him. Once tracked a man over a hundred miles."

"The detective or the dog?"

Grupper chuckled. "The dog. Speaking of which, I guess we should get going. I understand we're after a couple escaped mental cases?"

"Psychiatric patients, yes. Does Carter need a personal item to get the scent?"

"He doesn't need it—especially since I understand we're going to be tracking through desert—but it won't hurt. You have an idea where the trail starts?"

"Follow me." Catherine gave Grupper the torn sheet she'd found and a T-shirt that Theria had worn, then led him and Carter down the hall and out the fire exit.

Once outside, Grupper knelt and let the dog sniff both items. Carter took his time, snuffling deep into the folds of the cloth.

"Human beings have somewhere around five million olfactory cells," said Grupper. "A bloodhound has forty times that crammed in their nose."

Carter began casting about on the ground. "Our chances are good," said Grupper. "Good time of day for tracking, not that big a lead, not a lot of other scents to interfere. We'll find them."

"Let's hope so," said Catherine.

Carter lunged forward, straining at his leash, and they set off. The sun was just rising, and Catherine slipped on her sunglasses. Grupper did the same.

The ground was rocky and bare, with only the occasional sage bush to break it up. Carter seemed intent, sometimes keeping his nose to the ground, sometimes lifting his head to sniff the air.

"Scent hounds track in two different ways," Grupper said as they walked along. "When they've got their nose down, they're following the actual trail of footprints—more specifically, the little bits of dead skin that every person sheds, no matter how bundled up they are. When the dogs lift their heads, they're picking up those bits of skin in the air—and the warmer the air gets, the more the dead bits rise up. The floppy ears and wrinkly jowls help; they work kind of like a big scoop, collecting those bits as they drift past."

"I see. And the slobber?"

The dog handler grinned. "Some people say that the drool gives off steam, which helps lift the skin particles into the air. Me, I think it's their secret weapon. You haven't seen the havoc dog drool can wreak until you've seen a hound shake his head on a hot day."

The sun was low, but the temperature was already beginning to rise. Catherine wondered if John Bannister and Theria Kostapolis had any water with them; she doubted it.

Carter stopped, his head up, his tail quivering. After a second, he resumed moving forward with his nose to the ground.

"What was that about?" asked Catherine.

Grupper shrugged. "Hard to say. It's not just their nose that's sensitive; dogs can hear things people can't, at both the upper and lower ends of the spectrum. Humans can't hear much above twenty thousand cycles per second, but canine ears can go all the way up to forty-five. Lower, too—Saint Bernards can hear down in the subsonic, which tells them when a snow pack is shifting and about to avalanche. Some say that's the reason dogs get uneasy before an earthquake, too—they can hear the rocks grinding away at each other as the pressure builds up."

"You know, you talk about your dog the way a car buff talks about engines."

Grupper laughed. "I guess I do. Well, they're damn amazing animals. I figure if I'm going to work alongside one, I should know what makes it tick. Suppose that makes me a canine geek."

Catherine smiled. "There are worse things to be."

"All right, you want to hear something really amazing? It sounds pretty out there, but I swear to God it's been documented."

"As long as you're not about to tell me about a golden retriever who's the Second Coming, go ahead."

"Dogs can also detect certain medical conditions. Seizures, blood-glucose levels, even cancer."

"I've heard of that, actually. Makes sense to me—I mean, any kind of serious disease is going to cause biological changes, right? A dog is probably just picking up on the difference in the way someone smells."

"Sure," said Grupper. "That's exactly what it is for diabetic patients or people with a tumor. But a seizure is a brain event, and dogs seem to be able to detect it *before* it happens. How do you explain that?"

Catherine shrugged. "I can't. But then again, my ex used to have a dog that would always know when he was on his way home from the bar, regardless of day or time. She'd get up and stare at the door, and about ten minutes later he'd roll in. I used to call her my drunk detector—too bad she couldn't tell me how wasted he'd be when he showed up."

"Dogs are great, but they're no substitute for a good divorce lawyer."

"Amen," said Catherine.

The Nevada Neurological Studies Institute was southeast of Las Vegas, and the rocky, sage-brush-dotted terrain gradually gave way to a more lush landscape of deciduous trees and marshy grass.

"They're headed for the wash," said Catherine, stopping and uncapping her canteen. She took a long drink; the sun was up and blazing now.

Grupper did the same, pouring a small amount of water into a collapsible pan for Carter first. The hound sniffed at it, then ignored it, straining at his leash; he had no time for petty details like hydration. "Mixed blessing, I guess. Good for them, bad for us."

Catherine nodded and took another drink. The Las Vegas wash was a twelve-mile-long urban river that funneled runoff from several creeks and the city proper. The wash was mainly a slow, meandering body of water that supported a lot of marshy wetlands at its banks and where it eventually drained into Lake Mead. While it could prove a godsend for two dehydrated, hyperthermic patients staggering out of the desert, it could be difficult tracking them through it.

"Carter can smell a cadaver under twenty feet of water," said Grupper, "but a corpse tends to stay in one place. A moving subject in moving water is another story."

"If we're lucky, they stuck to the banks," said Catherine. "If they decided to go for a swim in the river, our luck might have just run out."

"Well, it is hot as hell out here. They might want to take a dip just to cool off."

"If they see it as water and not molten lava."

"Excuse me?"

"I'm told our escapees are undoubtedly hallucinating. Whether they see us as saviors or devils probably depends on what shape they're in when we find them."

They continued onward. "Saviors or devils, huh?" said Grupper after a moment. "That's kind of funny."

"Why's that?"

"Because of where bloodhounds come from. See, they wouldn't even exist—not in their current form, anyway—except for a religious vision. Guy named Hubert, real party animal who also happened to be the son of the duke of Guienne. Like a lot of hunters, he liked to booze it up while he was out stalking game with his dogs; on one particular hunt, he saw a white stag with the image of the cross between its antlers. The stag told him it was time to stop carousing and get serious with the Lord, and Hubert decided to become a monk.

"But you know, love of dogs gets in your blood. Hubert couldn't give his up—he just switched from hunting to breeding. Wound up producing what we call bloodhounds today. They were known as Saint Hubert hounds for the longest time, and they became about as popular with European royalty of the time as the purse-size accessory dog is with today's aspiring bimbette."

They could see a line of green ahead of them: cottonwood trees. *At least we'll get some shade,* Catherine thought.

But that wasn't all they found. She saw a flash of blue through the trees, and as they got closer, she identified it as a plastic tarp.

"Looks like we're not alone," said Grupper. Carter had his head up now, casting around before resuming course—straight toward the tarp.

The tarp was part of a crude shelter, made from old cardboard boxes, metal barrels, and scrap lumber. A fire pit surrounded by stones and topped with a grille from a stove or fridge was located a few feet from the structure's entrance, and some ragged clothes hung from a length of clothesline between two trees. A three-wheeled contraption built from old bike parts and a shopping cart was parked under a lean-to made from another tarp.

"Complete with carport," said Catherine. "Somebody lives here, that much is obvious. Hello? Is anybody home?"

No answer. They could hear the river now, only a few feet away but hidden behind a thick stand of bulrushes. Carter was already skirting the edge of the rushes.

Catherine cautiously stuck her head inside the entrance to the shelter. "Anybody here?"

She withdrew a second later. "Empty. Which means our homesteader must have gone for a walk, because his wheels are still in the garage."

"Actually," a voice said from the bulrushes, "there's a second possibility."

Anarchic hand—or alien hand syndrome—showed up in sixty percent of people with CBDS. It was a neurological condition in which one of the patient's limbs appeared to take on a life of its own, entirely beyond its owner's control. It would perform actions that ranged from inappropriate—such as public masturbation—to dangerous, including instances where the hand actually attacked the body it was attached to.

Bannister's symptoms had become self-reinforcing. He frequently hallucinated that his hand was a clawed, scaly monstrosity and took to binding it to his torso to prevent it from acting.

"Subject has formed an emotional bond with another patient, TK, in a surprisingly short period of time," was noted at the end of the file. "While nothing was done initially to discourage this, it now appears that the relationship is contributing to a case of SPD (shared psychotic disorder) in both patients. Considering their individual case histories, I'm recommending they be separated and have no further contact with each other."

It was the last entry in the file. Ray put it down and picked up the one labeled "Theria Kostapolis."

He stopped almost immediately. "Cotard's syndrome?" he said aloud. He looked up from the file. "My God," he said softly.

6

GREG AND SARA SURVEYED all of the evidence they'd collected from the Panhandle, spread out before them on the crime lab's layout table.

"Where do you want to start?" asked Greg.

"How about I take the mummy wrappings and you take the guard's uniform?"

"Fine with me."

Sara starting cutting the long swathes of gauze into more manageable strips, while Greg dug the bloody clothes out of the evidence bag. "There's a lot of material here," said Sara. "We got the new DNA extraction kits in, right?"

"Yeah," said Greg. "There's a stack of them over there. Haven't had a chance to try one out yet, though."

"No time like the present."

DNA could be hard to isolate, but the technology was getting better all the time. The development

Sara was about to try worked on the principle of ionic charge; essentially, coated magnetic beads were added to the sample, which then had its pH lowered. This caused the ions in the beads to become positively charged and the DNA to bind to them.

They worked in silence for a while, both concentrating on the tasks at hand. Greg took samples of the blood from the clothes, then processed them for epithelials as well.

"Okay," he said. "Done with the clothes."

Sara looked up. "I'm still working on the bandages. You want to take a look at that fiber you found?"

"Sure." He got the sample ready and slid it under the lens of a microscope. "It's synthetic," he said after a moment. "Looks like spun polyester, with some kind of coating, maybe a polymer. I'll run it through the infrared spectrometer."

Greg carefully cut a short piece off the fiber, mixed it with dry salt, then shaped the mix into a disk. When the disk was exposed to infrared radiation, the rock crystals of the salt would act as a prism, breaking the rays into a spectrum that the machine would measure and analyze.

"I think I've got an ID," said Greg at last. "It's spun polyester coated with nitrile butadiene."

"Synthetic rubber," said Sara. "You get a hit in the database?"

"I have. It's from a fire hose."

"There are fire hoses on every floor of the Panhandle."

"Going to get exemplars now." Greg slipped out of his lab coat.

"I'll go with you—we can drop off the DNA samples with Wendy on the way."

Greg carefully clipped a stray fiber from the fire hose on the spool, then examined it closely before popping it into an evidence bag and closing the glass door set into the wall of the hotel corridor. "Well, that's the last one," he said to Sara. "I've taken samples from every floor."

"You don't look happy."

"I'm not. I'll double-check at the lab, but I can already tell none of these is going to match. The fiber I found was made using a process called through-the-weave extrusion, which coats the fabric of the fire hose with the rubber. These hoses are older models—I can see just by looking that they don't have the rubberized coating. Probably a cotton-polyester blend."

"So the fire hose didn't come from here. Has there been a fire here recently?" asked Sara.

"I'll check with the fire department."

"I'll check with the front desk."

They headed down to the lobby, Greg pulling out his phone in the elevator. A few quick questions ascertained that the only calls the fire department had responded to from the hotel in the last year had been medical, and no one with an industrial-strength fire hose had hauled one up to the roof.

In the Denali on the way back to the lab, Greg said, "Why a fire hose?"

Sara shrugged. "Why not a fire hose?"

"Very zen. What I mean is, I can see someone using a fire hose out of necessity—if there's no rope handy, you grab the nearest thing that'll do. But not only was there no hose available on the roof, they didn't use the nineteen closest options, either. So why go to the trouble of bringing something bulky, heavy, and specialized like a fire hose to a roof?"

"To put out a fire?" Sara smiled.

"Except the only fire was on the ground—the burning dirigible."

"Maybe the dirigible didn't land where it was supposed to."

Greg frowned. "So bring a hose to the roof as fire insurance? I guess they could have used the pool for the water supply, but they'd still need a pump."

"And a couple of fire extinguishers would probably do the same job a lot easier."

"True. Which puts us right back at square one— why a fire hose?"

After returning to the lab, Greg had verified that none of the samples he'd taken from the hotel's fire hoses was a match to the fiber he'd found on the roof. He'd spent the next hour examining photos of the tool marks they'd discovered on the windowsill and pipe before sitting down at a workstation and inputting data. "Check this out," he said.

"Simulation?" asked Sara, looking over Greg's shoulder at the screen.

"Hypothesis," he said. "Here's the layout of the rooftop, including the penthouse bedrooms." The screen showed a wireframe, three-dimensional graphic. "Here's the pipe that was bent. Here's the tool mark at the edge of the roof. And here's the tool mark on the window frame."

"If there's a pattern, I'm not seeing it."

Greg hit a button, drawing a thin red line from the roof to the pipe to the window. "Try this. What if those tool marks were from clamps attached to pulleys?"

"If they were, the force being exerted would be in this direction," she said, tapping the screen.

"Which is exactly the direction the pipe was bent in," he said. "I think the fire hose was run through a pulley system and used to lower or raise something onto the roof."

Sara frowned. "To quote a friend of mine, why a fire hose? I mean, wouldn't rope or cable be much more effective?"

Greg shrugged. "Only one way to find out. You up for a re-creation?"

"Does it involve me dangling off the edge of a roof?"

"Only if you ask nicely."

Greg stood on top of a two-story-high metal scaffold set up in the CSI lab parking lot. "Okay," he called down. "You ready?"

Sara looked up at him, shading her eyes from the sun, and called back, "Ready!"

"I'm not," said Nick, strolling up. "What's going on, guys?"

"We're trying to re-create the scenario that took place on the roof of the Panhandle," said Sara. "Minus the burning dirigible and bears roaming around."

"Yeah? Mind taking me through it?"

"Ask Greg—it's his theory."

Nick quickly scaled the scaffold and stood beside

Greg on the plywood that was standing in for the top of the hotel.

"Hey, Nick. Just in time."

"Looks like. What's the plan?" He eyed what Greg had set up.

"Well, to start with, I found some heavy-duty vise clamps that matched the tool marks we found. Then I located the widest pulleys I could find and attached them to the clamps. The clamps are now in the same positions relative to each other that they would have been on the roof—pipe, edge of roof, windowsill."

"And you've got a fire hose running through them."

"We found fibers from a fire hose on the windowsill. I think it was used to haul something up or down the edge of the roof—something heavy. I did stress tests on a pipe of the same diameter, and we're talking something in the neighborhood of three hundred pounds. That's what I've got attached to the other end of this hose." Greg patted the winch beside him. "I don't know how far—or in what direction—the weight was hauled, but I figured I'd start by trying to pull something up two stories."

"Let her rip," said Nick.

Greg signaled down to Sara once more, who gave the all-clear and stood back. The fire hose was tied in a knot around one end of a cargo net loaded with sandbags, which began to rise once Greg activated the winch.

But not very far. After only a few feet, the load yanked to a halt.

"Whoa! Turn it off!" said Nick.

Greg killed the power and walked around to where Nick was examining the pulley attached to the pipe. The hose had moved sideways, off the pulley and onto the axle, where it had jammed.

"Huh," said Greg. "Guess I didn't position it correctly. Give me a hand unjamming it, and we'll try it again."

They did—and came up with the same result. Going up or down, the hose wouldn't travel more than a few feet before running off the pulley and getting jammed.

"Well, so much for that," said Greg glumly. "The hose has no problem bearing the load, it just doesn't like the gear."

Nick clapped him on the back, "Look at this the way Thomas Edison would have. 'I have not failed—' "

"—I've just found a thousand ways that won't work,'" Greg finished. "Sure. One down, nine hundred and ninety-nine to go . . ."

7

ACCORDING TO THE SECURITY LOGS, the fire alarm that had been tripped at the Panhandle was in a recessed corner no more than fifty feet away from the elevator where the alleged bear attack took place. Nick reviewed the camera footage for that area of the casino and wasn't surprised when it showed a security guard strolling up and yanking the lever before calmly walking away. Nick was pretty sure the man was wearing a wig, a fake mustache, and prop eyeglasses.

Archie walked in while Nick was studying a screen shot of the phony guard's face. "Hey, I know that guy," Archie said.

Nick swiveled on his chair. "You do?"

"Sure. I just spent the last few hours staring at a very blurry, red-tinted version of his face. Maybe I don't know his name, but I feel like we've become close. I call him Gorylocks."

"Cute. Does that mean you've managed to clean up that footage?"

"Some. Take a look at this." Archie slipped a disk into a workstation and sat down next to Nick. "Okay, the first thing you notice is that the bear drops down. Previously, it was on its feet, giving old Gorylocks a big ursine hug and pretending to chew on his neck."

"Pretending?"

"Yeah. See over there? That's where one of the gore hoses was planted; you can see it sticking out of his collar and flopping around later."

Archie tapped a key. "Okay, now that the camera has been gooped, he gets down to business. It's still really blurred, but it looks to me like he just hit a button on the control panel."

"Yeah, going down. He wanted to get to the basement level before security could lock down the elevator again."

"Then he does a face plant—playing corpse for when the doors open. As soon as they do, the bear lumbers out. But then—" Archie hit another key, freezing the image. "See? He put his hand out, to the base of the open elevator door."

Nick nodded. "He's holding the safety guard in, so the door stays open."

"Right. And he just stays like that, while the bear herds everyone out to the fire stairs. Once everybody's gone—"

"He gets up," said Nick. "And—aw, you're kidding."

"Yeah, he pulls out what I can only assume is a more concentrated version of what's already all over the lens and sprays some more on. The only thing you see after that is more red. Sorry."

"It's more than I had a minute ago. Thanks, Archie."

"Hey, Hodges," said Nick, walking into the trace lab. "You finished looking at the blood sample I sent you?"

Hodges crossed his arms and smiled but said nothing.

"What?" said Nick.

Hodges's eyebrows went up. His smile stayed put.

"Hodges, I don't have time for this—"

"Ah, but *my* time is infinite, is that what you're saying?"

"Noooo—"

"Then why, oh *why*, would you send me a sample to analyze that clearly should have been sent to DNA?"

"Because I didn't want DNA, Hodges. I wanted to see if there was something in it that shouldn't have been."

"Then you could have asked for a tox screen."

"I'm not looking for a drug."

Hodges's smile was replaced by a suspicious frown. "And you're not trying to pull a gag? Do a little hazing on the newbie?"

"Hodges, you've been here longer than I have."

"True . . ." He stroked his chin.

"Look, Hodges, did you find something unusual or not?"

"All right, I'll take this at face value. But if I hear even a *hint* of a punch line involving a fairy tale, I *will* have my revenge." Hodges strode over to a table and grabbed a piece of paper. "Here. I refuse to be your straight man."

Nick took the paper cautiously, then scanned it quickly. "This is from the bear attack?" he said.

"Yes. *Three* bears, right? I'm not thick—though *this* certainly was."

"Hodges, this says it wasn't human blood at all. It came from a pig."

"That's correct. Three bears and three little pigs, right?" He looked triumphant. "I'm sorry, did I ruin the joke by figuring out the structure? Sorry, but that's what I *do.*"

Nick sighed. "For the last time, Hodges, there's no punch line. The interior of that elevator was sprayed in pig's blood, because our missing guard was never wounded in the first place. The attack was a fake—if the joke's on anyone, it's on me."

"Oh. I was wondering why there was corn starch in the blood instead of porridge. Seemed like a real missed opportunity, theme-wise."

"It was there as a thickening agent. The intent was to coat the lens of the security camera, preventing anyone in the security office from seeing what was happening. I guess unadulterated blood didn't do a good enough job."

"No," said Hodges thoughtfully. "But this mixture wasn't too thick or too thin. You might say—"

"Don't do it, Hodges—"

"—that it was *just right.*"

Nick was starting to get a sense of the case. Someone had gone to a lot of time and trouble to create not one but two illusions: a man dying in a fiery aircraft crash and another mauled to death by a bear. He might not know where the miniature zeppelin came from, but the bear's origin was a lot easier to trace.

The bears all came from the same place, an animal-rescue ranch just outside Henderson owned by a man named Nazar Masterkov. Nick did a little research on the history of the ranch before getting into his Denali and driving out there.

The Bruin Rescue Ranch had been established five years ago specifically for circus bears, though it did some rehabilitation work with zoo animals as well. It was a nonprofit organization, and its partnership with the Panhandle had apparently been planned from the start—the hotel had been built at the same time the ranch was established.

A long, narrow road led from the highway to the ranch's front gate. Nick stopped the Denali, buzzed the intercom on the metal post, and identified himself. The gate swung open silently and he drove inside.

He pulled up outside a low, sprawling house with a Spanish-style red tile roof and parked. There was no large sign over the front door to tell him he was in the right place, but the ranch wasn't a tourist attraction; other than the daily shows at the Panhandle, they seemed to have little contact with the public.

A woman walked out onto the covered front porch. She was tall and broad-shouldered, her dark hair tied back in a ponytail. She wore tan shorts, a khaki shirt, and hiking boots; her legs were tanned and muscular.

"Yes?" she said. "How may I help you?"

"Nick Stokes, Vegas Crime Lab. I was wondering if I could talk to someone about the incident at the casino."

"I'm Nadya Karnova," she said. Her accent was more Texas than Russia. "I'm in charge of the bears, so I guess the person you want to talk to is me."

There was a padded bench and two chairs on the porch; she sat down and motioned for him to do the same.

"Let's start with the bear that attacked the security guard," said Nick, taking a seat. "What can you tell me about it?"

"Her name is Brownie. She never should have been in the rotation to begin with—that was our first mistake."

"Why not?"

"For one thing, she wasn't a circus bear. They're used to crowds, used to being transported. Brownie's from a zoo and was originally captured in the wild; she's with us because she was displaying maladjusted behavior in her old home."

"What sort of behavior?"

"Pacing, bar biting, swaying. They're all signs a bear isn't happy."

"So why was she on display?"

Nadya shook her head. "That's just it—she wasn't supposed to be. Bureaucratic error; one of the handlers misread a form."

"Uh-huh. Where's Brownie now?"

"Still recovering, in our medical facility. How's the man she attacked?" Her voice was worried.

"He'll live. Would it be possible to see Brownie?"

"Yes, of course. Follow me."

She led him down the steps and around the corner, down a dusty cement walk to the half-dome shape of a massive Quonset behind the house. "This is our main environment," she said over her shoulder. "Most of our bears come from places that aren't quite this dry or hot. We like to make them as comfortable as possible."

She pulled open a reinforced steel door, letting out a puff of moist, cool air. Nick followed her inside.

It was like stepping into a rain forest. Fir and spruce trees reached to the ceiling, which was mostly glass. The air smelled of damp moss and pine. Nick stopped and looked around; even in a city that prided itself on creating artificial environments, the illusion was impressive. The forest stretched out before him, Nadya already twenty feet down the path that wound through it.

"I feel like I'm on my way to Grandma's house," Nick said as he trotted to catch up. "Maybe I should have worn red today."

She laughed. "Don't worry, you're in no danger of being eaten. This part is fenced off—it's purely selfish, for our own enjoyment. A small perk for all our good work."

The path ended at three white rectangular trailers parked side-by-side. Nadya entered the one marked "Medical."

The trailer's interior was lined with cages, though only two of them held bears. One was lying on its side on a bed of straw and barely looked up; the other sat on its haunches and studied them intently.

"As you can see, Brownie's still a little groggy." She knelt beside the cage and peered at the bear. "Poor thing. I hope she won't have to be destroyed."

Nick came over and stood beside her. "I don't see any blood on her claws or fur."

"Our veterinarian cleaned her up while she was tranquilized. He didn't want the smell to disturb the other bears."

"Of course." Nick paused. "So, how did you get into this line of work? Pretty unique."

"Oh, it's in my blood. My family has been working with bears for generations—training them, mostly. You know, government work."

"Excuse me?"

She laughed. "Sorry, it's an old family joke. When the Communists took over in Russia, it was decided that the circus was the 'people's entertainment'—something everyone could enjoy or even participate in. Lenin nationalized all the circuses in the country, even created circus schools that were run by the government. That's my background—my great-grandmother even met Lenin once."

Nick glanced around. "This seems pretty far from the big top."

"I'm less interested in exploiting animals than helping them. It's led to more than a few interesting discussions around the dinner table, believe me."

The door opened behind them. A man Nick judged to be in his seventies stood in the doorway. "Nadya, what's this? We have a visitor, and you didn't tell me?"

She quickly stood. "I didn't want to bother you.

Mr. Stokes, this is Nazar Masterkov, the owner of the ranch."

Masterkov put out his hand and Nick shook it; the man's grip was firm. "Mr. Stokes." He eyed Nick's baseball cap with its CSI logo. "You are investigating the unfortunate accident at the casino?" His English held no trace of an accent.

"That's right. Can you tell me who was in charge of transporting the animals that day?"

"That would be Mischa," said Masterkov. "He's very upset by the whole ordeal. He works very closely with the animals."

"I understand the bear that attacked wasn't supposed to be on the rotation for that day?"

Masterkov glanced at Nadya. "That's right," he said. "An oversight on Mischa's part. He blames himself for the whole thing."

"Could I talk to him?"

"Of course," said Masterkov. "I believe he's out in the main enclosure right now. Nadya, can you give him a call?"

"Sure." She dug a cell phone out of her pocket and flipped it open.

"Bears are such amazing animals," Masterkov said. "I have always admired them. So clever and so strong. Did you know that of all the predators in the wild, there is only one brave enough to hunt the bear?"

"Human beings?"

Masterkov grinned and shook his head. "I said in the wild, young man. No, the tiger is the only beast fierce enough to stalk and kill a bear for food—and even a tiger would hesitate before attacking a grizzly or polar bear."

Nadya snapped her phone shut. "He'll be here in a few minutes," she said.

"You can run along," said Masterkov to Nadya. "I'll keep our guest company—that is, if you're finished with her?"

"Done for now," said Nick. She gave him a quick smile and left.

"There is a famous Russian folk tale," said Nazar. "*Morozko*. Do you know it?"

"No, sir, I'm afraid I don't."

"It's about an arrogant young man named Ivan. Trying to impress a young girl, he attempts to kill a mother bear and her cubs with his bow. The wizard who gave him the bow sees this and is so appalled he changes Ivan's head into that of a bear." Masterkov grinned, showing off teeth so even and white Nick doubted they were real. "After that, Ivan is alone. People fear him, even though all he wants to do is repent of his crime and help them."

"People can be like that."

"Yes. Appearances can be deceptive, can they not? As someone in your line of work must surely know. And despite the fearsome appearance and reputation of the bear, they are really solitary, shy creatures. To force such creatures to perform for the delight of an audience by riding bicycles or pretending to dance has always seemed disgraceful to me. Man is not the only animal to value his dignity or his freedom."

"I agree," said Nick.

The door opened. Nick recognized the man with

the short gray beard who entered as the same one he'd seen supervising the removal of the bear at the casino. He was dressed much the same as Nadya Karnova, in tan shorts, a khaki shirt, and hiking boots.

"Hello," the man said. "I am Mischa Korolev." Unlike the others, he had a pronounced Russian accent. "How may I help you?"

Nick introduced himself. "What I need from you, Mr. Korolev, is to tell me what happened when the bears got loose."

Korolev shook his head. "Was my fault. The bear that went rogue, she should not have been there. I was doing routine transfer from truck—rolling cage down ramp to loading dock—when suddenly, there is fire in the sky."

"The dirigible."

"Is that how you say? Yes. I am distracted, the bears are upset. Brownie charges the door; it hits me and knocks me down. The other two follow her out, and they head into the building through the doors of loading dock. I block doors open beforehand to make rolling cage through easier, and they go straight through to casino."

Nick made some notes on a pad. "Okay. So you chased after them?"

"Not right away. Bumped head on floor, was not awake for few minutes. Bears already gone."

"What about the other two bears? Ever have any problems with them?"

"No, no. Both from circus, very tame, very calm. They follow Brownie out of curiosity. No trouble rounding them up."

Nick nodded and closed his notebook. "All right,

that's about all I need for now. I'll be in touch if I have any more questions."

"*Da.*"

Masterkov showed Nick to the front door. "We're deeply sorry about this," he said. "My condolences to the family of the man who was attacked. If there's anything else you need to know, please contact us immediately."

"I will," said Nick.

On the drive back to the lab, Nick thought about what he'd learned. Someone was lying, that much he was sure of. If the bear attack had been faked—and all of the evidence pointed to exactly that—then there was no way the phony security guard had set it up with a dangerous bear. He would have used a trained bear, one used to wrestling with a human as part of an act. So either Brownie wasn't the unstable wild animal her handlers claimed she was, or someone had switched bears without anyone noticing.

There was one essential player still missing. Nick probably could have talked to him while he was at the ranch, but thought the interview might go better if it happened at the lab. Bears weren't the only animals that preferred to meet challenges on their own turf.

"Dr. Villaruba," said Nick. "Thanks for coming in to the lab. Sorry I missed you at the ranch."

Dr. Villaruba was a short man with wiry black-and-gray hair and pale blue eyes that never seemed to stop moving. He glanced from Nick to the door to the recording equipment set up for the interview. "Not at all, not at all. I'm very busy, as I'm sure you are. Not that I mind giving a statement, you understand."

"No, of course not—"

"Just eager to get back to the animals."

"Right. Well, this shouldn't take too long." Nick shuffled through a few papers in front of him, then studied one intently for a moment without saying anything.

"What would you like to know?" Villaruba said at last.

"Hmmm? Well, I guess we should start with some background. How long have you worked for the ranch as their veterinarian?"

"Not that long. Six months, give or take."

"You work there full-time?"

"Oh, no. I have my own animal clinic in Vegas. But I do put in a good twenty hours a week at the ranch."

"You have a lot of experience with bears?"

"I'm no expert, no. But the ranch advertised for someone and I thought it would be interesting to work with some larger animals, so I applied. Big difference from cats, dogs, and parakeets."

"I'll bet. How about Brownie? How familiar are you with her?"

"Uh, not very. I examined her when she first came in, of course. She seemed healthy."

"Any behavioral problems?"

"She has a history of being overly aggressive. I certainly wouldn't have recommended she be put on display in the casino."

Nick nodded. "I understand you checked her out once she was returned to the ranch after the attack?"

"Yes. She was still tranquilized."

"You cleaned her up? Removed the blood from her fur and paws?"

Villaruba blinked. "Well, yes. I thought the smell of human blood would get the other bears worked up. Was that a mistake?"

"Technically, it's destroying evidence in a criminal case. That's definitely a mistake."

Villaruba swallowed. "Am I in trouble?"

Nick didn't answer. "Are you familiar with the Panhandle Casino?"

"Not really. I mean, I've been there. I've never examined the bear habitat, though."

"Really? That's kind of unusual, don't you think?"

"I never thought about it. I see the bears out at the ranch."

"Sure. So you don't know the route the handler takes when he moves the bears from the loading dock to the habitat?"

"What? No."

"The service corridor is pretty much a straight shot, but it does go right past the kitchen. Bears have a pretty good sense of smell, right?"

"Yes, very."

"But all three ignored the kitchen and went right through into the casino. Seems like pretty strange behavior."

"That *is* strange. But like I said, I'm not an expert on bears."

"So you say," said Nick. "And *that's* pretty strange, too."

8

CATHERINE STARED AT the wall of green bulrushes in front of her, her hand creeping to her holstered gun. "Las Vegas Police," she called out. "Step out where I can see you."

"I'd rather not," the voice said. It sounded young, male, and embarrassed. "See, I was going for a swim, and my clothes—well, they're hanging up right behind you."

Catherine glanced at the clothesline. "Uh-huh. Tell you what, why don't I toss your clothes to you, you put them on, and then you come out so we can talk?"

"Sure. I'm, uh, over here." A hand shot up near the edge of the bulrushes. Catherine picked a pair of jeans off the clothesline and threw them over.

A moment later, a man in his twenties with a scruffy black beard and a scrawny, hairy chest stepped into view. "Hi," he said. "I'm, uh, Mark Viceroy."

"Hi, Mark," said Catherine. "You live here?"

He hesitated before answering. "Not really. I'm just staying here for a while. It's temporary."

"We're looking for a man and a woman, Mark. Anybody come by in the last few hours?"

Mark blinked at her. "Uh, no."

Catherine sighed. "Look, they're not in trouble—not unless we don't catch up to them. Both of them have serious medical conditions; they escaped from a hospital, not a jail. Covering for them isn't helping anyone, including them."

Mark looked at Carter. "Never saw a bloodhound used to find hospital patients before."

"You'd be surprised at what he can find," said Grupper amiably. "Maybe I should have him nose around your campsite, see if there's anything interesting."

Mark blinked again. "Uh, they came through here a few hours ago. Guy with his arm in a sling and a woman, right?"

"You talk to them?" asked Catherine.

"A little. I was up making some coffee, and they came walking in out of the dark. They seemed kind of out of it."

"I'll bet. Tell me everything they said and did—don't leave anything out. This is important."

Mark pushed his wet hair out of his eyes. "Okay. Lemme see . . . I asked if they wanted to sit down, have some coffee. They didn't want any, asked for water instead. The guy kept staring at the fire like—I don't know, like it was going to bite him or something. I could tell he wanted to leave, but he wouldn't until she'd drunk some water."

"They tell you their names?" asked Catherine.

"No, and I didn't ask. The way I figure it, there's kind of a code out in the middle of nowhere—either you're there because you don't want to be around anyone else, or you're lost. Either way, you're probably better off offering someone a space at your campfire than asking them who they are or what they're doing."

"That's very polite," said Catherine. "But we're only a few miles away from Vegas—this isn't exactly Death Valley. What *did* they say?"

"Well, funny you should mention death. They asked me how long I'd been here, and when I told them about a month, the guy asked me how I died. I didn't know how to answer that, you know? I mean, I've hung out with schizophrenics on the street—you say the wrong thing, they'll flip out on you. I didn't want to wind up with a hatchet in my skull."

"So what did you tell him?"

"That I didn't remember. That seemed cool with him. The woman, she hardly said a word the whole time. Not until she stood up and said it was time to go—then you could tell who was in charge. He thanked me, and then they walked right into the wash—it's pretty shallow around here, only up to your waist."

Catherine nodded. "So they crossed over to the other side and kept going?"

Mark shrugged. "Beats me. You can't really see anything with the rushes that line the bank, and it was still dark. I thought I heard splashing moving upstream for a while, so they might have stayed in, waded ashore farther up."

Grupper sighed. "Well, the trail ends here. I can see if Carter can pick it up farther down the wash, but if they stayed in the water we're probably out of luck."

"Thanks for your help," Catherine told Mark. "You do know that all the runoff from the city flows through here, right? The wetlands at the far end act like a filter, soaking up a lot of contaminants before they reach the lake, but this close to Vegas? You wouldn't catch me swimming here."

"Better than the desert," said Mark. "Or the streets."

"Unfortunately," said Catherine, "that seems to be the direction that our subjects are headed in."

Even an hour before dawn, the sidewalks are crowded with lost souls. Most are simply rotting corpses, shuffling along mindlessly, cameras thumping hollowly against their exposed ribs, mildewed bottles or cans clutched in their bony fists; but not all. Bannister spots a werewolf in a Gestapo uniform, a bloodstained meat cleaver in one immense, furry paw. Even hell has a police force.

"Take my hand," he whispers to Theria. She does so, not out of any affection but because she's learned it's easier simply to do what he says.

They walk along, hand-in-hand, Bannister struggling to turn his stiff-legged shamble into a more acceptable limp. He knows Theria has no sense of self-preservation—for that matter, neither does he, not really—but Bannister does have something that has replaced it: a sense of purpose. Being pounced on by a member of lycanthropic law enforcement will hinder that purpose, and thus must be avoided.

He hopes that his demon hand will be enough to disguise him, that Theria won't simply collapse into a boneless heap as she sometimes does. He wishes he could have known her in life; from what he can tell, she was quite beautiful.

The werecop lets them by, giving them no more than a suspicious snort as they pass. Bannister wonders what they smell like to such a creature.

"There," Theria whispers, pointing at a massive building with huge white pillars out front. A bronze statue of a Roman gladiator holding a sword in one hand and a severed head in the other guards the entrance; the eyes of both swivel to watch them as they enter.

"Why here?" he asks.

"It's a mausoleum, isn't it?" she says, as if it were self-evident. "It's where I belong."

He cannot argue with her logic. They enter.

The aisles of the Roman complex are made of marble, veined with scarlet. Golden gutters line either side, filled with a sluggish mixture of gore and sewage.

Slaves seem to be the coin of the realm, dead-eyed men and women in rags chained by the neck and hauled from game to game. A line of them are attached to the brass rail of an elaborate marble bar, the bartender a monstrous demon with the head of a warthog. He glares at Bannister and Theria with tiny, red-rimmed eyes, trying to decide if they're customers or property.

More warthog demons, most wearing togas, man the games of chance. The most popular seems to be a steep-walled, sandy pit set into the floor, ringed with seats; slaves are forced to fight armored gladiators for their lives. Each gladiator has a specific rank and crest, and they fight in teams. Bannister watches a Jack of Skulls and a Queen *of Knives beat a slave with a crude "17" tattooed on his forehead to death using three-lobed clubs.*

The dead slave is hauled out of the pit with meathooks and dumped on a trolley. A steady stream of trolleys departs from the pits to a huge central area with row after row of troughs; the bodies are chopped up and dumped in the troughs, where pigheaded demons in bloodstained togas devour them greedily.

"I can't leave you here," Bannister says. "You'll be devoured."

"Does it matter?"

"Yes, Theria. It matters. Not here."

After a moment, she nods. "Not here . . ."

A search up and down both banks of the river for a mile in either direction produced no results, and Catherine eventually had to give up and send Grupper and Carter home. She returned to the institute, found Ray, and sank into a chair—probably the same chair that Theria Kostapolis and John Bannister had sat in themselves, many times—shaking her head at Ray's inquiring glance. "No go, Ray. Bannister was trained to deal with surviving in a harsh desert climate, under combat conditions—it could be that he used that to throw us off. Tracking dog lost the scent at the Las Vegas wash."

Ray nodded. He looked as if he hadn't moved since the last time Catherine had talked to him, several open file folders in front of him on Wincroft's desk. "That's too bad. I've been delving into both patients' histories. I can't decide which one is more tragic."

"That bad?"

"I'm afraid so. There's a lot of material here, but I'll see if I can condense it for you. John Bannister is from a small town in West Virginia, orphaned as a child. Grew up in a series of foster homes, enlisted at eighteen and worked his way up to sergeant. He was stationed at a base near Tikrit as a bomb-disposal expert, specializing in IEDs, when he was injured. An explosive device he was trying to defuse set off a second device nearby, killing four members of his unit. He was in a coma for a week. His symptoms didn't begin to appear for another month or so—though whether or not they were triggered by the explosion is unclear."

"And the woman?"

"Theria Kostapolis. Her history is a little more—involved. She grew up in a very religious atmosphere—both her parents were devout Roman Catholics who lived on a farm in Pennsylvania. They were convinced Theria should become a nun. She didn't respond well to this, running away repeatedly from the time she was thirteen. Her parents tried to change her behavior with punishments that ranged from locking her in a shed to actual floggings. They withdrew her from school and taught her at home, a process that seemed to focus almost entirely on religious study. She was deprived of food, sleep, and comfort, apparently in an attempt to mimic the routines of certain monks."

"My God."

"Not mine. And apparently not Theria's, either—she managed to escape again, this time when she was sixteen. She had better luck, winding up in Pittsburgh and evading her parents for almost eighteen months. They finally tracked her down, living in a shared house with several other teenagers. She was working full-time at a fast-food restaurant, had a boyfriend, and was looking into re-enrolling in school."

"And then they dragged her back."

"Yes. According to her case file, she'd become what young people today refer to as a goth—you're familiar with the term?"

Catherine sighed. "I have a teenager, so yes. Lots of black clothing and eyeliner, pale skin, and a gloomy attitude. Think Dracula in studded leather with loud, depressing music."

"It's a subculture centered around a rather bleak worldview, one in which many traditional religious icons such as crosses or angels are subverted or used in an ironic way. I can understand why she'd be attracted to it."

"I'm guessing her parents didn't share her opinion."

"No. They had her boyfriend arrested for harboring a minor, took her back home, and locked her up. Then, realizing that in less than six months she'd legally be an adult, they played their last card. If she didn't agree to give up her lifestyle and join the church, they would send her to a missionary camp in Sierra Leone. They thought she'd be less likely to run anywhere if she was stranded in one of the most inhospitable, violent countries in the world."

"What did she do?"

"She started a fire, hoping to escape in the confusion. She suffered smoke inhalation and was hospitalized." Ray paused. "Both her parents died in the fire. She was charged with arson but found mentally incompetent to stand trial. After finding out she'd killed both her parents, she had a complete breakdown in the hospital. She's been institutionalized ever since, but it wasn't until about a year ago that she began to demonstrate signs of Cotard's syndrome."

"Is that serious?"

"Yes. I've read about it, but I've never personally encountered a case—it's an extremely rare disorder, one both fascinating and disturbing. Simply put, a person with Cotard's syndrome believes they are dead."

"Uh-oh."

"This can manifest in a variety of ways. Mild cases suffer from despair and depression, while extreme examples deny that they exist at all. The delusion can extend to surroundings as well; subjects sometime believe that not only have they died, but they've gone to hell."

"And this is a delusion that *both* of them now share?"

"I would say so, yes. Even before being exposed to BZ, Theria and John were beginning to show signs of SPD—shared psychotic disorder."

Catherine frowned. "Wait. They were already sharing delusions? How did that happen?"

"It can occur when a dominant delusional personality encounters one that's more pliable. Theria and John met in art therapy, an interest they both share. There's a series of sketches in both their files; seen side-by-side, they're very interesting."

Ray pulled a sheaf of papers from the file and laid them down one by one on the desk before him, then picked up a second file and did the same.

"These sketches were done by Theria Kostapolis," Ray said, indicating the ones on the left. "Her preoccupation with death is obvious. Coffins, skeletons, gravestones—the imagery remains consistent throughout."

Ray pointed at the first sketch to the right. "And these were done by John Bannister. The obsession with death is there, too, but in the beginning his drawings were much more violent—screaming faces, explosions, even dismembered or mutilated bodies. As time goes on, though, they become calmer; less dying and more death. Some of these depictions are almost pastoral."

"As long as you ignore the open graves. But yeah, I see what you mean." Catherine picked up one of Theria's sketches and studied it. "This one seems different."

"Yes. The art therapy was being directed by this point; she was told to draw something specific. In this case, the sun."

"So she drew a sunset." Catherine squinted at the picture. "It is a sunset, right? Not a sunrise?"

"I would agree with that assessment, as did Dr. Wincroft. But what's really interesting is this." Ray picked up one of Bannister's drawings and handed it to her.

"He drew a sunset, too," said Catherine.

"Yes. And those aren't the only ones; both he and Theria drew dozens of them. By the time Dr. Wincroft separated the two of them, the drawings they were doing were almost identical. It's important to note that Theria began doing them first, though—it seems that she's the dominant one. Even though Bannister is the one initiating action, his view of reality itself has been subsumed by Theria's."

"How does one come down with this—Cotard's?"

"It can show up in conjunction with another neurological condition, as a result of brain injury, or even simply because of severe depression, as seems to be the case with Theria. According to Dr. Wincroft's notes, she's come to believe that she died in that fire and has been in hell ever since."

"So we're not just chasing two escaped psychiatric patients—we're chasing two people who think they're already dead."

"That's about the size of it."

Catherine sighed. "Let's hope it's still a delusion when we catch up to them."

9

GREG STUDIED THE PULLEY in front of him on the light table morosely. "Maybe if we fold the hose in half?"

Sara sighed. "We tried that."

"But we could hold it in place by putting rubber bands or string around it at spaced intervals—"

"Greg." Sara grabbed his arm. "Let it go. A fire hose and pulley system do not good partners make."

He shook his head. "Okay, okay. The pulley system was pure speculation, anyway."

Sara smiled. "We should probably—"

"But the fire hose isn't. We *know* there was one up there, and it didn't come from the hotel. And the fact that we found a fiber on the sill means it must have gone out the window."

Sara started to speak, then stopped herself. "Okay, granted. How do you want to proceed?"

"Standard length for a hose of this type is fifty feet. Pulleys or not, that's a measurable range. I say we go back up to the penthouse and see if we can find anything within it."

"You're talking about the outside of the building?"

"If that's where the evidence is." Greg grinned. "And hey, you did say you wanted to hang off the top of a building."

"True, but I was thinking of something a little closer to the ground . . ."

They started with Greg taking a fifty-foot, weighted length of rope and dangling it from the penthouse window of the Panhandle. Sara stayed on the ground and snapped pictures with a telephoto lens while Greg slowly swung the rope from one side to the other. The downloaded photos, laid one on top of the other, provided a clear pattern of the arc the hose could have reached.

The next step involved a window-washing rig, a suspended platform lowered or raised by an on-board electric winch. Sara stepped from the roof to the rig without hesitation, then glanced back at Greg. "Coming?"

"Uh, yeah," he said. "Just double-checking my safety harness."

"I think you're up to quadruple-checking, actually."

"Safety first," he muttered, and stepped carefully onto the platform.

They had to work in sections, starting at one corner and making their way down, then moving the rig over when the section was done. They were looking for anything out of the ordinary—a tool mark, some transfer, a stray fingerprint on the glass. It was slow, painstaking work, the glass reflecting both light and heat. A gust of wind would shake the platform every now and then, and Greg would inevitably wind up glancing down as he grabbed a handrail; just as quickly, he'd look back up.

"Kind of nice up here, actually," said Sara. "Terrific view. If I was wearing a bikini, I could even get a tan."

"Uh, yeah," said Greg. He focused on the few square inches of glass directly in front of his face. "It's a terrific place to fall to your death. Leave behind a corpse with really good skin tone."

"You don't do well with heights?"

"Heights I'm fine with. This is to heights what trees are to fungus."

"It's not that bad. Twenty stories, right? A body falls at thirty-two feet per second every second. Approximately fifteen feet per story, so that's three hundred feet. Which works out to—"

"Just under ninety-five miles an hour by the time you crater."

She glanced at him. "That's pretty good."

"You have a funny definition of good."

"I meant how quickly you worked it out."

"I did the math beforehand. I like to be prepared when I'm obsessing about my imminent demise."

"You're doing fine."

"Sure. That's because in my head, I'm still at the lab, looking at a pane of glass I hauled in and mounted on a frame myself. Any second now, Hodges is going to walk up behind me and ask why no one ever makes a fresh pot of coffee in the break room."

"That's a smart technique." She paused. "I was

just trying to distract you, you know. Crunching numbers works for me when I'm trying to distance myself from a situation."

"Not for me. You should have stuck with your first attempt."

Sara frowned. "My first attempt?"

"You in a bikini. That stopped me from thinking about death for at least three, four seconds."

"You do know how to flatter a girl."

"I've got something," said Greg. "Look."

Sara peered at the window where Greg was pointing. "It looks like a toeprint," she said.

"Yeah. So unless one of the window washers likes working barefoot, I think we have a winner." Greg was already pulling out his print powder. "Now, if I can just capture this before the wind picks up again . . ."

He worked quickly, Sara shielding his body as much as she could as he dusted the print then lifted it with tape.

"Got it," he said triumphantly.

"You think it's the only one?"

"Let's keep going and see."

They found no more on the windows below, but their persistence was rewarded when they moved laterally, finding another on the window to the right. Greg was working on lifting it when the drapes abruptly opened and a woman in her underwear stared out at him.

"Uh, hi," said Greg. He smiled weakly and waved, then pointed to his CSI vest. "I'm not a, uh, peeping Greg. Las Vegas Crime—"

The woman scowled and pulled the drapes shut.

"Lab," he finished.

"Smooth," said Sara. "I bet she'll be back any minute to write her phone number on the window backward in lipstick."

"Absolutely. Spider-Man's got nothing on me . . . and speaking of which, I think we might be looking for a Spider-Woman. This toeprint's pretty small."

They kept going. The next window over held a cluster of prints, some of them overlapping. Greg lifted them all. "We've hit the end of the trail," he said. "Whoever it was, I think they touched down briefly on the other windows, then stopped here."

The drapes on the window were shut. "Well, we know where our next stop is," said Sara.

Archie Johnson found Nick in the hall just outside the AV lab, trying to coax a granola bar out of the vending machine. "This machine is not my friend," Nick muttered.

"No, but I am," said Archie. "Got something for you. I took a look at that remote you fished out of the pool."

"And?"

"No way it could have been used to control something as complex as a vehicle. It was a short-range radio broadcaster that sent one simple signal."

"An on-off switch. Any idea what it could have been used to trigger?"

Archie shrugged. "Could have been most any-thing. Even a vending machine." He smacked the glass of the machine, and the granola bar dropped.

"Thanks a lot, Fonz," said Nick with a grin.

Archie flipped up the collar of his lab coat as he walked away.

The hotel room with the toeprints on the window was registered to a Mr. Bela Giancarlo, who'd checked out shortly after the bears had been recaptured. Greg and Sara were in luck; the room hadn't been cleaned yet.

Sara unlocked the door with the card key and opened it. "After you," she said to Greg.

"Doesn't look like the bed's been slept in," said Greg.

"Bathroom looks untouched, too. It was only booked for one night, but nobody leaves a hotel room this pristine."

"They didn't. Look." Greg pointed at the carpet. The carpet was indented in four spots in a rectangular pattern. "Doesn't look like they believed in packing light."

Sara was already snapping pictures of the indentations. "So they brought something heavy with them."

"Or took something away." Greg inspected the window. It was divided in two, a square lower section and a narrow upper one. The upper one was designed to open inward, but only a few inches.

"I think this window's been tampered with," said Greg. "See? Scratches around the screws holding the top part in place."

"If you undid these from the inside, you could open the window all the way. It's narrow, but a small person could wiggle through."

"Like our barefoot woman. But going in or going out?"

"Going out gets her on the roof. Going in gets her *off* the roof." Sara shrugged. "Let's process the room and see what we find."

Greg started by undoing the same screws and examining the frame. "Well, well, well," he murmured. "I've got another fiber. And I'm willing to bet my next paycheck that it started its career as a piece of firefighting equipment."

"I've got a fine powder of some kind, over beside the indents." She carefully scraped some into a vial.

The rest of the search turned up nothing—their barefoot phantom had been more careful with her fingers than her toes.

"Security footage should tell us what the guy who rented the room looked like," said Sara as they packed up. "That and the credit card info should be enough to track him down."

"When we do," said Greg, "let's ask him how he feels about heights."

10

"I DON'T KNOW if this is such a good idea," said Ray.

He and Catherine stood outside a hospital room. The staff members who had been exposed to the nerve gas had been taken there for observation; many of them had slipped into unconsciousness and weren't expected to wake up for sixteen hours or more.

"I don't know what else to propose," said Catherine. "Search teams haven't been able to locate them. You thought studying their case files could give us some idea of where they might go—any suggestions?"

"I'm afraid not. All I can tell you is they're in a highly delusional state. There's no telling what they might do in any given situation, how they might react. It's quite possible they're in hiding."

"Then I say we talk to their doctor—he might have some insights. Right now, at least he's awake."

"True," Ray admitted. "And he could slip into a stupor at any time. There is an antidote for BZ; a shot of physostigmine is effective four hours after exposure and would counteract the acetylcholine-inhibiting effects quite rapidly. Unfortunately, Dr. Wincroft has a history of heart arrhythmia, which would preclude any such treatment."

"So he'll just have to ride it out." She shrugged. "I talked to him a few minutes ago, and he seemed lucid to me. I say we give it a shot."

"If you insist."

Ray followed her into the room. Wincroft was sitting up in bed, aimlessly plucking at the front of his hospital gown, and looked over as soon as they entered. "Visitors," he said. "Good. I was getting bored."

Ray stood back and let Catherine direct the interview. "Dr. Wincroft. I was wondering if you'd mind talking to us a little bit about two of your patients."

"Which two?"

"The two who escaped, John Bannister and Theria Kostapolis."

Wincroft nodded. "Of course. I'm sorry, my memory seems a little fuzzy at the moment. What would you like to know?"

"We're trying to figure out where they might go, how they might be thinking. Can you help us out?"

"I'll do my best." Wincroft frowned. "Unusual cases, both of them. Both of them presented with a host of symptoms. I'm having a little trouble concentrating . . . can you be more specific in the information you're looking for?"

Catherine nodded. "All right. Theria Kostapolis—

her file says she suffers from a condition that causes her to believe she's . . .well, dead. Any idea where she might head?"

"I would think that would be obvious. A graveyard."

Catherine glanced at Ray. "I suppose—"

"Ha! I'm just kidding," said Wincroft. "Sense of humor's important in my line of work. Bedside manner, laughter's the best medicine, keep them in stitches, right? Anyway." He frowned. "Theria Kostapolis is Greek. There's been a lot of tragedy in her family, which probably contributed to the syndrome. Cotard's is more common in women than men, and is often triggered by depression. Her history was no doubt a major factor in her depression." He paused. "In fact, it's no doubt influencing her actions now."

"I see. How about John Bannister?"

"Bannister. Very different case. He has, uh . . ."

"Corticobasal degeneration," said Ray. "Dementia with Lewy bodies."

"Dementia, yes. Bannister's dementia . . . very odd case. He actually believes he's a spiral staircase."

Catherine frowned, but Wincroft seemed completely serious. "A staircase?"

"Yes. Going around and around, from floor to floor. He'd invite people to step on him, try to twist his body into the proper formation. We finally had to sedate and restrain him."

Catherine gave her head a quick shake. "I thought he had something called reduplicative paramnesia—the belief that one location had been duplicated or transported somewhere else."

"Oh, yes, that too. Sometimes he was a spiral staircase at Disneyland, sometimes at a water-slide park or on a cruise ship."

"Those are all relatively upbeat places. I thought his delusions were darker, more similar to Ms. Kostapolis—"

"Well, of course they changed once—"

"Excuse me," interjected Ray. "I think I can clear up any confusion. Catherine, do you mind?"

She shot him a questioning look, but said, "No, Ray. Go ahead."

"Thank you. Dr. Wincroft, you mentioned Theria Kostapolis's history. Very tragic, don't you think?"

"Yes, very." Wincroft's face clouded over. "All that death."

"What do you think affected her the most?"

"It's hard to say—there was so much to deal with for such a young woman. But I'd have to put my money on Troy."

"The city," said Ray.

"Yes. It must have come as a terrible blow when it fell."

"I imagine so. It was hardly the only Greek tragedy, though."

"No, of course not. That business with Medusa, the Cyclops attacking Philadelphia, the Minotaur eating that presidential candidate . . . truly awful, all of it."

Wincroft seemed close to tears. Catherine opened her mouth, then shut it again.

"I understand that Bugs Bunny was also involved in the patients' escape," said Ray.

"Oh, yes. I should never have allowed them to correspond with him, let alone send away for that

Acme Rocket Pack. I'm just glad it didn't burn the whole place down when they flew away."

"Yeah, that's a real stroke of luck," said Catherine. "I think that's all we need for now, Doctor. Thank you for your time—you should probably get some rest now."

"As if I could sleep with all these dragonflies in here. Shoo! Go away!" He batted away an invisible bug in front of his eyes.

Out in the corridor, Catherine turned to Ray and said, "Okay, I've seen a lot of bizarre things in this job, but that was weird on an entirely different scale."

"It's called confabulation. The subject may appear lucid, even cooperative, but will try to justify the most outrageous statements. He isn't trying to lie to us—his mind is just working in a very different way. Any possibility suggested by our conversation will seem entirely credible, and he'll use whatever knowledge he possesses to rationalize and explain away the situation. If I went in there and set the bed on fire, he might thank me for putting on such an instructive display for his Cub Scout troop."

She sighed. "So anything he tells us will be worthless. Got it."

"It won't last forever. Concrete illusions—like the dragonflies he was seeing—tend to get smaller as the drug's influence lessens. Seeing insects is better than seeing snakes."

"Or wabbits," said Catherine.

Bannister knows that entering the palace is a mistake.

It's topped with minarets, the encircling high white walls spiked with rusting iron. Carrion birds perch between, calling noisily and occasionally flapping their large, ragged wings. Giant blind eunuchs with battle axes stand guard at the entrance, turning their empty gaze on every visitor who passes between them.

Inside, the thick Persian carpet underfoot is woven with an intricate design of goat-headed demons and flames, and it begins to writhe if Bannister's gaze lingers on it too long. But the air is cool and inviting, and Theria seems drawn to the place.

The rugs end where the dunes begin. They seem to go on forever, to fade into the distance beneath a merciless sun. Mirages dance on the horizon, flickering images promising wealth, comfort, food, drink.

It's a trap.

Bannister supposes they've been lucky so far. They're in hell, after all, and no one can travel forever in such a place before being made to suffer. It's what the place was designed for.

The cool air on his face is no more real than anything else. Bannister can feel the heat inside him, raging like a fever, and he knows that to set foot on that sand is never to return. They will trudge endlessly, salvation always mocking them just a few steps ahead. If they slow or stop, sandstorms will drive them onward, scouring the flesh from their bodies.

He grabs Theria's shoulder with his unbound arm. "No," he says.

"Let me go."

"You won't find any rest there. It's an illusion—"

"It's what I deserve."

"No." He pulls her around to face him, while his demonic limb begins to twitch, thumping elbow to ribs. "That's not true."

"I'm rotting inside. Let the sand cover my bones."

"You think it's that easy? That obvious? It'll never work, Theria. Look." He turns her roughly, points into the distance. "See? Jackals."

"I see them."

"They'll dig you up, do horrible things to you. I know, I've seen places like this. Traps, everywhere." He glances around, his nerves on fire. "IEDs. Snipers. Ambushes. You wouldn't think so much death could hide in so much nothing, but you'd be wrong. I was."

And now something flickers in the depths of her eyes. Recognition of his pain. It's one of the things that drew Bannister to her, that even in the midst of her own torment, she can recognize the suffering in him. Pain makes people selfish; that was a hard truth Bannister learned long ago.

But not Theria. She hasn't run from their prison out of self-interest—she's done it because Bannister asked her to. She's done it because Bannister needs to finish this one last mission, and she will not deny him. Bannister loves her for that, even though she's no longer capable of returning that emotion. He knows that, and knows it doesn't matter.

The demon coalesces out of a whirlwind of sand right beside them. Its skin glows like red-hot metal, and ram's horns curl from its forehead. It's wearing a tuxedo.

"Is there a problem here?" it asks pleasantly.

"No," says Bannister.

"Ma'am?"

Theria doesn't answer. The demon reaches for Bannister.

Bannister's training and reflexes take over. He hits the demon with his free hand, very hard, where the solar plexus would be in a human being. The demon grunts in pain and surprise, but before he can react, Bannister has stepped forward and slammed his elbow into the creature's snout. Thick ichor splatters from its nostrils. It falls to the thick carpet with a thump.

And then Bannister is running, dragging Theria along with him, his possessed arm flapping wildly with excitement. He hopes they can make it out in one piece.

Ray looked up from the file he was reading when Catherine knocked on the frame of his door. "Ray, one of our escapees just turned up."

Ray put down the file and got to his feet. "Which one?"

"John Bannister. Radio car picked him up on the Strip."

Ray grabbed his jacket and slipped it on as they walked. "What was he doing?"

"Just sitting at a bus stop, watching the crowds go by. Wouldn't have attracted any attention if he didn't have blood on his shirt."

"And Theria Kostapolis?"

"Still missing."

John Bannister, shackled and dressed in an orange jumpsuit, didn't look up when Ray entered. His gaze remained on the center of the table he was handcuffed to, though there didn't seem to be anything in particular to stare at. Ray wondered what it was Bannister saw.

Ray sat down on the other side of the table. "Mr. Bannister," he said. "My name is Ray Langston. I work for the Las Vegas Crime Lab, but I'm also a doctor. I was wondering if you'd be willing to speak with me."

No reply.

"Is it all right if I call you John?"

Nothing.

"John, I know you've been through a lot. I know about your medical condition and about the gas you've been exposed to. But you're safe now; no one's going to hurt you here."

Bannister's eyes flickered to the side, a quick evaluating glance, then back.

"I don't know what you're seeing right now," Ray continued, "or what you've experienced in the last twenty-four hours. But I'd like to. And in return, I hope I can make some of those visions go away. I can't promise to banish all of them, but I'll do my best to help you. I'll be your anchor to reality, if you'll let me."

Bannister swiveled his head slowly to look at Ray. Stared at him for a long moment. "So that's how you're going to play it. I mean, I knew he'd go back on his word—I'm not stupid—but I wondered what kind of approach would be used. *Admitting* that he lied is too honest, of course. Not in his nature."

"Who are you talking about, John?"

"Your boss. I'm a little unclear on exactly what to call him—why don't you pick one of his titles and we'll go with that?"

Ray frowned. "I'm afraid I'm at something of a loss, John. Can you humor me and pick one for me?"

Bannister sighed. "Sure. How about Lucifer? That's a classic."

"Lucifer. All right. Well, I don't work for Lucifer, John. I work for the Las Vegas Crime Lab."

"A crime doctor."

"If you like. I examine crime scenes instead of patients, but for the same reason: to get to the truth."

"Truth? There's no truth in hell. I was told we'd be left alone, and here I am in a cage."

"You're not in hell, John. You're in a police station. You escaped from a medical facility where you were being treated for CBDS, along with another patient. That's the truth—anything else you're experiencing is a hallucination."

"Except you, of course." There was the slightest hint of amusement in his voice.

Ray smiled. "I see the problem. But acknowledging that you might be hallucinating is the first step toward reality." He reached out gently and touched Bannister's left hand with his own. "Tactile illusions aren't usually a symptom with CBDS or BZ. You can feel that, can't you?"

"Yes. But I already know you're real."

"Good. I'll like to—"

"You're a real demon. I'm chained in a real dungeon." He yanked on the handcuffs for emphasis. The fingers on one hand twitched, spasming like a bug having a seizure. "This is really hell. I know why I'm here, too: you want to know where Theria is, so you can capture and torment her. We jumped through all your hoops—I'm sure you found it vastly amusing—and now you're tired of playing the game. But I won't tell you where she is." He met Ray's eyes defiantly. "And *that's* real, too."

Ray considered his next words carefully. Confabulation didn't necessarily mean cooperation; BZ symptoms or dementia could also produce hostility and combativeness.

"All right, John. I understand that you don't trust me. But think back. Don't you remember being a patient? Being treated by doctors?"

"I remember dying." His voice was flat and without inflection, but Ray knew that was simply another of the symptoms that the BZ produced. "They fooled me for a long time, telling me it was a clinic and that I was being treated, but Theria showed me the truth. I was already dead. I died in Iraq, but I brought something with me."

"What did you bring with you, John?"

"A canister of nerve gas. I stole it from a munitions dump. I think it was what killed me—that's why it crossed over with me. It must have leaked." He stared blankly ahead, his eyes wide and unblinking. "I died in my bed, in my sleep. That's where I hid it, under my bed. And then one morning I woke up and everything was different."

"The nerve gas you stole isn't lethal, John. It temporarily affects people's minds, but it doesn't kill."

"I kept the canister with me. Theria said whatever killed me still had power, even here. So I used it on the demons and we escaped."

"Tell me about Theria."

"Theria just wanted to rest. No more demons poking and prodding her, no more pointless tests, no more questions. I knew they'd never leave her alone, so I took her with me."

Ray nodded. "You were just trying to help her."

"Yes."

"Why?"

Bannister turned his head to look at Ray. He studied Ray for a moment but said nothing.

"She thought she was dead. If you both believed that, what was the point?"

"You wouldn't understand."

"Why? Because I'm supposedly a demon?"

"Because it doesn't make sense."

"Try me."

Bannister dropped his gaze back to the table. Ray waited; he could tell the man was mulling it over. At last, Bannister spoke. "It's not possible to lose everything. No matter how much gets taken away from you, you still have something left. That's the cruel part.

"Dying wasn't what I expected. It happened by inches. That day I woke up and everything was different—well, it took me a long time to *realize* that. Most things still seemed the same, only . . . flatter. Grayer. That's because none of them were real anymore, and I hadn't figured that out yet. But bit by bit, I started to see what they really were. Ugly, decaying, false. It wasn't like I had died, more like the whole world had died and the corpse was beginning to rot."

"Did that include other people around you?"

"There weren't any. Just empty husks. Pretending to be alive. But I didn't figure that out until I met Theria."

"What did she tell you?"

"That she knew she was dead. That she knew all of us were. And suddenly, everything made sense." Bannister paused. "The ones who kept us locked up didn't like that. The dead aren't supposed to know what they are; that's part of the horror. Once you know, there's nothing else they can do to you, nothing else they can take away. That's what Theria told me—but she was wrong."

"Because they took *her* away."

"Yes. And that's when I decided I had one last thing to do. Not for myself, but for Theria. And that's just what I did."

"What did you do, John?"

"I kept her safe."

Ray chose his next words carefully. "There was blood on your shirt when you were picked up, John."

"You want me to admit to something, is that it? Okay. I did it."

Ray felt something cold in the pit of his stomach. "I need more than that, John."

"The blood. It's not mine. I fought someone—some*thing.* One of the demons. I suppose he wants his payback, right? Go ahead, bring him in. I don't care."

"Where did this happen, John?"

"Some kind of Arabian desert wasteland—what does it matter?"

A casino with a Middle Eastern theme, perhaps? He'd have to check with any that might fit the description. "Was Theria hurt in the fight?"

This time there was no reply, no matter how long Ray waited. John Bannister, it seemed, had nothing else to say.

But the evidence did.

11

SARA SIDLE KNEW THAT not all cases were solved in the lab. The certainty of physical evidence was one of the factors that had attracted her to forensics work, but she was self-aware enough to recognize that this was personal bias; no matter how messy or imprecise, cases were ultimately about people and their choices. She tried to remind herself of that from time to time, when the temptation simply to concentrate on the science and ignore the human factor crept in.

Jim Brass helped her do that. You could always count on Brass to provide a pithy viewpoint on humanity, one that usually made Sara grin.

But not always—sometimes he was the bearer of bad tidings. "Sorry," Brass said. He reached across his desk and handed her the report. "Credit card was a fake. Hotels have been having problems with a ring cranking out phony plastic here in town."

She took the report and studied it with a frown. "Thanks, I guess."

She started to rise from her seat, but Brass waved her back down. "Hang on there, Speedy Gonzales. I might have something for you anyway."

She settled back down. "Oh? Like what?"

"Like I might have an unofficial lead to where said plastic was coming from."

She cocked an eyebrow. "Unofficial?"

"Well . . . more like a hunch. Nobody's been able to pin down a source for this particular outbreak of credit-card-itis, but a friend of mine in Jersey told me something the last time we talked. The boys in Brighton Beach have apparently been pushing into this market pretty hard lately."

"Brighton Beach? You're talking about the Russian mob?"

"The so-called Red Mafiya, yeah. That's why I called you in here to talk instead of just dropping this on your desk."

"Oh? Worried I might end up in a shallow grave with a hammer and sickle in my back?"

"That's communism, not crime. I just wanted to give you a quick rundown on the players in town so you're prepared for what you might encounter. If you've got a minute, I mean."

"Yeah, sure."

"Okay. First up is Grigori Dyalov—he's the big cheese, Der Kommissar, the local Stalin. Reports directly to Little Odessa. He's into prostitution, money laundering, bootleg DVDs, anything that'll turn a profit. Rumor has it he's ex-KGB, but that's not exactly rare with these guys. He's been around awhile, dozen years or so. Real hard case."

"Ever been busted?"

"Not in Nevada. He keeps enough layers between himself and his boys that nothing sticks to him. His number one guy is Boris Svenko, a Chechen with a nasty reputation. You get anywhere near him, be careful. He's got about as much respect for a badge as a Kalashnikov does for a bull's-eye."

"Got it. Anyone else?"

Brass pushed a sheet of paper at her. "Here. I made a list, but it reads like the cast of *War and Peace*. I can't pronounce half the names, so I won't try. You'll do better with a hard copy for reference than trying to memorize it all."

She picked up the list and scanned it. "Thanks."

"No problem. You got any questions, let me know."

Greg walked into the DNA lab and found Wendy Simms talking to Henry Andrews, the tox specialist.

"So what you're saying," said Wendy, "is that, essentially, *everything* is poisonous."

Henry, a somewhat meek-looking man in his twenties, said, "No. What I'm saying is that, potentially, almost any kind of *food* could be poisonous."

"Well, sure—botulism."

"I don't mean food that's spoiled or been laced with something. I just mean something that you were planning on eating. Meat, vegetables, whatever."

"So my honey-garlic chicken wings—"

Henry nodded rapidly. "Mountain laurel. Chickens that eat it don't die, but their meat becomes poisonous. Bees that collect nectar from its flowers—or from azaleas, oleander, or rhododendrons, for that matter—produce poisonous honey."

"An order of French fries?"

"Unripened potato sprouts contain *Solarum tuberoscum*. Related to deadly nightshade."

"A nice salad?"

Henry shook his head. "Don't get me started on greens. Monkshood, fool's parsley, hemlock . . ."

"Uh . . . French onion soup?"

"That's the stuff with the croutons on top, right? Well, right off the bat, you've got potential contamination of the bread from ergot or corn cockle. And do you have any idea how many lethal plants are mistaken for onions? Meadow saffron, black snake root—and if the cows that produced the milk the cheese was made from were grazing anywhere near white sanicle, forget it."

Wendy sighed. "Great. You know what, I'll just give up eating as a bad habit."

"There's always pie," said Greg.

"Pie?" said Henry. "Are you *insane*?" He shook his head as he walked away, muttering under his breath about elderberries.

"Ohhh-kay," said Greg. "Sorry to interrupt what seemed like a fascinating discussion, but I was wondering—"

"About your DNA results, right?" said Wendy. "From that security guard uniform?"

"Yeah. I already know the blood is from a pig, not a person, so don't worry about that. I'm more interested in the epithelials."

Wendy sorted through a pile of papers in front of

her on the counter and pulled out a sheet. "Yeah, I've got it right here. Already ran it through CODIS and didn't get any hits, but you might find it useful just the same." She handed him the sheet.

Greg's eyebrows went up as he read. "Huh. Our guard was disguised in more ways than one."

"Yes, she was," said Wendy.

Nick, Sara, and Greg sat in the break room and discussed the case over lunch.

"Okay," said Nick. "Here's what I've got so far. On the bear front, I went out to the ranch where they live and talked to the woman who runs the place, the handler in charge of the bear that supposedly attacked, and the owner of the ranch. I also brought in the vet who looks after the animals." He shook his head. "Somebody's lying to me. The vet seems clueless about bears in general, the bear that attacked may have been switched with another one—they claim it was an accident, but I'm not convinced—and all of the physical evidence of the attack was removed from the animal in question and destroyed."

"How about the dirigible?" asked Sara.

Nick took a swallow of his milkshake before answering. "Going to see Hodges after lunch for results from the mass spec. Archie says the remote we found in the pool couldn't have been used to control it—too unsophisticated. He thinks it was just a simple activation trigger."

"Like maybe setting off a firebomb?" suggested Greg.

"But why have that be a separate remote?" asked Sara.

"Yeah, it's messed up," said Nick. "How about you guys?"

"We found toeprints on the outside of windows within swinging range of a fire hose dangled from the roof," said Greg. "Pretty small prints—could be a woman. They led us to a hotel room, where I pulled another fire-hose fiber off the window frame."

Sara nodded. "We've also got some unidentified white powder from the room and evidence that something heavy rested on the carpet. Wendy's still running the DNA from the bandages we found in the penthouse."

"But we do have results from the bloody clothing," said Greg. "The blood might not have been real—well, not real human, anyway—but the epithelials from the uniform were. Our mysterious missing rent-a-cop is also a she."

"Huh," said Sara. "So we've got two unidentified women, and a plus-size guy on wheels wrapped to go."

Nick put down his burger and leaned back in his chair. "We've also got a phony clown in the air, a staged bear attack in an elevator, and a barefoot acrobat swinging from the top of a twenty-story building. Is anybody else seeing a pattern here?"

"Sounds like the circus is in town," said Sara.

"This is Vegas," said Greg. "The circus is *always* in town. The real question is, which one?"

Nick frowned. "Well, I've been running into an awful lot of Russian names so far—the people who run the ranch have family connections to the Moscow State Circus."

Sara glanced at him. "Really? The hotel room was

booked with a fake credit card, and Brass just told me the Russian mob in Vegas is probably involved in cranking out phony plastic."

"Russian circus, Russian crooks, Russian bears," said Greg. "There go all my Yogi and Boo-Boo jokes."

"There's a Russian circus performing at the Caribbean," said Nick. "I think I'll go have a little talk with them."

"Let us know what you find out," said Sara.

"Will do."

12

CATHERINE STUDIED THE CLOTHING and other items laid out before her on the light table. They were everything John Bannister was wearing or carrying when he was picked up.

She catalogued each mentally. *One short-sleeved shirt, bloodstained. One pair of blue jeans. One pair of socks, white. One pair of sneakers, white. One pair of boxers. One length of white cloth, tied in a loop. One wallet. Seventeen dollars and seventy-three cents in cash.*

"Guess hell doesn't have much of an economy," she murmured. She clipped a tiny amount of bloodstained cloth from the shirt.

She examined the loop of cloth next. Hospital linen, most likely from the ripped sheet she'd found in one of the rooms. She pulled out the evidence bag and compared the two pieces side-by-side; they matched.

She opened the wallet and looked through it. Driver's license, VA card, a few credit cards. An inkjet-printed picture, folded in four, of a smiling John Bannister in full combat gear posing with his unit beside a dusty armored vehicle. Nothing that gave any clue to where he and Theria Kostapolis had gone, what they'd done, or where she was now.

She examined the shoes next. They were cheap but almost new, with virtually no wear on them. The underside of one shoe had a bit of shiny material stuck in the tread. She pulled it out with a pair of tweezers and studied it: gold foil. She held it up to her nose and sniffed.

Chocolate.

She turned her head as Ray Langston walked in. "I just finished talking to John Bannister. He's still convinced this is some version of the underworld, making the officers who picked him up—and, by extension, you and me—demons. He wouldn't talk about the whereabouts of Theria, but I did get him to discuss the situation in more general terms."

Catherine nodded. "Demons, huh? Well, I've been called worse. You ask him about the blood on his shirt?"

"I did. Apparently, he was in an altercation of some sort. The only description he gave of the location was someplace vaguely Middle Eastern."

"Plenty of casinos with a desert theme. Any other details?"

"He claims he's being cheated by the devil."

"Really? What did he do, buy a used car from him?"

"He didn't give me any specifics, just implied there was some sort of agreement that was broken. I'm not sure what it means." Ray scanned the items on the light table. "How about you? Find anything revealing?"

"Maybe." She showed him the foil.

"Could be a candy wrapper from just about anywhere."

"I don't think so. Most commercial chocolate bars use foil with a backing of thin waxed paper, but this is just foil. The Orpheus Casino gives out chocolate coins wrapped in gold foil; you see the wrappers out front all the time."

"It's a start."

The Orpheus Casino featured an Arthurian theme, lots of stone parapets, suits of medieval armor, and serving wenches in revealing bodices. The fountain out front had a marble statue of the Lady of the Lake, holding aloft an Excalibur that seemed to be made of running water; it was a clever illusion, utilizing a transparent sword blade and carefully crafted fluid dynamics.

When Catherine and Ray entered, a woman dressed in Renaissance Fair finery tried to hand them each a gold coin. Catherine accepted hers, then grabbed Ray's when he said, "No thanks."

"I thought we weren't supposed to accept gifts," he said.

"Turn down chocolate? Yeah, right." Catherine glanced around. "I'm not sure why Bannister would go into a casino in the first place. From what he said to you, he was looking for a place for Theria to rest. Casinos are designed to inspire everything but."

"Maybe it wasn't his idea. Let's take a walk."

They strolled through the casino, keeping their eyes open.

"If they were here, I wonder what they saw," said Catherine. "I mean, Vegas is surreal at the best of times. I can't imagine what it would be like while being surrounded by constant three-dimensional hallucinations."

"Well, the type of dementia Bannister has produces hallucinatory images that aren't necessarily disturbing, and the BZ tends to generate imagery that's mundane as opposed to bizarre."

"How does that translate into being trapped in hell?"

"The problem is the *folie a deux*. Theria's condition makes her see the world through a much darker lens, and Bannister's psychosis has synchronized itself with it. The BZ is exaggerating this effect, amplifying what's already a powerful feedback loop."

"That almost sounds like telepathy."

Ray smiled and shook his head. "No. They've just become extremely attuned to each other's emotional cues, both subconscious and overt—body language, word choice, intonation. They're sharing a singular worldview, not a single mind."

"Too bad that view is terrible. Otherwise, it's almost romantic."

"It's obvious John Bannister cares deeply about this woman. The problem lies in his conviction that she's already dead; it means that ultimately, by trying to help her, he's going to do her harm."

"We always hurt the ones we love, Professor. That one holds true no matter where you are."

When a complete circuit of the place produced no

results, Catherine headed for the security offices to review surveillance footage, while Ray decided to go back and talk further with Bannister. "I'd like to try something," he told Catherine. "It may not work, but if it does, Bannister might be more forthcoming."

"Good luck." She took another glance around the casino. "Even if they were here, footage alone won't tell us what they experienced. In this case, the camera might not lie, but it won't be giving us the whole picture, either."

"We'll figure it out. The first step toward an accurate diagnosis is to gather as much information as possible, even if it doesn't make immediate sense."

"Same with an investigation: collect first, then analyze. But there's generally less time pressure when your vic is already approaching room temperature." She saw the look on his face and shrugged. "Sorry. Warped sense of humor is an occupational hazard in our line of work. It's easier to make jokes around a corpse—you don't have to worry about offending them. But I'm hoping Theria Kostapolis is still alive."

"If she is, I wouldn't tell her. It might hurt her feelings."

Catherine blinked.

Ray smiled. "You think CSIs are the only people with a bleak sense of humor? Try attending a pathology conference. I guarantee it's the only place you'll hear a knock-knock joke with a punch line involving necrophilia."

She smiled. "I'll see you later, Ray."

"I'll keep you posted."

*   *   *

Ray Langston found the "demon" Bannister had fought by checking police reports of disturbances at hotels within the last twelve hours. The doorman at the Sand Dollar Hotel described the man who attacked him as having one arm bound in a sling, with a woman who matched Theria Kostapolis's description accompanying him. Ray drove over to the Sand Dollar to talk to the victim.

Teddy Galloway was a big man, broad of shoulder and wide of gut, but the two black eyes and bandaged nose he now sported made him look like an oversize panda that had been mugged. He cradled a cup of tea in both large hands, seated on a bench outside the casino, and nodded glumly. "Yeah, he really caught me out. Looked like he was havin' some kind of squabble with his lady, and I guess that's between them and all, but I don't need that kind of stuff going on inside my crease."

"I'm sorry," said Ray. "Your what?"

"My crease. It's a hockey term, for that area around the goal. That's how I think of my job, like a goalie—gotta stay sharp, keep my eyes open for anythin' trying to get through that don't belong here. These two, they were already inside, but just because something's behind the net doesn't mean you ignore it, right?"

"I suppose not."

Galloway took a delicate sip of his tea, wincing a little at the temperature. "Anyway, I was keepin' an eye on them because they seemed a little off, but I sure wasn't expecting what happened. I mean, the guy was in shape and all, but he was walking with a limp and had his one arm in a sling. Last thing I thought was he'd get physical."

"What exactly happened?"

Galloway shrugged with one shoulder. "The guy was gettin' more and more upset, arguing with the lady. She seemed—that was the weird part, I guess. She just seemed really . . . I don't know. Down in the dumps, I guess, but that don't really cover it. Like her best friend just died or something. And when the guy grabbed her, I thought I'd step in, defuse the situation—and then *pow*!" He shook his head ruefully. "Guess I shoulda remembered goalies wear face masks, right?"

"And then they ran off?"

"Yeah. I didn't see which way—all I was seein' was stars."

"Thanks for your help."

They run.

They run through the zombie crowds, back under the harsh glare of the burning sun. They run between rows of black hearses driven by vampires, while crows with glowing yellow eyes chase them and scream obscenities in the voices of dead relatives.

They stop at last in an alley, a dark canyon of featureless gray concrete that stinks of garbage and urine. They crouch behind a Dumpster and try to ignore the rats that giggle like insane children.

"John," says Theria. "This can't go on."

"It won't. It'll be over soon, I promise."

"Listen to me, John." Talking causes her pain; he can see it in her face. "They won't let us go. We can't escape."

"Yes, we can. We got out of that place we were locked up in, didn't we? They're not all-powerful."

"But there's nowhere to go. We're in hell, remember? Every place will be just as bad as the last."

"Not every place."

John knows that even in hell, there's a hierarchy, and the being perched at the top of the heap won't be suffering at all. In fact, he'll probably be enjoying himself.

"We need to talk to the one running this place," he says.

He has never heard Theria laugh, but she manages the ghost of a smile now. "That would be Mephistopheles, John. I don't think he'll be interested in helping us."

"Maybe he'll cut us a deal. He's the Devil, isn't he? Isn't that what he does?"

"What could we possibly offer him? We have—we are—nothing."

"That's not true. We have our freedom, our ability to think. We know where we are, what's happening. None of the lost souls around us do. We can make that work for us."

"How?"

"We find something the Devil has, and we take it away from him. Then we bargain."

She reaches up to touch his face. Her hand should be cold, but it's feverishly warm. "You fight for me," she says. "Even here, where all hope is gone. I wish I had known you, before."

They huddle for a while, while John tries to think of a plan. He comes up with one after a while, a crude, un-subtle thing, but at least it gives them a direction, a reason to keep moving.

They leave the alley and go in search of Satan's palace.

John knows he'll recognize it when he sees it. It will embody more than just decadence or cruelty; it will radiate authority, age, permanence. Amid the bright crimson bloodiness and razored silver, it will seem as ancient and implacable as a mountain.

As soon as he sees the castle, he knows.

Weathered gray tombstones mortared together into a towering wall. An immense iron portcullis, guarded by metal dragons. A constant flickering thunderstorm looming overhead, replacing the glare of the sun with the flash of thunderbolts.

"This is it," he whispers to Theria. "Can't you feel it? Whoever runs this place does it from here."

She nods, but does not speak. Her previous words have all but exhausted her.

He leads Theria across the wooden drawbridge, his stiffened leg thumping with every step. His bound arm is trembling like a branch in a high wind. The dragons— one gold, one bronze—watch them with eyes like burning emeralds, but let them pass.

The interior is a dungeon, a vast, sprawling torture chamber lined with medieval devices. Screaming prisoners are pinioned to upright wheels that spin endlessly. Row after row of victims are lined up in front of iron-bound, head-high chests; all of them are chained like galley slaves to oars, shackled by the wrist to the long, heavy wooden lever projecting from the side of each chest. The slaves pull down on their levers, grunting with effort, hypnotized by the spinning sigils in front of their eyes. Hunchbacked women stomp by at regular intervals, carrying trays of steaming acid that they pour down the galley slaves' throats.

Bannister knows the place must be heavily guarded,

but he can't spot them until he looks up. Red eyes gleam from ledges high up on the walls; gargoyles track their every movement, stone claws flexing with barely restrained violence, ready to swoop down on batlike wings and tear Theria and him apart.

Bannister keeps looking. Most rulers are arrogant or proud, and the one who sits on the throne of hell must surely be both. Like all kings, he will be wealthy—and some of that treasure will be on display, not only to glorify the ego of its owner but to make the rest of hell that much worse by contrast.

And then he sees it.

It's on an elevated platform that turns slowly under bright spotlights. Only a velvet rope around the platform itself stands between it and him.

It's a car.

But like no car Bannister has ever seen. Its long, aerodynamic body looks like a cross between a Maserati and a rocket ship. It has razor-sharp fins on the back and a tangle of pipes jutting from the sides of the exposed engine like chrome intestines. The paint job is a black so deep that looking at it for too long gives Bannister vertigo; there are stars and galaxies and nebulae whirling around in there, buried beneath the glossy skin of the chassis.

The wheels look like snakeskin. The interior's a plush, obscene pink that almost throbs. It's a wet dream mated with a nightmare, a phallic monstrosity radiating lust and death; just looking at it makes Bannister think of smashing into a girl's boarding school at a hundred and fifty miles an hour.

And then he notices something else.

*   *   *

Catherine leaned forward and peered at the monitor. "Hold it," she told the security guard sitting beside her. "Right there. I think that's them."

Catherine had been looking at surveillance footage in the security center of the Orpheus for almost an hour before she spotted John Bannister and Theria Kostapolis. The pair were standing near the hotel's south entrance, staring at a display.

The guard, a black woman named Amanda with a close-cropped afro, froze the image. "They seem real interested in the Compensator," she said.

"The what?"

Amanda grinned. "Sorry. That's what we call it around here. It's some kind of high-powered prop for a new movie coming out. The hotel's got a big promotion going, going to give it away as a prize. We have to wipe the teenage-boy drool off it every night."

"Not the kind of thing I'd expect them to be interested in," Catherine murmured. "Wait. Did you see that?"

Amanda swore. "I did. I can't believe nobody caught that." She backed up the image and watched it again. "Aw, damn. Things are about to get ugly around here . . ."

"He just stole the keys," said Catherine. She turned to the guard with a look of disbelief on her face. "Why are the keys even in it?"

"They're not. I mean, they're just a prop with a shiny keychain from the Orpheus attached. But nobody should be able to just yank 'em out and walk away, not on my watch."

But that's exactly what Bannister had done.

*   *   *

The only reason he'd gotten away with it, Bannister knew, was that the king of hell thought no one would ever dare.

But he had. And now the small piece of metal with its attached bauble is deep in his pocket, while he walks back to Theria and tries to ignore the gargoyles he knows must be staring at him.

"What now?" she asks on his return. "We steal Satan's chariot? Go joyriding?"

"Now we find a place to hide the keys. And then—then we open negotiations."

"You're insane," she murmurs, but there's something like fondness in her voice. "And what are we negotiating for? Do you honestly think he'll let us go?"

"No. But I might be able to persuade him to leave us alone."

Bannister doesn't believe that, any more than he believes he can trust a deal made with the prince of lies. But he thinks there's a chance, a very small chance, that he can sacrifice himself and give Theria the peace she craves.

No matter what it costs him.

Catherine watched Bannister and Theria leave. "Why would they take the keys?" she said aloud.

Amanda shrugged. "A souvenir? Or maybe he was planning on coming back later and taking it for a spin."

Catherine thought about that. "You know, you just might be right. I need to look at some more footage."

Bannister and Theria returned less than an hour later, though they didn't behave the way Catherine expected. They gave the car a wide berth, spending some time wandering around the casino before finally going next door to the large restaurant attached to the complex. It featured medieval-themed entertainment, including jousts and a royal banquet.

Where, apparently, they requested an audience with the king.

Pawn shops in hell, Bannister thinks, prove that no matter how far you've fallen, the pit is deeper still.

He and Theria move slowly down an aisle packed to the rafters on either side with every sort of object: musical instruments, toys, furniture, art. There are more personal possessions, too: hands, legs, hearts, eyes. Bannister wonders what sort of twisted economy hell supports, what the denizens who traded away these things got in return—a few minutes' respite from agony? A cool drink of water? Or perhaps these items belonged to people still living, some sort of marker exchanged for success or riches in the material world, a little piece of someone's soul instead of a contract signed in blood.

It doesn't matter. What matters is getting the owner to make a deal with them.

The man at the front of the shop is difficult to look at. His head is an enormous spider, with thick, hairy legs hanging down on either side like dreadlocks. His eight eyes swivel to focus on them as they walk up.

"Can I help you?" he says.

Bannister places an item on the counter. It's an ornately carved antique music box, with a headless ballerina that twitches spastically when you turn the handle. Bannister stole it from a souvenir shop full of useless junk, all of it designed to remind the patrons where they were trapped: T-shirts with sayings like "Go to . . . here," and "What did I do to deserve this—oh, right."

"I'd like to pawn this," Bannister says.

The spider clerk picks the box up and examines it. His mandibles twitch in a very unimpressed way. "I don't know. Don't really handle much like this."

"Make me an offer."

"Well . . . I guess I could give you five bucks for it."

"Done."

Bannister doesn't know why hell even needs money—though he supposes that it might have something to do with it being the root of all evil—and doesn't care. It isn't the money that's important.

It's what he's hidden in the base of the music box.

"Your Highness?" said Catherine.

The man in the makeup chair turned around. "Hmmm? Not backstage, darling. Once I take off the crown, I rejoin the proletariat."

The king bore no resemblance to the Vegas performer usually associated with the name; this monarch was closer in appearance to Henry VIII, complete with ermine-lined robe, bushy beard, and large belly. His full title was King Oswald V, liege of Orpheus.

Catherine glanced around. Backstage at a theme restaurant looked pretty much like backstage anywhere—plenty of props, costumes on rolling racks, lots of little tables crowded with makeup and lit by a circle of bulbs around the mirror. She was used to more half-naked women and fewer men in tights, but that was the only major difference. That, and the smell of horse manure.

"I'm Catherine Willows, Las Vegas Crime Lab," she said. "I need to talk to you about one of your subjects."

"Humor me and call them fans. I haven't had subjects since I flunked out of community college."

"All right—two of your fans, then. A man and a woman."

"You'll have to narrow it down a bit. I get a lot of couples, especially on the weekend. All the men want to be knighted. Well, so do the women, but they mean something else."

"I think these two had something different in mind." Catherine showed the actor a still she'd pulled off the security feed.

The ersatz king's eyebrows went up. "Oh, *those* two. I should have known. At first, I thought they were Ren Fair types—you know, the ones who take this whole shtick *way* too seriously? Stay in character no matter what, usually ramble on for far too long in what they think is Shakespearian dialect? Sometimes I just want to pull out my cell phone halfway through and call nine-one-one—hello, I'd like to report a tragedy, this person's life is a *train wreck*—but those people usually dress like an explosion in a pirate's closet. These two at least *looked* fairly normal—though the guy with his arm in a sling was kind of twitchy. After listening to him for a minute, I decided they were both just high."

"What did they say?"

"Let's see." The king began to peel off his beard as he thought. "He wasn't as toadying as many people are. In fact, he didn't so much ask me for a boon as suggest a trade."

Catherine nodded. "I think I can guess what he offered."

"Really? Then you're doing better than I did,

sweetheart." He frowned and rubbed his now bare chin. "He claimed to have something I wanted—'a key of great value' is how he put it. When I asked to see this key, he said he wasn't stupid enough to have it on him—he'd hidden it somewhere I'd never find it, but he'd tell me where it was if I gave him what he wanted. I tried not to show how disappointed I was."

"What did he ask for in return?"

"Peace."

"That's it? Peace?"

The king sighed. "If only it were that easy . . . you'd be surprised how many people ask for that. I used to say that *my* kingdom hadn't declared war on anyone recently, but that's just not enough for some people. So I sent them on a quest."

"You're kidding."

"No, no, quests are very popular. I just make them up on the spot. Some of my friends say I should have little maps printed up with clues and whatnot, but who am I, Long John Silver? Kings assign quests, not scavenger hunts. Besides, I enjoy the creative aspect. I told this one couple to—"

"Where did you send them?"

"I didn't send them *anywhere*, exactly. The point of a quest is to accomplish something, not just go somewhere. Let me try to remember what I told them . . ." He frowned at himself in the mirror as he picked up a cloth and began to clean the makeup off his face. "Ah, that's it. I said that peace is a precious commodity, but I would grant it if he could prove his heart was true, yadda yadda yadda."

Catherine shook her head. "I'm afraid I'm going to need more than *yadda yadda yadda*."

"You want details, huh? Let me see, let me see . . . I told him he had to do three things—I usually ask for three things, it's so *Grimm's Fairy Tales*—and the first one was to demonstrate his faith. In a completely nondenominational way, of course; the last thing you want to do is offend the clientele. Anyway, I said he had to demonstrate his faith in *her,* which is always a big crowd pleaser."

"Demonstrate how?"

"I always leave that up to them—it's show biz, you don't want to get bogged down in details. Next was, let's see . . ."

"Charity?"

He rolled his eyes. "Please. This is *Vegas*—charity is just a line on your income-tax deductions. No, I told him he had to demonstrate *loyalty.* To her, obviously, but I was willing to go with a sports team or the good old US of A if I thought that was the way the wind was blowing. And loyalty to me and my court is always implied—management gets upset if I don't toss in a corporate plug every now and then. Go ye forth and spend the coin of the realm at our fabulous games of chance!

"And the last one was hope. Same thing, that he had to not only share his hopes with her, he had to *commit* to those hopes. Big whoops from all the ladies in the house on that one."

"Okay. How did he react to these . . . pronouncements?"

The king peered into the mirror and squinted,

then dabbed at the corner of one eye. "He was kind of weird about the whole thing. I told you I thought he was on drugs, right? He seemed okay with the faith bit, and he was definitely onboard for loyalty, but when I mentioned hope, I got a little worried. He sort of tensed up, you know? I thought he might go all French Revolution on me."

"What about the deal he was offering? The key he said he had?"

"Oh, that. You know, for a second, I thought he was coming on to me. But then I saw the look he gave her, and realized that he definitely wasn't talking about his room key. In any case, I told him that upon the successful completion of his tasks he could keep the key, and I'd grant him the peace he was after as well."

"Very generous of you."

"I thought so." The king smiled and settled back on his chair. "After all, what's the point in being royalty if you can't bring a little happiness to the people?"

Faith, Catherine thought. *Where do you go to demonstrate faith when you're trapped in hell?*

Catherine herself put more faith in science than religion; the last religious act she'd performed was to light a candle in a church after her father died in her arms. Her relationship with Sam Braun had been rocky at times, but she still missed him. He'd been larger than life to Catherine even before she discovered she was his daughter, and the void left after his death was just as big.

Faith in Vegas usually boiled down to the belief that the next big win was just around the corner or that the lucky streak was never going to end. Mirages, about as real as the illusions crafted by magicians on the Strip—or the hallucinations that danced through the minds of Theria Kostapolis and John Bannister.

Faith in *her,* King Oswald had said. Where did you go in Vegas to demonstrate your faith in another human being?

She thought about the dozens of wedding chapels on the Strip as a possibility and after a moment rejected the idea. Getting married was the opposite of faith—it was demanding a declaration of love in writing, actual physical evidence as opposed to an intangible belief. Faith was something you could demonstrate through your actions, but saying "I do" in front of an Elvis impersonator didn't qualify.

To demonstrate faith in another person meant taking a risk, it meant entrusting that person with your own fate. How did you do that when you were already convinced both of you were dead and in hell? When you'd already lost everything, what was left to risk?

Each other.

After their audience with the king of hell, Bannister gives the claim ticket from the pawn shop to Theria.

"Here," he says. "You need to have this."

"Why?"

"Because it's power, Theria. Whoever holds this ticket holds the keys to Satan's chariot, and that means something. If worse comes to worse, maybe you can use it as a bargaining chip. I have the feeling that demons are used to making deals, even behind their master's back."

"We've already made our bargain."

"But we might fail, Theria. I might fail. If that happens, you need to have something as insurance."

Again, that pale shadow of a smile. "And if I betray you? Make a deal of my own, sell you down the river?"

Bannister smiles back and presses the ticket into her limp hand. "You won't. I know."

"No, you don't." She closes her hand gently around the ticket and his own fingers. "But you believe you do. You believe in me. *And so the first task is done . . ."*

13

Nick Stokes had always loved the circus. Not because of the animals, which he always felt vaguely sorry for, or the clowns—which he found creepy—but because of the acrobats. What they did seemed almost superhuman, and when his parents refused to let him build a trapeze in the backyard, he settled for spending a summer teaching himself how to juggle and walk on stilts.

The troupe that was performing at the Caribbean Hotel and Casino were an offshoot of the Moscow State Circus, but that was hardly unusual—that was the generic name once used by every traveling circus that toured outside Russia. These performers called themselves the Red Star Circus, and their poster claimed they were "the Royalty of Russian Circus performers."

Although the actual performances took place in the hotel's amphitheater, the circus itself—or at least the larger animals—was housed in tents and trailers in the hotel's parking lot. A tall chain-link fence kept the curious at bay, but Nick's CSI badge got him past the burly security guard without a problem.

Unlike many circuses that had gone the Cirque du Soleil route, the Red Star still featured animal acts. A man in coveralls led a lumbering elephant right past Nick's eyes, and he couldn't keep himself from grinning; even the occasional clown in full makeup walking past didn't seem so bad.

But it wasn't clowns or elephants he'd come to see. It was the acrobats.

The performers themselves were staying in rooms in the hotel, but Nick thought he might get lucky just by wandering around. That's what he told himself, anyway; the truth was, he was enjoying the experience. His work ethic wouldn't let him goof off for long, though. After only a few minutes, he sighed and got directions to the performers' dressing rooms, in the hotel itself.

Nick eventually found himself in a long corridor backstage, looking for a particular door. Once he located it, he knocked, and a voice told him to come in.

The first thing he saw on entering was a woman in a leotard on a chair in the middle of the room. Not sitting, though—she was doing a handstand, one hand on the chair's back and one on the edge of the seat. The chair was at an angle, too, balanced on its back two legs.

"Uh—hi," said Nick.

The woman didn't even look at him. "Yes? If you have something for me, please put it down and go."

"That'll be hard to do, since what I have are questions."

The woman's toes were together and pointed straight at the ceiling. She slowly brought each of them down, in opposite directions, until they formed a straight line parallel to the floor. "Questions about what?"

"Questions about what you were doing last night at around one A.M."

"Last night? It was my night off—the show's dark Sundays. I was in my room, sleeping."

Nick glanced around the room. Costumes on a rack, makeup table, a couple of tumbling mats in one corner. He walked over to the makeup table. "Can anyone verify that?"

She brought her legs together once more, until they were pointed straight up again. "I was alone, if that's what you mean. Why? And who are you, anyway?"

"Nick Stokes, Las Vegas Crime Lab. I'm investigating an incident at the Panhandle." The mirror above the makeup table had a picture stuck in the frame; it was a publicity shot of a group of acrobats, all of them dressed in green and balanced one atop the other to form the outline of a Christmas tree. The one on top with the star on her head was the woman he was talking to.

"I'm Marta Golovina—but I suppose you already knew that." She brought the chair down onto all four legs with a thump, then swiveled her body around so that she was suddenly kneeling on the seat. "And I suppose the hotel could verify I was in my room—don't they have security cameras all over?"

Nick studied her for a moment before replying. Marta Golovina seemed to be in her forties, but her body was as muscular and trim as an Olympic sprinter. Her hair—short, dark, and black—was streaked with gray, but the only wrinkles her face held were around her deep green eyes.

"Yes, they do—which means I shouldn't have any trouble doing just that." He tapped the photo on the mirror. "Can you tell me who this is, please?"

"That's my niece, Alisa. She performs with me, as does her sister."

"I'm going to need to speak with her."

"Why?"

"Because," said Nick, "it appears she's been moonlighting as a nurse."

Alisa Golovina stared coolly at Nick over the interview table, her body language alert but relaxed. She was in her early twenties, her blond hair cut very short and dyed purple on the sides. "I'm not sure why I'm here," she said.

"Because of this." Nick handed her a still from the video feed of the penthouse elevator. It showed a nurse with long black hair behind a wheelchair that held a large man swathed in bandages. "That's a nice wig, but this is clearly you."

"So?"

"You don't deny it?"

"Why should I? Playing dress-up isn't illegal."

"How about your partner here? Why's he all bandaged up?"

"He cut himself shaving."

"Right. And the wheelchair?"

"All that shaving tired him out."

"Sure. Lot of area to cover. What were you doing at Andolph Dell's party in the first place?"

She shrugged. "What reason is there to go to any party? Have some laughs, have some drinks."

"You weren't invited."

"Really? *Someone* let us in. Maybe you should be blaming him."

"Hey, nobody's blaming anyone for anything. I just have a few questions."

"That's good, because I just have a few answers. I'll let you know when I run out."

"Who's the guy in the wheelchair?"

"My boyfriend. Sorry to break your heart, but it would have happened sooner or later."

"What's his name?"

"Bronislav Alexandrei. Or, as he's better known, the Strongman of Minsk."

Nick's eyebrows went up. "He's a strongman? As in circus strongman?"

"He tried being a strongman for Wal-Mart for a while, but it didn't work out."

"So you—a professional acrobat—and your strongman boyfriend crashed a party dressed as a nurse and a skiing accident."

"What can I say? We lead such mundane lives, we need to make our own entertainment."

"Uh-huh. You know, nobody noticed your boyfriend leave."

"I'm not surprised. For a strongman, he's remarkably forgettable."

"Security cameras don't show him, either."

"Maybe they just missed him. He's short."

"Witnesses described him as being quite large."

"It's the bandages. They add a few pounds."

Nick paused. "Miss Golovina, I'm going to have to ask you to take off your shoes."

"Oh? Funny, you don't look Japanese."

"We found a toeprint at a crime scene. I could go to the trouble of getting a warrant, but considering where we found the print—and your profession—I don't think that would be terribly difficult to obtain."

"That won't be necessary. I don't want to make any trouble." She smiled. "Or should I say, I don't want to step on anyone's toes?"

After he'd printed Alisa Golovina's toes, Nick took the prints away to compare against the ones Sara and Greg had found on the hotel windows. Golovina had agreed to wait until he returned, which surprised him; she seemed awfully blasé about the whole thing.

Hodges intercepted him before he reached the print lab. *"Guten abend, mein herr."*

"I'm sorry?"

"Sprechen sie Deutsch? Nein?"

"Hodges, I'm kind of busy. I don't have time for a *Hogan's Heroes* moment."

"Then how about two minutes' worth of *Hindenburg*?"

"You have the mass-spec results from the dirigible wreckage?"

"Jawohl, mein Kommandant." Hodges handed Nick

the sheaf of papers he was holding. "I did a little research on zeppelin fires for comparison and discovered some interesting things. Did you know that some people's analysis of the *Hindenburg* disaster state that the whole thing burned in sixteen seconds? Most people put it at closer to thirty—between thirty-two and thirty-seven—but there's no clear consensus."

"And how does that relate to our crash?"

"Hydrogen—the gas used in the *Hindenburg*—burns quickly. Helium—the gas most often used in lighter-than-air craft today—isn't flammable at all. What I found was traces of both."

Nick studied the papers Hodges had handed him. "Huh. Not a lot of helium, either. But enough to slow the rate of the fire. I have footage from a number of cell-phone cameras that caught the whole thing, and it took the dirigible a good three minutes from the moment it started to burn until it stopped."

"A nice, even-burning fire. Good for marshmallows."

"But bad for clowns. The question is, what does it mean for an acrobat?"

"I can tell you what it meant for the one aboard the *Hindenburg.*"

"There was an acrobat aboard the *Hindenburg*?"

"Yes, a vaudeville performer named Joseph Spah who was filming the landing while onboard. When the fire started, he smashed the window with his camera and jumped out—let's see you do *that* with a BlackBerry. Dropped about twenty feet and only twisted his ankle; both he and the film survived."

"Lucky guy."

"Maybe, maybe not. One of the theories about what caused the accident was a bomb, and Spah was one of the suspects. He made frequent trips during the flight into a freight room near the stern of the ship, ostensibly to feed his dog; he could have used the time to plant an incendiary device."

"Sounds pretty circumstantial to me."

"True. But he was also heard making anti-Nazi jokes during the flight."

"Are there any other kind?"

Hodges considered this. "Good point. And if there are . . . I know *nuhssing. Nuhhhhhhhhsing* . . ."

"Thanks for your help, Schultz."

"Well, Miss Golovina," said Nick. "I just compared your prints with the ones we pulled off several panes of glass. You mind telling me what you were doing eighteen stories above the ground on the wrong side of a hotel window outside the Panhandle?"

"Vodka."

"Vodka?"

"Yes. The bar at the party didn't carry my brand, so I thought I'd just swing by my room and pick up some."

Nick grinned and shook his head. "That's a very entertaining excuse, but you'll forgive me if I don't believe you."

She pretended to pout. "We Russians are very particular about what we drink. Where we drink it and with whom, not quite so much. Besides, the elevator wasn't working."

"You couldn't take the stairs?"

"Where's the fun in that?"

Nick thought about mentioning the fire hose but had a better idea. "How'd you manage it? You always carry a few dozen feet of rope with you when you go to a party?"

She studied him for a second before answering. "Depends on the party."

"Miss Golovina, I'd appreciate some straight answers."

"Then you're asking the wrong person. I'm also a contortionist."

Nick sighed. "I could have you arrested for fraud. Your hotel room was rented with a phony credit card—"

"Did I say *my* hotel room? My mistake. I was trying to *find* my hotel room, but they all look the same from the outside. I might have accidentally wound up in someone else's room—but I didn't take anything, I swear. Not even from the minibar."

"There's always trespassing."

She gave him a mock frown. "Trespassing? Oh, no. My life is over. Take me away to prison, please."

"Not just yet. What were you doing while the big fire show was going on outside?"

"What, the burning balloon man? Unfortunately, we missed it. We were enjoying a little privacy in one of the bedrooms. Quite the show, from what I heard."

"Oh, it was. Only about three minutes long, but there's all kinds of things you can do in three minutes, isn't there?"

"If you're flirting with me, Mr. Stokes, I should warn you that Bronislav is a very jealous man."

Nick met her eyes, and now there was no smile

on his face. "You're very charming, Miss Golovina. But one way or another, I will get to the bottom of this."

"Never say that to a trapeze artist," she said. "It's bad luck."

14

RAY LANGSTON ARRANGED to have John Bannister transferred from a holding cell to a room in Las Vegas General Hospital; he was still restrained, but at least he was in a medical facility. Cortico-basal degeneration was a serious disease, and Ray was worried about Bannister's health. In less than twenty-four hours, he'd been exposed to hypothermia, dehydration, hyperthermia, and nerve gas.

There was a treatment for BZ exposure, but Ray was reluctant to try it. Physostigmine increased the concentration of acetylcholine at synapses, effectively counteracting the anticholinergic effect of the gas, but Bannister's doctors had been treating his CBDS with a cocktail of atypical antipsychotics; adding a cholinesterase inhibitor might temporarily increase his lucidity but worsen other physical symptoms. Bannister had been through enough—Ray didn't want to stress his body any more than he had to.

But Bannister's life wasn't the only one at stake.

Bannister's hand twitched in the padded restraints when Ray entered the hospital room, but otherwise Bannister didn't react to his presence at all.

"Hello, John. I hope you're feeling better. The saline they've been giving you intravenously should have helped with your dehydration."

Bannister's gaze remained fixed on an indeterminate middle distance.

Ray put down the tray he'd carried in. It held a vial of physostigmine, some antiseptic swabs, and a hypodermic. "I'm going to give you a shot, John. This is a drug known as Antilirium; it will temporarily suppress the effects of the nerve gas you were exposed to. I'm afraid I'll have to give it to you as an intramuscular shot instead of through your IV; it's safer if it diffuses into your bloodstream slowly."

Bannister's eyes flickered to Ray for the first time. "Temporarily?"

Ray filled the syringe from the bottle. "Yes. BZ produces symptoms that last up to ninety-six hours; the Antilirium is only effective for about an hour. You'll have to have another shot every sixty minutes until the gas wears off—"

"Why bother?"

"Because, John, you're under the influence of a powerful drug. It's clouding your judgment and ability to make decisions—"

"What decisions would those be? Whether or not to turn my head to the right or the left? I think my days of making decisions are over."

"You might not feel that way in a minute, John."

Ray swabbed one of Bannister's shoulders before

he gave him the shot; Bannister didn't resist or react.

"It'll take a minute or two to have an effect."

"This is a farce."

"How so?"

"You say I'm under the influence of a drug that distorts my view of reality. You give me another drug to restore my view of reality. Tell me, what happens when I don't have any drugs in my system at all?"

"You'll still be suffering from CBDS, John. That's not going to go away. You'll still have dementia, confusion, memory loss, and even hallucinations."

"Right. So like I said, why bother? Reality is just another station on this line, and I missed my stop a long time ago. You don't want to admit this is hell? Fine, I won't argue with you. But what difference does it make *what* label you slap on it? It'll all change anyway." He made a sound that Ray supposed was an attempt at a laugh. "Things keep changing, ever since Theria . . . ever since the last time I saw her. This room, the bed, your face—none of it stays the same from moment to moment."

"Are you sure? Look around, John—you should be experiencing a little more stability by now."

"Stability. Because the snakes have disappeared, and the room isn't on fire anymore? Yes, that's quite the improvement."

"I need to talk to you about Theria, John." Ray pulled a chair over and sat down. "I was hoping you might have a different perspective once the Antilirium took effect."

"Ha. Antilirium. Great name." Bannister shook his head, as if trying to clear it. "I do feel a little different. Less . . . murky."

"I'm glad to hear that."

"Ha!" Bannister barked. "This is . . . I get it, I really do. This is *funny*."

"What is, John?"

"What you gave me. You want me to tell you where Theria is, so you gave me *truth serum*." His smile was terrible. "Truth serum in hell, to find the only true thing in this place. That's what Theria is, and that's why you want her so badly—but you'll never have her. *Never*."

Ray frowned. Despite the injection, Bannister's worldview was still firmly entrenched. Without Theria's delusions reinforcing his own, Bannister would probably eventually regain some semblance of sense—but Ray didn't know how long Theria had, or if it was already too late.

"Then tell me one thing, John. Tell me one thing, and I promise you I won't torment you any longer."

Bannister studied him suspiciously. "What?"

"Is she *intact*, John? Is she still in one piece, or did you think that hiding her in more than one place would keep us from her?"

Bannister reacted the way Ray hoped he would. The widening of Bannister's eyes, the sharp intake of breath—it was shock and revulsion, too immediate to be anything but honest. "I wouldn't—no. No, you bastard, she's still in one piece, and she'll stay that way for eternity. You'll never find her, you'll never disturb her. She's at peace, where *nothing* will ever touch her again."

"For both your sakes," said Ray, "I hope that *isn't* true."

15

Nick surveyed the charred and broken debris lying on the light table in front of him. The wreckage of the dirigible, including the melted remains of the clown mask.

He looked for the cause of the fire first. The remains of a small thermocouple seemed the most likely culprit, and he found bits of melted plastic and wire that could have been part of a radio receiver. The electric motor that drove the propeller at the back was still mostly intact, as was the battery that powered it and the chain system that made it appear that the clown was pedaling. The frame had been built mostly out of lightweight wooden materials, almost all of which had been destroyed by the fire. All that was left of the clown's body was a puddle of melted plastic and some scraps of charred paper jumpsuit.

He examined a wooden cross-piece that had survived. It wasn't held together with wire or screws—it had been carefully cut and then glued together, probably to save weight. He separated the pieces, then took photos of both and samples of the dried glue. He dusted every piece of the wreckage large enough to hold a print but didn't find any.

It was obvious that whoever built the dirigible knew what they were doing, not just in constructing a remote-control aircraft, but in the use of pyrotechnics. The crash had been specifically designed to draw the attention of the people at the party and hold it for at least three minutes. But why?

Nick didn't have any answers yet—but he thought he knew where he'd find them.

The Red Star Circus, according to its Web site, had been formed in 1921. It had originally featured a number of equestrian acts as well as tumblers, clowns, magicians, and trained bears. Many of its performers could trace their circus roots back to the eighteenth century, and those roots remained strong; entire families were conceived, raised, and married under the big top, three-ring dynasties born with spotlights in their eyes and sawdust in their blood.

Circus acts these days relied less on trained animals and more on spectacle, but the Red Star remained stubbornly old school. It still featured elephants, lions, and tigers, plus the usual assortment of clowns, trapeze artists, jugglers, and animal trainers.

But no bears.

One of the things Russian circus tradition had been big on was illusion; an entire ring had been dedicated to it in the Moscow State Circus auditorium. The Red Star didn't have an illusionist, but with a little digging, Nick discovered the site did credit one Illarion Shayduko as being in charge of "fireworks and pyrotechnical effects."

Nick wondered if that included incendiary clowns—and decided he'd better go see for himself.

Nick found the pyrotechnics expert in a trailer inside the fenced-off parking lot of the Caribbean Hotel, tucked beside the elephant pens. He knocked on the door and was rewarded with a grumpy "What?"

"I'm looking for Illarion Shayduko."

"Come back later, unless you want to get blown up."

"I'll take my chances."

There was a long pause. Nick was about to knock on the door again, when it creaked open. A man with a shock of wiry gray hair and a stubbly beard peered at him over a set of wire-rimmed glasses. "Yeah? What's so damn important?"

"Nick Stokes, Vegas Crime Lab. I was wondering if I could ask you a few questions."

The man frowned at him. He was dressed in faded yellow pajamas and an oversize pair of army boots, unlaced. He clutched a soldering gun with a wisp of smoke curling from the tip in one hand, and a cigarette in the other. "Sure, okay, come on in. This isn't going to take too long, is it?"

"No, sir." Nick followed the man inside and shut the door behind him.

And was immediately sorry he had. The atmosphere was thick enough to see, tobacco smoke and solder and burned plastic; Nick's eyes started to water, and he felt a coughing fit coming on.

The trailer was crammed with electronics gear, boxes marked with explosives symbols, and stacks of engineering magazines. Shayduko sat down at a table covered with various tools and electronics and began to solder a component into place in the guts of what looked like an old radio.

Nick looked around for a place to sit, didn't see one, and decided to stay on his feet. "Mr. Shayduko. I understand you're in charge of pyrotechnics for the Red Star Circus, is that right?"

"If you mean I'm the one they run to when they want pretty fireworks at the end of their number, then yes. Also the one they blame when they miss their damn cue and get a face full of colored smoke instead of a dramatic backdrop."

"That's show biz."

"That's a gigantic pain in my backside, that's what that is. What can I do for you?"

"What do you know about zeppelins?"

"Pointy on one end, full of gas in the middle, pointy again. What else?"

"Did you hear about the one that crashed and burned last night?"

"No, can't say I did." He waved a hand around without looking up. "I'm in here most of the time. Different states, different cities, but the same damn four walls. I might as well be a turtle."

"Well, one went down in the parking lot of the Panhandle. Maybe twenty feet long, controlled via remote, filled with a hydrogen-helium mixture. Sound familiar?"

Now Shayduko looked up. "No," he said flatly. "What, you think I *know* something about this? I build props for animal trainers and trapeze artists, not the Montgolfier brothers."

"Did I mention the pilot was an inflatable dummy in a clown suit?"

Shayduko scowled. "Really. Well, if he was dressed as a clown, then I guess the whole *circus* must be guilty. You should take all of us away and lock us up. Make sure you bring extra-large handcuffs for the elephants."

"I'm not making any accusations, Mr. Shayduko, just looking for some answers."

Shayduko's scowl lessened slightly. "Well . . . that's your job, I guess. Circus folk can get a little touchy, you know—we don't have a real good history with law enforcement."

"I understand. And frankly, the use of an inflatable clown tells me someone's trying to point the finger at you in a very unsubtle, obvious way. Me finding that someone would be a good thing for you, wouldn't it?"

Shayduko nodded grudgingly. "You got a point. Sorry. But what do you want me to say? I don't know anything about this."

"Maybe you don't, but somebody does—and that somebody is probably not far away. How would you feel about showing me around? I promise I won't go making any wild accusations."

Shayduko put down his soldering iron and considered what Nick had just said. After a moment, he leaned across the table and pulled the plug out of the wall. "Okay, okay. But I don't have that long, you understand? I got a job to do."

"Thanks. I appreciate it."

What Nick wanted was an excuse to poke around the circus in the hope of uncovering more evidence, but he had to admit that getting an insider's tour was more of a thrill than he'd expected.

"Over here are the elephants' quarters," said Shayduko, gesturing with a cigarette as they walked along. "I prefer elephants to people, most days. Better memories and better manners, most of them. Of course, there are always exceptions."

They stopped to let a trainer go by, leading one of the massive gray beasts. It studied Nick with an eye higher than his head as it lumbered past.

"That elephant has already killed two men," said Shayduko.

Nick took a step backward. "Excuse me?"

"People have no idea. At one time, about ten years ago, there were maybe forty killers out of four hundred working elephants in North America. People think an elephant kills someone, it gets puts to sleep, yes? But they are talking about an animal worth a hundred thousand dollars. An elephant will have to kill three, maybe four people before a circus even thinks about getting rid of it. Then it gets sold to a zoo or a nature park or maybe a circus in Mexico—they are always desperate for elephants. Even then, it will probably kill again before it's finally put down."

"You're kidding me," said Nick. He watched the elephant slowly stomp away.

"No, no, I'm serious. There was even a list going around for a while, which places had a dangerous elephant—you can't always tell by the animal's name, owners can call them whatever they want. Like any criminal, hey? Move to another state, change your name, go back into business."

Nick shook his head. "You'd think losing a hundred-thousand-dollar investment would be small change compared with a multimillion-dollar wrongful death suit."

"Penny wise, pound foolish. Elephants are smart, but even the smartest person can make bad decisions. Some elephants, I think they react the same to murder as some people."

"How's that?"

"They like it. They do it once, see they got away with it, they do it again."

"You're saying there are elephant serial killers?"

Shayduko shrugged. "Sure, why not? There are elephant cops, you know."

"Okay, Mr. Shayduko, now I know you're putting me on."

"No, no, Mr. Stokes. I'm very serious. A big animal like a pachyderm, you have to have a way to keep it under control. What many elephant trainers do is to take the biggest, strongest elephant and train it to be a bully. To attack the other elephants on command. If one of them gets out of line, the bully elephant is sent in to discipline it. And that's exactly what it will do."

Cages of big cats were lined up under shade

structures, most of the animals sprawled out motionless in the heat. A tiger paced back and forth restlessly, glaring at Nick with a baleful yellow eye as they walked past. "I've noticed you have no bears," said Nick. "Seems odd for a Russian circus—isn't the bear act kind of your trademark?"

Shayduko tossed his cigarette butt away and pulled another one out of a slim silver case before answering. "We used to have many bears. But now they are retired."

"Why's that?"

Shayduko lit another cigarette, then waved it in the air irritably. "Why? Yogi Bear. Winnie the Pooh. Smokey and Paddington and Teddy Ruxpin. In Russia, the bear is seen as a source of great power, great pride; performers like the great Gosha were national heroes. Here they are silly cartoons for children, and when people see bears performing, they react as if we are torturing their childhood. They want bears to be cuddly and harmless and two-dimensional."

"You sound a little bitter."

"Do I? It's early yet—a few more cups of coffee, and I'll really get going. We Russians don't have blood, we have poison cut with vodka."

"So public pressure made you get rid of the bears?"

Shayduko expelled a gloomy cloud of smoke. "I suppose. They are well cared for, but I know for a fact they miss performing. They live on a ranch outside the city now."

"The rescue facility. I know, I was just there."

Shayduko glanced at him, his eyes narrowed. "Oh? You think perhaps a bear was behind your flaming zeppelin? I've seen them do many clever things, but that might be a little much."

"The crash triggered an escape by three of the bears as they were being transported to the casino. One of them might have attacked a man."

"A zeppelin crash and a bear attack? Now I think you're the one not being serious, Mr. Stokes."

"It's all over the news, Mr. Shayduko. Kind of strange that an old circus hand like yourself hasn't heard about it."

"I told you, I never go out."

"Haven't seen a newspaper, turned on the TV, checked the Internet?"

"Newspapers are for wrapping fish, TV is for morons, and the Internet is something young people use to steal music."

Nick was going to ask whether or not Shayduko was completely friendless as well but thought better of it. He thought he knew the kind of answer he'd get.

They finished the tour of the animal area with the stables, which housed horses, donkeys, goats, and pigs. "I have to admit," said Nick, "pigs are one animal I wouldn't associate with the circus."

"Maybe not in America—here all they think pigs are good for is ham hocks and pork chops. But pigs have a proud tradition in the Russian circus."

"A proud tradition of what?"

"Political satire."

Nick grinned. "Of course."

"I mean it! Pigs are smart, trainable, and come with a built-in reputation. You dress a pig as a local politician, everyone knows what you're trying to say.

Of course, these days it's more likely to be a teenage singer or a movie star, but the idea's the same."

"Sounds pretty subversive for something sponsored by the state."

Shayduko smiled with nicotine-stained teeth. "Ah, you know a little bit about our history, eh? Yes, it's true that while the Communists were in power the circus was sponsored and controlled by the Kremlin. But we folk of the *tsirk* have been around long before the Revolution, and we're still here after it's folded its tents and left."

Shayduko dropped his cigarette and ground it under his boot. "Before Lenin took over, the *skomorokhi*—the clowns—would poke fun at the tsars and the ruling elite; afterward, they had to be much more careful. Everything they did was scrutinized for the slightest trace of antigovernment sentiment. Can you imagine trying to get laughs like that? Like trying to do ballet with a load of bricks on your shoulders."

"Can we take a look around inside?" asked Nick.

"I don't know, they're very busy. It's probably not a good idea."

Nick shrugged. "Your call. But I'd hate to have to come back here with a warrant—that's the kind of thing that can hold up or even cancel performances."

Shayduko sighed. "Yes, okay. Just stay close to me and don't bother any of the performers, all right?"

They entered the hotel through a door big enough to drive a truck through. The performing space was only large enough for a single ring, but the ceiling was high enough to accommodate a trapeze. Three acrobats were rehearsing overhead, two of them swinging side-by-side from the same bar.

But that wasn't what caught Nick's attention. At the far side of the arena was an oversize cannon, painted a lurid purple with red stars running the length of the barrel. "Is that what I think it is?" Nick said, a wide grin on his face.

"Absolutely. We're declaring war on Utah and using that to shell the Mormons."

Nick was already striding toward it. "A human-cannonball act. I didn't think anybody did those anymore."

"The classics never die. They just get a new coat of paint and a hip-hop soundtrack."

Nick stopped in front of the cannon and peered into the barrel. "Man, this is great. When I was a kid, this was number one on my list of future careers."

"Don't be too eager. The attrition rate is more than sixty percent—mostly by missing the net at the other end. There was one famous act, the Zacchinis, who thought they'd shake things up by doubling the danger—they used two cannons, one at either end of the arena, firing simultaneously. You'll never guess what happened."

"They didn't."

"They did. In midair. Both of them survived, but one broke her back." Shayduko slapped a hand on the barrel. "It's a lot harder than you might think, even when you don't have to dodge a family member going the other way. First of all, the cylinder that launches you is compressed into the base of the barrel at a pressure of two hundred pounds per square inch. When that gets released, it throws you into the air at around seventy miles an hour. You'd better have strong leg muscles, because you have to keep your body as straight and aerodynamic as possible to control your trajectory."

Shayduko walked around the other side of the cannon, then pointed to the net set up against the opposite wall of the arena. "If you don't hit that, you're pretty much a stain on the wall. But just hitting it isn't enough; you go into it headfirst, you'll probably snap your neck. So you have to turn in midair, just enough that you land your back instead of your front."

"Okay, I'm reconsidering."

Shayduko chuckled. "Oh, and sometimes the g-forces make you black out for a second. Or so I'm told."

"Don't believe a word he says," said a voice from the bleachers. "He's a terrible liar."

Nick looked up. A man sat sprawled out in a seat a few rows up, holding one hand to the back of his neck. He wore only baggy black shorts and sneakers, his lean chest bare and hairless. His hair was short and chestnut-brown, his features sharp.

"Fyodor," said Shayduko. His voice was neutral. "Shouldn't you be out drinking?"

Fyodor took his hand from behind his head, and Nick saw that it held a bag of ice. "Got an early start today," said Fyodor. "Already done."

"Such an industrious lad," said Shayduko. "Mr. Stokes, this is Fyodor Brish. He's our walking, talking ammunition."

Fyodor winced and moved the bag of ice to his shoulder. "Talking, yes. Walking, I'm not so sure."

"Rough night?" asked Nick.

"No more than any other," said Fyodor. "It's not being fired out of a cannon that's hard on you—it's the sudden stop at the end."

"I'll bet. You do the pyro for this, too, Mr. Shayduko?"

Shayduko nodded. "The compressed air does all the work, but I throw in a few fireworks to give it a bang and some smoke. You show people a big gun, they want to hear a big boom."

Nick nodded. "Well, I've taken up enough of your time. Thanks for showing me around."

Shayduko shrugged. "My pleasure. Good luck with finding your mad zeppelinist."

By the time he got back to his Denali, Nick was frowning. Something was nagging at him, but he wasn't quite sure what.

He was halfway back to the lab when it hit him.

"Well, well, well," Nick murmured, staring at the monitor in the AV lab.

Greg walked up behind him. "Pictures from the penthouse party?"

"Yeah. I pulled these from cell-phone footage of the dirigible. See that guy in the corner?" The man Nick pointed to was out of focus and half turned away.

"Yeah, so?"

"So I think I know who he is—and he's definitely not on the guest list."

"If he wasn't on the guest list, how'd he get in?"

"You're not going to believe it. I'm not sure *I* believe it. In fact, I have to verify his identity before I even say it out loud." Nick got up and headed for the door.

"Where are you going?"

"To talk to a man about a bathrobe."

Greg shrugged, then went looking for Hodges. He found him in the break room, drinking from a water bottle and leafing through a newspaper. "Hey, Hodges—you finish the analysis on that powder yet?"

Hodges didn't look up. "In case you hadn't noticed, I *am* on a break."

"I was just wondering—"

Hodges sighed. "Yes, yes, I'm finished. I take it you're talking about the powder you found in the hotel room of the Panhandle and not one of the million *other* random powders I'm expected to identify on a daily basis?"

"Well, yeah."

"Mostly silica and calcium carbonate, with some sodium, magnesium, and iron. If you want the exact figures, you'll have to wait another"—Hodges glanced at his watch—"seven minutes to get them. Oh, the suspense."

"Silica, sodium, magnesium, iron—that sounds like diatomaceous earth."

"Or in other words, tiny little ground-up fossils. The calcium carbonate, on the other hand—"

"—could have come from all sorts of sources: eggshells, snails, seashells, even pearls. The question is, what were they doing together?"

"It's not that I don't care," said Hodges. "But I'm going to pretend I don't for the next . . . six minutes."

* * *

Ian Stackwell was off shift, so Nick got his address from the security office and went to see him at home.

Stackwell lived in a modest five-story apartment building at the edge of town. The voice that answered the buzzer was female and sounded half-asleep. "Yes? Whuzzit?"

"Sorry to disturb you, ma'am. I'm with the Las Vegas Crime Lab, and I need to speak to Ian. Is he there?"

"He's sleeping."

"Can you get him up? It's important."

"Yeah, yeah, okay. Come on up."

The door buzzed and unlocked. Nick took the creaking elevator up to the fourth floor, where a five-year-old in a cowboy hat tried to shoot him repeatedly with a stick. "Bang! Bang! Bang!"

"Bulletproof vest, pardner." Nick tapped his chest. "Better luck next time."

"But I shot you in the *head*," the boy said with implacable logic.

"Uh—bulletproof head?"

"Nuh-*uh*," the boy said, then ran down the hall and around the corner.

Nick knocked on Stackwell's door. A sleepy-eyed woman in a nightshirt opened it and asked to see his ID before letting him in. "He's getting dressed," she said, stifling a yawn. "You want some coffee?"

"I'm good, thanks."

Ian Stackwell walked out a moment later, barefoot but wearing jeans and a black T-shirt. "Mr. Stokes," he said, offering his hand. Nick shook it. "What can I help you with?"

"Sorry to bother you at home, but I was hoping you could take a look at a photo for me." Nick pulled out a publicity still he'd pulled off the Web. "Does this guy look familiar?"

Stackwell took the picture and studied it. "Yeah. This is the guy who vouched for the man in the wheelchair and his nurse."

"The one in the bathrobe, right?"

"Yeah. Who is he?"

"Someone who went to a lot of trouble to go for a swim," said Nick.

Nick wasn't gone long. Back at the lab, he'd gone straight to a computer terminal and begun working, and it had been another twenty minutes before he'd even talk to Greg—who was now regarding his fellow CSI skeptically.

"Let me get this straight," said Greg. "You're saying this guy cannonballed into a rooftop pool. *Literally* cannonballed."

"I know how crazy it sounds. But the guard ID'd him—and the research I've done says it's possible."

Greg crossed his arms. "Convince me."

"All right. The world record for being fired from a cannon is a hundred and eighty-five feet. Usually the cannonballer lands in a net, but sometimes he lands in water."

"I'm guessing that the water usually isn't in a pool twenty stories up."

"There's a new casino being built right beside the Panhandle, but construction's been suspended because of financing problems. Want to guess how tall it is?"

"Just a little taller than the Panhandle—I noticed it when we were on the roof."

"You happen to notice how far away its roof was?"

Greg thought about it. "I'd say around a hundred and fifty feet."

"Within firing range."

"But it's still twenty stories up. How do you get a cannon up there in the first place?"

"I don't know," said Nick, "but maybe we should go have a look."

There was no guard at the gate surrounding the casino construction site, but the chain on the padlocked gate had been cut and then draped back in place.

"Doesn't seem to be any security around," said Greg.

"Hard to justify guarding a half-finished shell when you can't pay the construction crew." Nick pulled the chain aside and opened the gate. He and Greg walked in.

Other than some fast-food garbage blowing around, the place seemed devoid of any human activity. The only piece of heavy equipment still present was a crane, perched on the roof like a gigantic yellow praying mantis. A tangle of steel girders lay rusting in the sun, while a small mountain of stacked concrete blocks rose beside the fence. Bits of cast-off lumber and PVC piping littered the ground.

"I think I've got something," said Greg. He nudged a large, curving piece of plastic with his foot.

Nick walked over and joined him. "Looks like pieces of a pipe."

"Yeah, a big pipe. From the arc of this piece, I'd say that when it was intact, it would have to have a diameter of at least two and a half, three feet."

Nick studied the ground around the shard. "Look at this—the pieces are scattered in a circle radiating out from this point."

"Impact crater?" Greg looked up. Twenty stories above them, the hook of the crane dangled at the end of a thick steel cable.

"Could be. The cannon is basically just a big cylinder of compressed air with a single piston, right? Pretty easy to fabricate. You could even charge it somewhere else, haul it out here on the back of a truck, then use the crane to hoist it into position."

"Okay, then—how do you aim?"

Nick rubbed the back of his neck. "It'd be tricky, but it could be done—especially if you had years of experience in doing the same thing over and over. Know how they get the range just right for a real human cannonball? They fire a test dummy that weighs exactly the same as the flesh-and-blood payload."

"I guess it would be pretty easy to set up once you had it on the roof."

"Sure. Use a sighting laser to get an accurate distance reading . . ."

Nick trailed off. He and Greg looked at each other.

"We are *so* doing a simulation of this," said Greg.

Nick grinned.

*   *   *

A search of the abandoned construction site produced something else of interest: several empty gas cylinders on the roof.

"I think we've found the launch site for the dirigible," said Nick. He glanced around. "Makes sense—plenty of space up here to inflate the envelope and less of a chance anyone will notice when you take off."

"Then all you have to do," said Greg, "is make it a hundred and fifty feet straight across to the party. The dirigible itself is black, which lessens the chance anyone will see it from the street. And once everyone's watching one act—"

"—act number two steps onto the stage."

"Except nobody's supposed to notice his entrance. While the entire party is watching an inflatable clown go down in flames, this guy is making a water landing in the pool."

Nick shook his head. "After which he climbs out, grabs a robe and a towel from poolside, and saunters up to the guard watching the elevator—just in time to vouch for his two friends downstairs."

"One hell of a way to crash a party, you gotta admit."

"Sure—but why? So far, there doesn't seem to be any reason to go to all this trouble. Nothing was stolen, nobody was hurt."

"The casino's rep took a hit," Greg pointed out. "Maybe that's what this is all about."

"I don't know. The bear attack, maybe. But this was all done just to get three people—four if you count the missing security guard—on the roof of the Panhandle."

"Where they apparently did nothing but a little freelance acrobatic work."

Nick nodded, a frown on his face. "I think I know what the remote we found in the pool was for. It was the trigger for the cannon."

"So he had it in his hand the whole way, then dropped it on impact?" Greg thought about it. "Having the cannonball launch himself probably means our little troupe was running low on manpower. We've got four people so far, plus whoever was controlling the dirigible."

"Who'd need line of sight for the aircraft. The controller would have to be in a place to see both the launch site and the far side of the hotel."

"There's another hotel right across the street. The controller could have been in any of the rooms facing this way, with a joystick in one hand and a pair of binoculars in the other."

Nick nodded. "Obviously this is getting more insane by the moment. Let's process this site—maybe we can get a print from one of the cylinders or the chain they cut. I'll check out the crane, too. They had to have used it to hoist the cannon into position."

"I'll take a closer look at the impact site, if you don't mind." said Greg. "Frankly, I'm getting kinda tired of rooftops."

There were certain things you just shouldn't do when you were drunk, Sara thought as she pulled into the parking lot of the strip mall. Driving was at the top of the list—as she'd learned, to her own regret—cleaning your gun was a close second, and calling an ex was probably number three. It said a lot about Vegas that besides the almost unlimited opportunities for alcohol abuse, you could also rent an exotic vehicle or drop by a shooting range to fire an AK-47. Nobody had come up with a reliable way to make money off number three, but it was probably only a matter of time.

She wasn't sure where getting a tattoo ranked on that list, but it had to be in the top ten—which was undoubtedly why Vegas had more than its fair share of tattoo parlors.

The storefront she parked in front of was called Grinning Bastard Ink. The sign was elaborate and colorful, no doubt painted by the resident artist, and featured many skulls, roses, crosses, and red-skinned, horned devil-women. But that wasn't what caught Sara's eye; at one end of the sign was a small representation of a church with three steeples, and at the opposite end was a pirate with an eye patch.

When she pulled the glass door open, the wave of cold air that met her was almost like walking into a freezer; the owner apparently didn't care for Nevada temperatures. Or maybe, she thought as she stepped inside, he just preferred working on frozen meat.

The shop was long and narrow, the walls lined with tattoo designs that ranged from cute to grim, from prosaic to exotic. An autoclave stood on a stainless-steel table at the back, next to a sharps container with a decal identifying it as medical waste. There was a tattoo bed and two tattoo chairs, one of which was occupied; several bright lights on tall, adjustable stands stood guard over the single customer, a scrawny-chested man with his shirt off and a nervous expression on his face. His hair was ginger flecked with gray, a prominent bald spot on top, and he looked as if he was having second thoughts about what he was doing there.

"Hi," said Sara. "Is the owner around?"

"Uh, he just went into the back to get something," the man said. "He'll be right back. Can I ask you a question?"

"Usually, that's my line. What about?"

The man handed her a piece of paper with a design on it. "Do you think this will look good on my chest? I mean, is it *me*?"

She took the paper and studied it. "Hmmm."

"Well?"

"I think it might be a little much."

"Really?"

"No offense. I just met you, so maybe I'm way off base. Just my gut reaction."

The man nodded, the worried look on his face now deeper. "Yeah. Yeah, no problem, thanks for being honest."

"Maybe you should give it a little more thought?"

"I think you're right." The man got to his feet and grabbed his shirt from a nearby hook. "Thanks. Uh, when he comes back, can you tell him—"

"I'll handle it, no problem."

The man practically ran out the door. Sara smiled, shook her head, and put the picture down on a table crowded with gleaming equipment.

A door at the back opened. A man with long, shaggy black hair, three chins, and a double-wide build squeezed himself through the doorway, carrying a bottle of ink in one hand; Sara guessed he must weigh close to three hundred and fifty pounds. He shuffled forward, frowning when he saw that his customer was no longer in sight. "Dammit," he said, his voice deep and scratchy. "I knew he was a rabbit when I laid eyes on him. Spends forty-five minutes trying to pick a design, then bolts when my back is turned. I should be able to use anesthesia, like a dentist. Or maybe leather straps on the chair."

"You can blame me. I'm afraid I didn't have a high opinion of his choice."

The man smiled at her. "Yeah, me neither. Didn't think he had the style to pull it off, but once he finally settled on something, I wasn't gonna argue."

"Well, the teddy bear was all right, but the cherubs were overkill."

"He had bad skin, too. I'd much prefer to work on something else." His smile got a little wider. "I'm Barry, by the way. I own this shop. You have something in mind?"

"I do. *Vory v zakone.*"

Barry's smile slid off his face. "That's not really the kind of thing I do."

"Sure it is, Barry. Oh, I'm sorry, I didn't introduce myself. Sara Sidle, Vegas Crime Lab. Jim Brass told me to look you up."

"You got some ID?"

She produced it. He took it and studied it intently, front and back, before giving it back. "If that's a forgery, it's a damn good one," he said. "Okay, so you know Brass. I still don't do those kinds of tattoos."

"That's okay—I'm here for information, not ink.

You've done that kind of thing in the past, though, right?"

Barry sighed. "Just a second, all right?" He shuffled to the front of the store, locked the door and flipped over the "Open" sign. Then he made his way back, where he eased himself onto a wide stool. "Okay. Yeah, I've done some work for the *Bratva na peeski*. Not a lot—they prefer to do their own stuff, usually while behind bars." He shook his head. "But some of the younger guys appreciate a more professional touch. In prison, they use a sharpened guitar string attached to an electric razor for the needle, and for ink they mix burned shoe rubber with their own piss. I can understand the attraction of a more modern approach, though there's a certain blurriness to that kind of tattoo that's very distinctive. I've managed to duplicate it with my own tools, but don't ask how—it's a trade secret."

"I'm more interested in the canvas than the art. I'm looking into a fake-credit-card ring, and I'd like to know a little bit more about the players before I start digging. Brass gave me the heads-up on some of them, but he felt you might have a more up-to-date perspective."

"He did, huh? Look, no offense, but talking about these guys is more than a little dangerous. I owe Brass, but—"

"Melinda."

Barry stopped. His eyes got wider, then narrowed. "He wouldn't . . ."

"Oh, he definitely would. He said to mention the name if you dragged your heels, so I did. Can we move on, or would you like to take a few minutes to grumble?"

"Yeah, yeah, fine. Where you want to start?"

"Grigori Dyalov."

"Right at the top, huh? Major badass. Runs the local operation, totally ruthless. Used to be a colonel in the KGB, did a lot of really nasty stuff in Chechnya. There's a story going around that his favorite way to execute political dissidents was to drag them behind a horse. To make sure the horse ran fast enough, he'd set the person on fire. To make sure the fire didn't go out too soon, he'd use kerosene."

"Scary stories are a dime a dozen. Every mob guy I've ever run into has at least one."

"I'm just sayin'. The other thing I heard is that he used to be a real high-level spook—you know, the Cold War, espionage, real James Bond stuff. They say that's why he's never been busted—he's got too many contacts, even here in the States."

"So he's Dr. No *and* the Godfather?"

Barry shrugged. "Hey, a lot of those KGB guys joined the mob when the Kremlin tanked. They got the skills, the contacts, the experience—where else they gonna go for a paycheck? Dyalov's whole crew is either ex-KGB, Spetsnaz, or both. Those guys would stick a knife in your eye just to have a place to hang their hat."

"Spetsnaz—that's their elite commando unit, right? Like Navy SEALs or the Green Berets?"

"Yeah, minus the bragging and swagger. Spetsnaz don't talk about how good they are—they just show up, kill everyone, then leave. Spetsnaz training focuses on toughening you up—they basically beat the crap out of you every day until you learn to ignore pain. I'm talking electric shocks, going for long swims in freezing water, all kinds of abuse. Not just physical, either—they'd send recruits to morgues or even car crashes, make them haul around dead or dismembered bodies. Get them so used to death that it didn't shock them anymore—just another day at the office."

"Guess I must be part Russian, then—you know you're a CSI when you catch yourself yawning at an autopsy. So what's Dyalov into?"

"The usual. Prostitution, money laundering, drugs, extortion. Identity theft is a big one these days. I hear they've been cranking out a lot of bad plastic."

"Any specifics?"

He hesitated. "I had these two guys come in here last week; one of them wanted a pirate put on his chest. Told me if I made it look like Johnny Depp, he'd beat me to death with a crowbar . . . anyway, in this community, a pirate tattoo means you've committed armed robbery. This guy already had a church with two steeples, so he'd done at least two years in prison."

"What's the tattoo for credit-card fraud? An American Express logo?"

"That's funny. I'll suggest that the next time one of those psychos shoves a gun in my face and tells me to do a good job."

"Sorry. Who was this guy?"

"His friend called him Ilya, didn't catch the friend's name. They talked in Russian while they were here—guess they thought I wouldn't understand. I'm not real fluent, but I know a little."

"What'd they say?"

"Something about a new shipment of plastic. Not a lot of specifics, but Ilya mentioned something about a souvenir shop on Fremont."

Sara nodded. "Thanks, I appreciate that. It'll give me something to go on, anyway." She walked over to the wall and eyed one of the designs. "Think this would look good on me?"

"Depends where you want it," said Barry. "Tattoos are like real estate. Location, location, location."

"Yeah. Speaking of which, where were you last night, around midnight?"

"Me? Here, working late. Why?"

"Don't suppose you own a wheelchair, do you?"

He frowned. "No. I use one of those electric scooters sometimes. What, somebody see a guy my size sprinting away from a crime scene?"

"Not exactly. Thanks for the help—I'll tell Brass you say hi."

"Melinda. He *would* bring that up . . ." she heard him mutter as the door swung closed behind her.

16

FAITH, LOYALTY, AND HOPE. Those were the three things King Oswald had asked for in return for granting the peace John Bannister and Theria Kostapolis were seeking, and Catherine wasn't sure where to find any of those three particular virtues in Vegas.

Although she'd rejected the idea that Bannister and Theria might try to prove their faith in each other by getting married, Catherine realized that proving their loyalty was another matter. Marriage was a binding contract stating flat out that the two people involved would remain loyal to each other, and in Vegas it was about as difficult to obtain as a bus transfer—though sometimes the transfer was good for longer.

They would have had to get a marriage license first, a procedure carried out at City Hall. She hadn't found a marriage license among Bannister's personal effects, but it was possible Theria had kept it.

A few minutes online with a civil-records database confirmed it: John Bannister and Theria Kostapolis had obtained a license earlier that day, though they hadn't exercised the option of an immediate civil ceremony. Which meant they must have visited one of the many wedding chapels Vegas had to offer—but which one?

She tried to put herself in their place. Trapped in hell, forced to undergo a ceremony that would seem bizarre and surreal no matter what the actual environment—would they choose the chapel carefully, or simply opt for the closest choice? She doubted Theria would choose anything connected to the Catholic church—not unless a twisted version appealed to her on some perverse level. Despite having apparently given up on life, Theria was obviously a strong-willed person; it had taken the death of her parents to finally stop her constant attempts to escape. Then, even after surrendering to guilt, she'd proven strong enough to get Bannister to see the world the way she did.

It was hard to say which way she'd decide to go. Catherine decided the best approach was to tackle the chapels based on proximity to the license bureau, and keep her eyes open for anything that leaped out at her.

"Thank you. Thank you verra much," said Elvis, waving as the bride and groom drove away. Catherine pulled up to the drive-in kiosk, her driver's-side window already rolled down.

"Hey, little lady," said Elvis. "Where's the lucky man? Takes two to tango, y'know."

"Sorry, I'm not quite ready to hang up my blue suede shoes." She pulled out her CSI identification and showed it to him. "I was wondering if you'd married a couple named John Bannister and Theria Kostapolis earlier today."

"I marry a lot of people. Kind of the point of a drive-through chapel, you know? Volume."

"They might not have been in a car."

Elvis frowned. "Hey, I don't do walk-ups. I have my standards, you know?"

"Can you check your records, please?"

"All right, just hold on."

He disappeared inside. Catherine knew this was a long shot, but she'd already canvassed every chapel in a ten-block radius with no luck.

A drive-through chapel presided over by Elvis wasn't the strangest Vegas wedding option, but it was close. She wondered about the people who chose to join their lives via someone impersonating a dead pop star in a venue that aped a fast-food restaurant. It was quintessentially American, she supposed—the rock-and-roll lifestyle, movie stardom, car culture and cheeseburgers all in one convenient package. But marriage was supposed to be about commitment, wasn't it? Not instant gratification?

She sighed and told herself to lighten up. Next thing she knew, she'd be telling those damn kids to get off her lawn.

Elvis came back, shaking his head. "Nope. Sorry, nobody by that name."

She thanked him and pulled away. There was already another car with a grinning couple in it right behind her, the woman wearing a plastic tiara, the man in a bright green cardboard tophat. "Oh, a *formal* affair," she muttered.

Damn kids. Get off my lawn. I have a gun.

The whole idea of marriage had been gnawing at her. Not marriage in general, but the idea of getting married in hell. It made no sense. What did you do, get a demon to preside over your ceremony? Elvis was bad enough as a symbol for commitment, but throw in a set of horns and a forked tail, and the whole thing went straight past mockery to out-and-out grotesque. Anything conventional would be warped and twisted by their symptoms—as would anything unconventional. They'd gone to the trouble of getting a license, no doubt as proof for King Lucifer Oswald, but how would they go about actually tying the knot in a way that would be meaningful to *them*?

She thought about it as she drove. An official marriage license was simply permission from authority. To actually marry, they'd have to seek confirmation from a *higher* authority—but not the authority of hell itself, because hell represented deceit and suffering. Catherine supposed she could make a case for marriage being the same thing, but she shouldn't let her own history color her judgment.

Was there such a thing as a higher authority in hell, other than the Devil himself?

"Well, I'll be damned," Catherine muttered. "And so, apparently, were they."

She was in a coffeeshop with free WiFi, her laptop open on the table in front of her. A little surfing through a few religious-studies sites had produced some surprising information; there was, in fact, an aspect of hell—according to some theologists, anyway—that remained untainted by the evil around it. It was referred to as "Abraham's bosom," the place where the righteous dead awaited Judgment Day. Exactly why they were waiting was a matter of some debate; some scholars believed it was a place for those who died before Christ's time and therefore had no chance to be redeemed. It was also said that during the three days Christ was dead, he went down to hell to collect these souls and take them up to heaven.

If that scenario were true, none of the scholars seemed to have any idea what happened to the place after it was vacated. And Abraham's bosom was very definitely a separate place, cordoned off from the rest of hell by either a wall or a chasm; maybe it was just sitting there empty, waiting for Satan to foreclose on the mortgage, or maybe it had already been turned into timeshares for the upwardly mobile demonic elite.

Or maybe it wasn't empty after all. Some accounts seemed to depict the righteous dead as the patient sort, preferring to wait until Judgment Day before heading into the light. Abraham's bosom was supposed to be a kind of paradise unto itself, which would explain why its occupants were reluctant to leave. Why join the general population when you already have a cozy little private estate of your own? True, the howling of the damned might take a little getting used to, but if paradise ever got boring, you could head into downtown Hades on a Saturday night.

"The righteous dead," said Catherine aloud.

"'Scuse me?" her waitress said.

"Oh, nothing. Sorry." *Just trying to figure out where a couple of crazy kids would go to get hitched in the underworld . . . and I think I might have figured out what they were looking for.*

Theria Kostapolis's religious indoctrination had included lots of studying. She'd be aware of Abraham's bosom and what it meant. If you were looking for a good man to pronounce you man and wife in hell, there was really only one place you could go.

All Catherine had to do now was find it.

There were numerous ravines in Vegas, many of them running through the golf courses that clustered around the edges of the city like green lily pads around the shores of a lake. Catherine thought one of them might qualify as the chasm that was said to separate Abraham's bosom from the rest of hell, and she was studying maps on the large wall screen in the AV lab when Archie walked in. "Hey, Catherine. Looking for someplace in particular or just using the equipment to do some real estate shopping?"

"Hi, Archie. I'm trying to figure out where a hallucinating couple suffering a psychotic break with reality might go to get married."

Archie raised an eyebrow. "Well, they're in the right city. Looks like you're checking out golf courses—they're going with a big outdoor ceremony, then?"

"Maybe. I'm actually looking at ravines—the golf

courses are incidental. A lot of people do get married on them, but I can't see my pair going that route. I'm looking for something a little more enclosed."

"An enclosed ravine? The only place I know of like that is out at the Desert Springs Reserve: they've got an interactive exhibit in the Mojave Room that re-creates a flash flood down an arroyo. It's pretty cool."

"No, what I'm looking for is an enclosed space *beside* a ravine. Someplace—I don't know, the opposite of most of Vegas. Quiet, serene, peaceful."

"A spa?"

"Not unless they offer an escaped-psychiatric-patient discount."

"Oh, your crazies are on a budget? Well, the Nature Preserve at the Lincoln Hotel is free—"

"Wait. That's it—Lincoln. *Abraham* Lincoln." She grinned. "Archie, you're the best!" She was already out the door and halfway down the hall.

"You're welcome!" Archie called after her.

The Lincoln Hotel was shaped like a horseshoe, its U-shaped building wrapped around a glass-roofed, three-story-high structure filled with exotic plants, birds, and a series of interconnected ponds, streams, and waterfalls. It was open to the public and mercifully free of the upbeat music piped to almost every public space in and around the Strip. It was intended to be an oasis of calm in the midst of frenzy, and it did its job well.

Catherine stood on a wooden bridge that arched over a gently burbling stream, looking around and trying to see the landscape through the eyes of John Bannister and Theria Kostapolis. Would they still have seen horror, or would their minds have gone along with what Theria had learned as a child— what, in some cases, she'd had beaten into her?

The mind always looks for an escape. Especially in the harshest circumstances. The concept of a sanctuary within Hades itself . . . it must have been a powerful idea to a young child trapped in her own hell. And if Theria is the dominant one of the two, that belief would have communicated itself to Bannister, made him see it the way she did.

Yes. They'd come here, she was sure of it. All she had to do now was prove it—and hope that they'd left some clue to their next destination.

She crossed over the bridge and walked down a path at random. An exhausted-looking tourist couple were sprawled on a bench, dressed in shorts, sandals, and T-shirts; they both had their eyes closed, sunglasses held in lax hands, listening to the birdsong.

She glanced from side to side as she strolled, alert to anything out of the ordinary. The place was laid out in a very open way, with nowhere a traveler looking for a more permanent resting place could conceal herself. Theria might have been here, but she hadn't stayed. Hotel security would have seen to that, though so far both patients had proven adept at avoiding the authorities.

The question now was, who would have performed the ceremony?

They wouldn't have approached a random tourist. They would have wanted someone who belonged here, one of the righteous dead—which meant an employee. She was headed for the hotel to talk to human resources when she suddenly stopped.

Beside the path, a shaft of sunlight fell on a monk.

He was kneeling beneath a palm tree, working on the flowered border. The top of his head was smooth and brown, with a band of hair that encircled it just above the ears. His hooded robe, Catherine saw as she took a second look, was really just a brown blanket thrown around his shoulders, bunching up at the back of the neck.

"Excuse me," she said.

The man looked up with eyes that were brown and mild. "Yes?" His face was wide and friendly, with a short, neatly trimmed mustache.

"I was just—do you always wear that blanket?"

The man chuckled. "I get cold sometimes, especially in the morning. Then I forget to take it off. It's a silly habit, I know."

"Have you been working all day?"

"*Sí*. I have."

Catherine pulled out a picture of John Bannister and Theria Kostapolis. "Have you seen these two?"

The gardener's eyes widened with recognition. "Ah! Yes, the lovers. They were very sweet—a little strange, but sweet."

"What happened?"

"They approached me as I was working. They asked me if I was—how did they put it?—if this place was my home. I laughed and said I spent so much time here, it might as well be."

"Did they ask you for anything?"

The gardener smiled. "Oh, yes. They asked me to marry them. I tried to protest that I was not a priest, but they were very insistent."

"So. Did you?"

The man shrugged. "I thought, what was the harm? All they wanted was a few words, and words arc free. So I laughed, and I put my hands on their heads, and told them they were married." He shook his head. "They seemed very . . . troubled. I thought maybe I could make them smile."

"Don't be too hard on yourself. They weren't looking for happy."

"Oh, I make the man smile. The woman, she still seemed sad."

"Did they tell you anything about where they were going next?"

The gardener frowned in thought. "Not really. I made a joke about the honeymoon, and the man said they had high hopes for it. That's all."

"High hopes?" said Catherine.

"*Sí.*"

She wished she had the same.

17

Nick dusted the inside of the crane's cab for prints and lifted a bunch. He'd have to call the construction company for exemplars so he could eliminate anyone on the work crew.

Greg collected all of the shards at the impact site, then bagged the cut chain on the gate as well. They took it all back to the lab.

They surveyed everything they'd collected, laid out on the light table: white plastic fragments of various sizes and shapes, the chain, the empty tanks.

"Well," said Nick, "tests on the cylinders confirm that they held hydrogen and helium, which supports our theory of the dirigible being launched from the construction-site roof. But these fragments of pipe are the only evidence of an air cannon."

"They must have just dropped it from the roof and picked up whatever they could from where it landed," said Greg. "There's so much other junk lying around, they probably figured no one would notice a few pieces of shattered plastic."

Nick frowned. "Still, it's a little sloppy. Considering how elaborate this whole setup is, it's hard to believe they'd slip up on something like this."

Greg shrugged. "Doesn't surprise me, actually. People with grandiose schemes never want to think about cleaning up afterward; they're all about the 'big picture.' Good thing, too—makes our job easier."

"Let's hope so."

They went to work, examining every shard for evidence. Greg carefully dusted each piece, hoping to find a usable print; Nick concentrated on looking for transfer or tool marks.

"You know, I used to love the circus as a kid," said Nick. "I always wanted to be a trapeze artist."

"Not me," said Greg. "Actually, I always found the whole thing kind of creepy. When I think of circuses, I think of bearded women and guys with no legs."

"Those are carnivals, not circuses. Circuses haven't done freak shows in a long time."

"Really? I wouldn't be too sure about that. I just read about a circus in Italy that was using two Bulgarian women as live bait in animal acts."

Nick put down his shard. "Live bait?"

"That's the best description I can come up with. Two sisters, one nineteen and one sixteen. The circus owners forced one of them to swim in a tank with live piranhas and the other to handle snakes. One had to be treated for snake bites and constriction injuries; the other one had a medical condition that meant she had to avoid swimming in cold water. That didn't stop the owners from forcing her head underwater in a tank they kept just above freezing."

Nick shook his head. "That's not a circus. That's just human cruelty on display."

"More like indentured servitude. The sisters' parents worked for the circus, too, and all of them were paid virtually nothing and given tiny, filthy living quarters. Most of their wages went to what their employers called 'operating expenses.' "

"Wish I could say I'd never heard a story like that before," said Nick. "Young girls from a Third World country, made to perform dangerous or degrading work for little to no pay, given a place to live that was little more than a dirty cage? Unfortunately, I've seen that play out a few too many times."

"Human trafficking," said Greg. "Yeah. And when they busted the owners, they actually seemed surprised. Like, 'Hey, it wasn't like we'd put them on the street or anything.' "

"Guys like that just don't get it. Not until guys like *us* catch them."

"Which is why I'd much rather be in a lab than under a big top."

Nick smiled. "That's hard to argue with. Guess I picked the right profession after all."

They found no usable prints, but the shards did yield a number of tool marks, as did the chain. "Looks like they used a Dremel tool to cut the pipe to size," said Nick.

"The lock was snipped off," said Greg. "Metal

shears of some kind. If we can find either the shears or the Dremel, we've got a case."

"I think I've got a pretty good idea where we should look for them, too. The only problem is getting a judge to sign off on a search warrant based on this evidence. I mean, even I have a hard time believing in this theory."

Greg shrugged. "All we can do is try."

The Honorable Judge Alden Mayerling was not known for his patience. A tall man with ebony skin and a lean, bony face, he was called Judge Skully behind his back by both prosecutors and defense attorneys alike. It had as much to do with his attitude as his appearance—Judge Mayerling was about as skeptical as they came.

He stared at Greg Sanders and Nick Stokes where they sat on the long, black leather couch in his chambers. He put down the warrant request he'd just finished reading, then pushed it away from him with one finger. "Gentlemen," he said, his voice as deep and serious as a grave, "I have to congratulate you."

Greg swallowed. "Thank you?"

Nick cleared his throat, then said, "Your Honor, I know our evidence is a little . . . *unusual,* but—"

Mayerling held up a skeletal hand, and Nick stopped.

"Unusual? Let's see if I have this right. You want to search a circus trailer."

"Well, yes—" Nick answered.

"Because you believe you'll find tools and/or supplies linked to an arson in a Las Vegas parking lot."

"That's right," said Greg.

"So far, all eminently within the domain of sanity. Now, the arson; this was caused by a small-scale zeppelin—piloted by a robot clown—that crashed and burned. Said zeppelin was launched from the roof of a nearby construction site, for the express purpose of distracting the attendees of a rooftop party at the neighboring building." He paused and looked at them, one at a time. Nick did his best to smile, while Greg coughed and looked away.

"Yes, sir," said Nick.

"Distracting them from the human cannonball."

"I know how it sounds," said Nick.

"The human cannonball being fired a hundred and fifty feet through the air, twenty stories up."

"It's really not that far-fetched," said Greg weakly.

"Thereby landing in the pool at the party without being noticed, allowing him to give two of his accomplices entry to said party." The judge paused, looking at them expectantly.

"Correct," Nick managed.

"Well, you've laid out all the details quite thoroughly—up to that point. Afterward, it gets a little vague. Perhaps you could clear up the reason for all of this elaborate subterfuge on the part of your suspects?"

"Not . . . really," Nick admitted. "We're still working on the reason for the crime itself. I mean, as CSIs, our job is to find facts, not uncover motivations—"

"The reason for the crime? I thought it was intended as a distraction."

"Well, yes," said Greg. "That's why the arson was staged. But that's only an incidental crime—the case is actually much bigger."

One of Mayerling's thin eyebrows went up. "Oh? And what sort of crime do you think this is ultimately leading to?"

"We . . . don't know," said Nick.

There was a moment of silence.

"And there were *bears,*" Greg blurted.

Mayerling's other eyebrow joined the first. Nick put his head in his hands.

"As I said," Mayerling continued, "congratulations. When it comes to getting a search warrant issued, I have seen attempts that were half-assed, attempts that were desperate, attempts that were based on logic so flimsy they could have been the basis for a Hollywood movie. I have also seen attempts at humor. This particular document, though, is the first time I have seen such a bizarre, completely improbable, thoroughly unbelievable set of circumstances so diligently and painstakingly documented. You two are either the most brazen con artists the Nevada legal system has ever seen, or just had the bad luck to draw the strangest case ever to cross my desk. In either case, I can't find fault with your facts—they may be outlandish, but you've supported your conclusions every step of the way. I'm going to give you your search warrant."

Nick raised his head. Greg opened his mouth, then shut it again. "You are?" he said.

"I may be a hard-ass, Mr. Sanders, but that doesn't mean I have a closed mind. Good luck."

Sara took another bite of her veggie burger, grimaced, then put it down on the passenger seat next to her. "These things were definitely not made to be eaten cold," she muttered.

She was in one of the lab's Denalis, parked down the street from the souvenir shop Barry the tattoo artist had pointed her at. She'd been watching the place for a while, seeing tourists come and go. Every now and then, someone would wander in who didn't seem to belong; sometimes these people would come back out in a few minutes, sometimes they stayed longer. One didn't come out for almost an hour, and he hadn't appeared to have bought a thing. She knew these customers were probably going upstairs, to the real business the souvenir shop was only a front for.

Sitting in a vehicle and observing wasn't all that different from her old habit of monitoring the police band on a scanner at home, something she used to do as kind of a hobby. But observing was about all she could do without a warrant, and a few sketchy-looking customers wasn't enough to call a judge.

So she'd called someone else instead.

She needed to find whoever had rented that hotel room in the Panhandle. Locating them, Sara suspected, would uncover even more—including a motive for the whole chain of events.

But so far, all she had were suspicions. She needed evidence.

A rap at the window got her attention. She turned to see Jim Brass standing there, bending down. She rolled down the window.

"Hey, sailor," said Brass. "New in town?"

She sighed. "No, but I am a little out of my depth. Thanks for coming by."

He opened the door, picked up the burger from the seat, and got in. "You kidding? Grissom would have my brain in a jar if I let anything happen to you. So where's the plastic factory?"

"A few doors down. Over Les Vega's Gift and Boutique."

"Les Vega? Cute. Barry steered you here?" Brass eyed the burger and said, "You know, these are terrible cold."

"Yeah, well, I don't have a lot of experience when it comes to stakeouts."

Brass shrugged. "Waste not, want not." He took a bite of the burger. "So, I take it you have no real reason to bust the place."

"Not a one. I was hoping you might have an idea."

"I might. You know what's good on a stakeout? Pizza. Keeps forever, good cold, lots of protein. Easy to eat with one hand. You can even get it delivered, though I wouldn't recommend that while sitting on someone's house. Tends to be a bit of a giveaway."

"I'll remember that for next time."

Brass popped the last bite of the burger into his mouth. "Hey, you ever do that thing where you order a bunch of pizzas to somebody else's place? The height of college humor. Nothing says funny like wasting a bunch of cheese, dough, tomato sauce, and the delivery guy's time."

"No, I don't think I ever did."

Brass mock-frowned at her. "The pizza gag's an evergreen, but even an evergreen needs updating now and then. Can you hang on a second? I'll be right back."

By the time Sara opened her mouth, he was already shutting the door. She watched him walk up to one of the men lining the sidewalk handing out cards that advertised local escort services and hold out his hand.

Brass did the same thing for every one of the card vendors, walking to the end of the street and then turning around and coming back. He got back into the car and fanned them out in front of him like a magician displaying a trick. "Hey, this is just like collecting baseball cards," he said. "Except a lot cheaper, and every player is an All-Star. Well, okay, they only have stars over certain parts, but those are pretty important parts—"

"Jim. What does this have to do with a Russian identity-theft ring?"

"Identity theft? Oh, no, I think you're mistaken. What's going on above that souvenir shop is obviously a house of ill repute—which, despite the beliefs of certain uninformed tourists, is still illegal in Clark County. Why, I'm sure I saw five—no, six— obvious prostitutes all go in there at the same time."

He studied the handful of cards critically as he pulled out a cell phone. "Now, the question is, which six . . . how about this one? She looks friendly."

Sara grinned.

The cards all promised prompt service, most within twenty minutes. They waited until the last one arrived—a tardy twelve minutes late—before they got out of the Denali and walked over to the souvenir shop. By that time, the people over the shop had figured out what was going on and had escorted the confused escorts back down the stairs, where they milled in an irritated, scantily dressed knot in the doorway, complaining loudly about cab fare and waving their cell phones in the air.

"Ladies, ladies," said Brass, holding his hands up for calm as he approached. "There's obviously been some sort of mix-up. Maybe I can help?"

Their reaction was varied. A few tried to gauge his value as a replacement customer, one or two immediately transferred all blame—quite rightly—to him, and the others tried to bolt. Brass stopped them by pulling out his badge. "Hold it, ma'am. You, too. Did you all just come from upstairs?"

The replies were both loud and contradictory, but Brass just nodded. "I see. Well, clearly, I'll have to check this out as a possible unlicensed and illegal establishment. If you girls wouldn't mind waiting here, I'll be right back."

He nodded to Sara. She pulled out her gun, and so did Brass.

By the time they set foot on the stairs, most of the girls had vanished; the ones too clueless to leave were being dragged by the arm by those with more experience.

The stairwell was dim, illuminated only by a single flickering fluorescent. They were halfway up when the door at the top opened and a large, bearded man appeared in the doorway. "I thought I told you whores—" he began.

Brass leveled his gun at the man with one hand and put a finger to his lips with the other. He'd slipped his ID into his outside breast pocket so the badge was visible.

The man stared at them for a long moment. Brass

took another quick step up, hugging the far side of the wall while Sara stayed flat against the other.

The man dove backward, out of sight.

"Las Vegas Police! Nobody move!" Brass yelled, leaping up the last two steps. Sara was right behind him, and when she reached the top of the stairs she stayed low, throwing herself prone on the floor.

Quick scan of room: table heaped with cellophane-wrapped bundles the size and shape of decks of cards. Several open laptops, some kind of machine like an oversized waffle maker. Couch with torn upholstery against one wall, galley kitchen in back, thin man with glasses and surprised look on face standing beside fridge. Bearded man snatching something lying on chair—

Gun.

Brass fired first. The bullet took the man in the chest, knocking him backward. The gun, a machine pistol, tumbled from his hands, landing at the feet of the thin man. He had a sandwich in one hand.

"Don't move," snapped Brass.

The man swallowed. "Can I put my sandwich down?"

"Sure," said Brass. "See, that's the advantage of a stakeout versus a criminal enterprise. We get to send out for pizza, while they're stuck in here making sandwiches. What is that, baloney?"

"Corned beef."

Sara got up carefully, covering Brass while he cuffed the man still standing. She moved to the bathroom door—it was open, and there was nobody inside. "We're clear."

"Well, corned beef is pretty good," Brass admitted. "Come on, we'll go down to the station and discuss the relative merits of French mustard versus German. You're Russian, you should have an interesting perspective."

"I'm not Russian. I'm from Carson City," the man said.

"Yeah? Well, welcome to Vegas."

Illarion Shayduko yanked open the door to his trailer and glared at Nick and Greg, a cigarette dangling from his lips. "What now?"

"Mr. Shayduko," said Nick. "I've got a search warrant for your trailer and workshop. Can you step outside, please?"

Shayduko squinted at Nick, took a long drag from his cigarette without moving his hands, then exhaled the smoke through his nose. "I wondered when you would be back," he said. "One moment." He slammed the door shut.

"Mr. Shayduko?" Nick called out. "I'm going to have to ask you to open the door, *right now*. You can't—"

The door swung back open. Shayduko had thrown a ratty bathrobe on over his yellow pajamas, the same ones he'd been wearing the last time he and Nick talked. "Don't get all excited, Mr. Stokes. You think I've never been rousted before? I'd like to put on my slippers, too—or are you afraid I'm smuggling contraband in the toes?'

"Uh—go ahead."

He slipped them on and shuffled down the steps. "There. Go ahead, do your worst. You can't make it any messier than it already is."

Shayduko stayed outside with a uniformed officer while Nick and Greg entered the trailer. Greg glanced around at the piles of incendiary devices, random electronics, and tools. "This could take a while."

"We're looking for anything that might match parts from the dirigible, or tools that could have been used to build it or the air cannon," said Nick.

"And the bolt cutters or metal shears that were used to break into the construction site." Greg nodded. "What say I look for tools and you take supplies?"

"Sounds good to me."

Nick concentrated on searching for wood glue; matching a sample to what he'd collected from the zeppelin remains wouldn't necessarily be conclusive, but it would be a start.

"I think I got something," said Greg finally. He held up a case for a Dremel Moto-tool, a handheld powered cutting device that rotated a bit at speeds of up to 37,000 rpm. Different bits could be used for many purposes: drilling, polishing, sanding, carving. There were even bits that let it function like a reciprocating saw, router, or planer.

Greg opened the case. "Well, the basic unit is here, but I don't see any of the cutting heads—just a grinder and a polisher."

"Keep looking."

Nick collected several bottles of glue. Greg found several small pairs of wire cutters but nothing larger.

"You know, I'm seeing a basic problem," said Greg. "There's no way he could have built the dirigible here. There isn't enough room."

"That's why the warrant also listed his workshop. He might do electronics here, but he has to have a bigger work area somewhere else. Can't build props for tigers and elephants in your living room."

"Any idea where it is?"

Nick hesitated. "Not exactly. But it's got to be on the grounds, right? He's going to be using power tools, lumber, maybe sheetmetal—no way he can keep all that hidden."

"Yeah, you're right. He's a legitimate craftsman, he'll have a legitimate workshop."

They went back to searching. "Well, well," said Nick, opening a tool box he'd just pulled out from under the bed. "Look at what I found." He held up a long-handled pair of bolt cutters.

"Great. Maybe our luck on this case has finally turned."

"What workshop?" Illarion Shayduko said. He smiled at Greg with nicotine-stained teeth and leaned back against the wall of his trailer. "What you see is what you get. I do all my work right here."

Greg glanced at Nick, who crossed his arms. Shayduko tossed his cigarette onto the ground, where it continued to smolder. "I'm telling you," Shayduko said, "I don't have a big fancy workshop."

Nick shook his head. "You can't expect us to believe you build all the props you need in there."

"I don't do set design—we outsource for things like that. This is Vegas, you know? Plenty of experienced people to build backdrops or platforms or what-have-you. You think an artist like myself would stoop to mere *carpentry*?"

"Forgive me for not taking you at your word," said Nick. "But I think we'll have to verify that before we can say we're done."

"Go ahead," said Shayduko. He took a step forward, crushing out the smoldering butt with the heel of his slipper. "Talk to anyone you want. They'll all tell you the same thing."

"We'll see," said Nick.

"I can't believe everyone told us the same thing," said Nick.

"We *were* warned," said Greg.

They were driving back to the lab with their samples. They'd had no luck locating Shayduko's workshop. Everyone they'd talked to, including hotel staff, insisted that work of the type they described was all handled by outside contractors. If Shayduko had been working on a remote-control zeppelin, either no one at the circus had seen him doing so or no one would admit to it.

"I know circus people are tight," said Greg, "but trying to keep a project like that under wraps would be difficult. And the people who work for the hotel are in and out all the time—you'd think somebody would have seen *something*."

"You know, they would have had to do more than just build the thing. They would have had to *test* it, too. Since Vegas hasn't been exactly rife with UFO reports in the last few weeks, they didn't do so out in the open."

Greg nodded. "That means a large, enclosed space to fly it around, like the amphitheater the circus performs in. But didn't we just rule that out?"

"That's not the large, enclosed space I'm talking about. I'm talking about the bear habitat out at the Bruin Rescue Ranch." Nick gave Greg a quick description of the place. "I didn't get a look at the other side of the fence, but it would be perfect—isolated, self-contained, spacious."

"And with its own set of oversized, furry security guards. You're right, it sounds perfect." Greg paused. "But the search warrant we have is only for the circus. We can't just go in and search a wildlife sanctuary without probable cause."

"I know, I know." Nick sighed. "Well, we got lucky once. If the stuff we just collected doesn't pan out, we might have to try again."

Judge Mayerling sighed, then put the book he'd been reading down on his desk. He looked at Nick, then at Greg. "I didn't expect to see you two back here so soon. I take it you didn't find what you were looking for?"

"No," said Nick. "None of the tools we collected matched the tool marks on the evidence. Same thing with the glue. But we're pretty sure we know why."

"The circus doesn't have a woodworking shop, per se," said Greg. "So we think the construction of the dirigible happened at the enclosed bear habitat at the Bruin Rescue Ranch."

"I see. And your reasoning for this is?"

"The bear attack was clearly faked," said Nick. "The bears came from the ranch, which has family ties to the Red Star Circus. This kind of elaborate operation would have needed a large, private area to hold practice runs—the building the bears are housed in is perfect."

"You're also asking for a DNA sample from one Bronislav Alexandrei, but I'm unclear as to why you think he'll be a match to the traces you found in . . . gauze wrappings?"

Greg nodded. "Alexandrei is the circus strong-man, Your Honor. Video footage of one of the suspects as well as the physical evidence indicate someone of above-average size and strength. He fits the bill."

Mayerling frowned. "Searching a trailer is one thing; going into an EPA-protected site is something else. If this doesn't produce results, what are you going to ask for next? You can't run tests on every woodworking shop in town."

"I know that, Your Honor," said Nick. "But this zeppelin had to have been built and tested some-where. If that place is the Bruin Rescue Ranch, we'll be able to prove it."

Mayerling sighed. "All right, I'll grant the war-rants. But if you don't find anything, don't come back to me again."

"Thank you, Your Honor," said Nick.

Mischa Korolev met Nick and Greg at the front door to the habitat. The bear handler did not look happy. "Yes?" he said.

"We've got a warrant to search the premises," said Nick, handing him the paper.

Korolev read it carefully. "Yes. All is in order.

You can come in." He stepped back and let them through the door.

Greg took a deep breath through his nose. "Ah. Man, it's like a mountain forest in here—this is great."

"Environment is carefully controlled," said Korolev. "Temperature, humidity, length of daylight. We take good care."

"Nobody's saying you don't," said Nick. "As the warrant says, we're looking for woodworking equipment. You must have some sort of tool shed or workshop?"

"Yes. Come with me." Korolev turned and marched away.

He led them to an area in a corner of the habitat, right next to the fence that walled off the bears' living space. It looked oddly out of place, simply a platform and three five-foot-high walls standing in the middle of a forest. "This is where things are built," said Korolev. "Is not my job—I know very little."

"Thanks," said Greg, putting down his CSI kit. "We'll take it from here."

"If you could wait outside?" said Nick.

Korolev nodded and left without another word.

"I don't know," said Greg, looking around. "I'm not seeing a lot of power tools. Hand saws, hammers, screwdrivers, clamps—the biggest thing they've got is a chainsaw."

"Well, all of the individual pieces were delicate," said Nick. "The zeppelin was built for lightness, not durability. I'm more interested in finding a cutting head for that Dremel."

They got to work. Between them, they found

wood glue and numerous cutting implements, though no Dremel cutting heads turned up.

"All right, we're about finished here," said Nick. "Ready for the hard stuff?"

They went outside and found Korolev, sitting in a lawn chair and talking to the uniformed officer posted outside.

"All right," said Nick. "We've checked over the workshop. Now we need to see the rest of the habitat."

Korolev got to his feet. "Excuse me?"

"Where the bears live," said Nick. "It's in the warrant—we have access to all areas."

Korolev frowned. "It is not safe."

"You go in there, don't you?" asked Greg.

"Bears know me. Before I can let you in, there are some bears that must be isolated. Might take some time—if bear is stubborn, not much can be done."

"You'd better get started, then," said Nick. "We'll watch."

Korolev glared at them, then stalked inside. Greg and Nick followed as Korolev led them to the interior gate that divided the two parts of the habitat. He opened it with a key, stepped inside, slammed it closed without a word, then stomped off into the trees.

"You think he's going to destroy evidence?" asked Greg.

"He's had plenty of time to do that already. No, I think he's just annoyed that we're disrupting the bears' routine."

"You have no idea how right you are," said

Nadya Karnova, walking up behind them. "Mischa's more protective of his animals than a mamma grizzly is of her cubs."

"We'll be as quick as we can," said Greg. "We just don't want to be turned into bear chow while we're working."

"Oh, little chance of that," said Nadya. "Bears are pretty easygoing, all things considered. When you're that big, there aren't a lot of things you feel threatened by."

"Size isn't everything," said Greg. "I mean, even a bear can be stung by a bee."

"Sure," she said. "They just don't care. Once a bear gets into a honeycomb, he'll keep on eating until it's all gone, no matter how many times he gets stung. He'll eat more than just the honey, too—bee larvae, even the bees themselves. It's all more protein to him."

"Guess every diet has its price," said Nick.

She grinned. "Ain't that the truth. It's always a question of payoff versus pain, I guess. Bears are omnivores, just like humans, so the range of what they'll eat is pretty amazing. There was a bear adopted by a Polish Army unit in World War II that was famous for eating cigarettes."

"That couldn't have been good for him," said Greg. "Nicotine's a poison."

Nadya shrugged. "Well, he was a Syrian brown bear, and he died at the age of twenty-two. That's pretty good for the ursine family. Grizzlies only last fifteen to twenty years in the wild."

Korolev abruptly reappeared. "Okay," he said,

unlocking the gate. "Problem animals mostly contained."

"Mostly?" said Greg.

Nick clapped him on the shoulder, and they went inside.

"I will stay with you," said Korolev. It wasn't a question. "For your own safety."

"Fine," said Nick. "Just don't get in our way."

They did a slow, thorough canvass of the entire space. Bears stared at them from behind wire gates set into the walls, seemingly curious about their unexpected guests.

They found a clearing close to the far wall, a relatively open space with deep gouges on the nearby trees where bears had been sharpening their claws. Greg knelt and said, "Look at this. Sawdust."

"We spread it here sometimes," said Korolev. "The bears like to roll around in it. It reminds them of their circus days."

"Sure," said Nick. "I'll bet there were all kinds of things in this clearing that reminded them of the good old days. None of it's here now, though, is it?"

Korolev met Nick's eyes blankly. "Only memories," he said quietly.

18

"Say 'ahh,' " said Greg.

Bronislav Alexandrei glared at him from the other side of the interview table. "And if I say *no* instead?" said the strongman.

Greg swallowed, holding a tiny cotton swab on a stick as if it were a magic wand that could protect him. Alexandrei was a big man, all muscle; his shaved head was tattooed with an intricate, curving dragon, the open jaws breathing twin jets of fire that curved over both his eyebrows. His features were surprisingly delicate, his nose small and his eyes large; the overall effect was of a baby who had wandered into a tattoo parlor by accident after falling into a vat of steroids.

"Then I'll be forced to ask again, even more politely," said Greg. "Please?"

"Hmmph. You know, I can bite an iron nail in two."

"I have absolutely no doubt of that."

"Let's get this over with." Bronislav opened his mouth.

Greg took the buccal swab as quickly and carefully as possible, and didn't realize he'd been holding his breath until he was finished. "Okay," he said, bagging the swab. "Thank you for your cooperation."

"What cooperation? You had a warrant."

"That's true." *But I* don't *have an elephant gun loaded with tranquilizers, a professional wrestling organization that owes me a favor, and those gas grenades they used on King Kong.* "All the same."

"You've got my DNA. Can I go now?"

"Not just yet. I have a few questions."

"Go ahead. I don't have anything to hide."

"I understand you and your girlfriend attended a party last night."

"Who told you that?"

"Your girlfriend."

"Oh." Alexandrei crossed his arms, which was a bit like watching two redwoods trying to embrace. "Well, she must have been talking about someone else. I wasn't there."

"Really. So the DNA I just took isn't going to match the DNA we pulled off the bandages left behind at the scene?"

"Don't see how it could."

Greg studied the man, puzzled. Alexandrei seemed awfully sure of himself. Of course, the ability to tear a phone book in half anytime you felt like it probably bestowed a certain amount of self-confidence, but still . . .

"So where were you last night?"

"In my hotel room, asleep."

"You have any way to verify that?"

"No. I was alone."

Greg nodded. "Thank you for coming in, Mr. Alexandrei. I'll be in touch about those DNA results."

"I'm sure you will." Alexandrei grinned, revealing teeth that were small and white and perfect. "But I don't think you'll be happy."

Nick watched the strongman leave, then joined Greg in the interview room. "Man, that guy's muscles have muscles. What do you think he benches? Four hundred, four hundred fifty?"

"It's not his upper-body strength that worries me. It's his attitude."

"What, did he threaten you?" Nick glanced over his shoulder quickly. "Don't let his size intimidate you. I've seen you face guys a lot scarier—"

"That's not it." Greg paused. "Well, okay, trying to stare down a guy who looks like he used to beat up the Hulk for his lunch money was a little nerve-wracking, but you're right—I've been in the same room with cold-blooded killers plenty of times, and size has nothing to do with how dangerous someone is. No, I mean he's denying being at the party with Alisa Golovina at all."

"Even after you took his DNA?"

"Yeah. Didn't faze him."

Nick sat down in the chair Alexandrei had been in. "Great. Another factor that doesn't add up."

"I know. So far, all we have is an elaborate plot to do—what? Embarrass the hotel? Make us look like morons? 'Cause I gotta tell you, I'm starting to feel like one."

Nick shook his head. "I know. None of the stuff we got from the circus or the ranch matched any of our evidence. I'm sure they were using the bear habitat as a staging ground, but they must have gotten rid of everything before we got there." He paused. "You know, somebody, somewhere, has got to be making money off this. Nobody goes to this much trouble otherwise."

Greg mock-frowned and said in a heavy Russian accent, "That is very capitalist attitude, comrade. Maybe it is all being done for the good of the state."

"If the Berlin Wall were still standing, I'd give that theory good odds, Gregor. This case has more Russians popping out of the woodwork than an old Rocky and Bullwinkle cartoon."

"No moose, though. Just bears. No viable suspects, either."

"Lack of suspects isn't our problem. Lack of suspects for our only real crime—the arson—is. I mean, anyone could have been remote-controlling that dirigible."

"Well, we're pretty sure we know who was fired out of that air cannon. Too bad we didn't find any prints or trace that could prove it. So what's next?"

Nick got up. "I don't know about you," he said, "but I'm going to go back over everything we've done so far. We must be missing something."

Greg got to his feet, too. "When in doubt," he said, "run in circles, scream and shout."

Nick stopped. "How does that apply?"

Greg shrugged. "It doesn't. I just couldn't think of something that rhymed."

"Oh." Nick paused. "Yeah, okay."

Greg stood in the crime lab parking lot, studying the mock-up they'd built of the Panhandle's roof. Pulleys were attached with clamps at the pipe, the edge of the roof, and the windowsill.

Nick walked up behind him. "You still working on your fire-hose theory?"

"Nah. I think I made a wrong turn there."

"Hey, it happens to everybody—"

"No, I mean a *literal* wrong turn." Greg pointed at the pulley mounted on the pipe that had bent. "We thought that something was being lowered or raised from the roof, right?"

"That's the direction the pipe was bent."

"Yeah, but what if there was another pulley? One over here?" Greg walked over to an empty section of the mock-up with a taped-off square marked "Elevator Machine Room."

"Well, that's in the same general area—it's to the left instead of the right, but the pipe would still bend the same way."

"And if we forget about trying to thread a fire hose through a pulley," Greg pointed out, "then we eliminate the jamming problem."

"So the hose was a completely separate thing—"

"—and the pulleys were used with something more conventional, like rope. Not over the edge of the roof, but into the elevator shaft."

"Where it was used to haul something up or

lower something down." Nick nodded. "We need to take another look at that roof."

"And that elevator shaft."

Greg squinted up at the roof of the elevator machine room.

"Can you see anything?" asked Nick from behind him.

"There's a lot of dirt and grease up here. Just a second . . ." Greg shone his flashlight on the cables that pulled the elevator up and down, then on the two massive pulleys that they ran through, bolted to a steel I-beam set into the concrete of the elevator shaft itself. "Wait a minute. I think I've got something, behind one of the pulleys. Yeah, there's something there. Tool mark, same as the others."

"So a pulley *was* clamped there. All we have to do now—"

"—is find out what was being hauled."

"And which direction it was going."

"And where it wound up."

"And who—you know, let's just focus on what."

"Good idea."

After they'd documented the tool marks with pictures, they headed down to the lobby. They'd already arranged with the hotel engineer to have the private elevator locked down on the main floor; now they had security let them into the basement offices via the regular one.

A few curious employees on their coffee break stood around and watched as they used a crowbar to crack open the sliding elevator doors.

"Couldn't they just press a button or something?"

a brunette in a dark business skirt and white blouse said.

The man standing beside her, dressed in a gray suit and sipping coffee out of a tall paper cup, shook his head. "Nah. They have to shut all the electrics down for safety. That way, they don't have to worry about the car coming down and, you know, squashing them."

"I think I saw that happen in a movie once. It was gross. Cut this guy right in half."

Greg did his best to ignore them. "Great," he muttered under his breath. "Now that I don't have to worry about plunging to my death, all I can think of is a big metal box hanging over my head. That, and Wile E. Coyote cartoons."

The doors popped open and Nick set the pry bar down. "This one's mine," he said. He shone a flashlight around the base of the elevator shaft; other than the shock absorber—a large piston mounted in an oil-filled cylinder that provided a cushion in case of emergencies—there was a variety of accumulated junk, things that had slipped through the crack between the floor of the car and whatever floor it had stopped at. Pens, key cards, pieces of paper, playing cards, change, combs, a butter knife, even a few casino chips.

"It's like the world's largest couch cushion," said Nick. "Most of this stuff has been here for a while—you can tell by the layer of dust and grease."

"Not all of it, though," said Greg. "Some of the stuff is cleaner than the rest." He pointed at one corner.

"I see it. Looks like a casino chip—newer than the others, though. And is that—"

"Blood," said Greg. "How much do you want to bet it turns out to be from a pig?"

Nick climbed into the shaft, picked the chip up with a gloved hand, and studied it. "Maybe," he said. "But so far, just about everything in this case hasn't been what it seems. I'm not ready to put my money on a winner just yet."

Jim Brass studied the man sitting across the interview table the way a gourmet chef would consider a side of beef. Brass's eyes were coldly analytical, but the rest of his face suggested that he was mulling over various recipes and couldn't quite decide on one.

The man's name was Leon James Governor. He was a college student with a certain amount of technical skill that he was using to help with tuition—at least, that's what Brass was sure he'd say to defend himself. The fact that he'd dropped out last year was no doubt just a temporary glitch, to be rectified as soon as he'd put a little hard-earned money aside. Leon had short, curly hair, wire-framed glasses at least ten years out of style, and the build of a scarecrow.

"Oh, if I only had a brain," Brass remarked.

Leon looked confused. It was a look he'd worn more or less since the first moment Brass had laid eyes on him, but they'd been together long enough now that certain subtle nuances of his bafflement had become apparent. The look he was wearing now, for instance, was the one Leon got when one of Brass's comments failed to register as being clever and/or witty.

"What?" Leon blurted.

"Never mind. How you doing, Leon?"

"I'm—I'm okay."

"Really? Seen a lot of people die right in front of you, have you?"

The look on Leon's face slid away from confused and toward queasy. "Uh—no."

"Oh, I'm sorry. I misspoke. What I meant to ask was, have you seen a lot of people *killed* right in front of you." Brass paused. "Well, have you?"

"No. No, I haven't."

"Well, if I'd run into you before today, I'd have told you to get used to it. Because these thugs you're working for, the Red Mafiya? They order assassinations the way other people order eggs. Scrambled, sunny-side up, fried . . . you get the idea."

"I don't—I don't know anything about a Red Mafiya."

"No? What language did you think your boss was yelling in? Pig Latin?"

"I don't know."

Brass nodded. "Sure. Just like you didn't know about all that phony plastic you were cranking out. You know, right now the crime lab is processing everything in that room, and we both know they're going to find your fingerprints all over the place. But I guess that doesn't really matter."

"Why not?"

"Same reason you won't have to get used to watching people get murdered in front of you. Well, you might have to watch *one*, but only if there's a mirror in the room."

Leon turned the volume on his confusion a little higher. Brass was starting to suspect it wasn't so much a lack of reasoning skills as a defense mechanism. "What are you talking about?"

"*Vory v zakone.* Know what that means? 'Thieves in law.' See, these guys live by a very strict code, and they kill anyone who breaks it. Did you know that in World War Two, members of the Red Mafiya in Soviet prisons were offered a deal? Enlist in the army and fight for Mother Russia in return for reduced jail time. Considering the conditions in some of those prisons, facing death on the front lines probably seemed like a pretty good idea."

"Let me guess. None of them took it."

Brass smiled gently. "Who's telling this story, you or me? No, there were Russians—even psychotic criminal Russians—who loved their country just as much as any other patriot. They joined up, fought the good fight—and then, at the conclusion of the war, the ones who survived were sent back to finish their shortened sentences."

Brass shook his head. "Unfortunately, the first rule of the code is *Never cooperate with the authorities.* Every last one of them was dead within a year—killed by their former comrades."

The confusion on Leon's face cranked up to new heights, pushed there by the terror bubbling up underneath. "Why are you telling me this? I mean, if you're trying to get me to cooperate, that's like the *worst* possible thing you could possibly say."

"Gee, you think so? I'm pretty sure I haven't played my ace yet."

Leon shook his head violently, as if he could

shake free all the horrifying thoughts competing for attention. "No. I'm not talking to you. No way."

"See, the guys you were working for aren't dumb. Evil, ruthless, and cruel, yes, but not dumb. I'm sure they already gave you some version of this speech before you ever saw a credit-card blank, and maybe they even spiced it up with some visual aids." Brass shrugged. "I would have brought in some slides, but our department's budget is tight. Besides, what's the point in trying to compete with a multinational criminal organization? They can afford to blow up a warehouse full of Lamborghinis just to make a point. Me, I have to fill out a requisition form if I lose a Sharpie."

Brass sighed and stared off into space for a moment. "Anyway, where was I? Oh, yeah, how completely screwed you are. As I was saying, the *zakone* boys play for keeps. That means that when a loose end—like you—is left dangling in the wind, they make sure to"—Brass made a scissoring motion with two of his fingers—"cut it off."

"But—but I'm not going to talk."

"I know. Dead men tell no tales and all that."

"No! No, I mean I'm not going to inform on them! They can't kill me if I don't talk!"

Now it was Brass's turn to look confused. He had no desire to compete with a master, so he kept it down around simple puzzlement. "Why not? Did I miss a memo? Was there a change in the official rule book? Oh, wait—there isn't one."

He leaned forward and favored Leon with a cold, completely humorless smile. "They can do pretty much whatever they want, Leon. The only reason you're still breathing at this very moment is because you're in police custody. And *now* I'm going to tell you the very, very worst thing I could possibly say to you at this moment."

Brass met Leon's eyes, but didn't say anything. The moment stretched out until Leon finally whispered, "What?"

"I'm letting you go," said Brass.

19

HIGH HOPES, CATHERINE thought. There was only one place in Vegas she could think of that would embody that phrase in literal as opposed to metaphorical terms.

She stood on the sidewalk—sorry, thc slidewalk—outside the Silver Spire and looked up. Way, way up. The Spire was the fifth-tallest free-standing observation tower in the United States, and looked like a gleaming rocket about to take off. The casino in the base, the rooms with their porthole-shaped windows, the restaurant named the Bridge at the very peak of the structure—all of it was designed around one theme: the future.

Can't have a future without hope—though some futures are grimmer than others.

Screams rose into the air as if to underscore her point. They came from the belly of the massive, semitransparent alien that pulsed its way up the side of the gleaming superstructure, suckered tentacles writhing with menace. It made the ascent every ten minutes or so; at the top, it was blasted with laser beams, which sent it ululating to its death far, far below. Then it was time for another bellyload of customers, another slow ascent, another fast plunge to its doom.

To the tourists who rode it, the Alienator was just another Vegas thrill ride, though it was one of the highest in the world.

But to John Bannister and Theria Kostapolis?

The ship reaches into the sky, a mile or more high. The creature that scales its heights is horrible, a continually shifting monstrosity that's hard to look at—not only because of the screaming souls dissolving in its transparent guts, but because it doesn't seem to be wholly of this dimension. It has a terrifying sort of depth to it that induces the same kind of stomach-tickling fear Bannister feels when looking down from an extreme height. Up and down it goes, never stopping, always feeding.

Both Bannister and Theria are familiar with the myth of Pandora, who opened a chest and set loose of all the world's evils. They understand the meaning of the myth, as well. The very last thing to leave the chest was hope, and the reason for that wasn't to give the story a happy ending. Hope is the greatest monster of all, the one that makes all the others worse simply by existing.

And that's exactly what this immense ship represents: the hope that one day, the residents of hell will be able to leave. It's visible from any point in the land, and clearly big enough to carry every last tormented soul to safety. Every time one of the damned sees its elegant, silvery shape, all that they've suffered—all that they have yet to suffer—seems unimaginably worse, because the possibility of freedom is right there in front of their eyes.

Bannister and Theria do not hesitate. They enter.

Catherine walked through the main entrance, a curving line of revolving doors made to look like transparent rocket tubes. Inside, the casino was laid out like the surface of a distant planet; the sky was a black dome overhead, projected images of at least seven moons of varying size and color moving at different speeds through a starry sky. The omnipresent chime and whir of the slot machines seemed both more natural and more alien in the setting.

The place is full of robots. One-armed robots, busy using their singular appendage to perform brain surgery on the blank-eyed subjects perched on stools before them. At second glance, Bannister realizes they aren't actually stools; they're a kind of four-legged docking station, a thick translucent cable plugging into the base of the spinal cord of the people sitting on them.

Bannister wonders what kind of bizarre fantasies are being fed to their brains. Are they living in an even worse world than this one, or are they experiencing scenarios where happiness is always just out of reach?

He thinks he knows the answer.

"Hope," Catherine muttered. "Demonstrating a commitment to hope, that's why they came here. That has to mean trying to escape from hell."

She headed for the elevators. She knew how crazy it would sound if she said it out loud, but if you were going to escape from Hell Vegas in a giant rocket, you obviously had to commandeer the flight deck. That would presumably be located in the nose of the ship, the restaurant known as the Bridge.

The elevator was made of glass, the soundtrack an upbeat version of "Major Tom." *High hopes,* she thought as the car surged upward and the ground receded. *High hopes . . .*

The fact that no one tries to stop them bothers Bannister a lot.

He knows they can't be the first to have tried this. He wonders, briefly, if the reason Satan has put up a gigantic beacon in the middle of hell is simply as a glorified bug zapper, with nothing but an agonizing, twitching death waiting at the top. Or maybe there's no fuel, the ship a grounded derelict kept gleaming solely for the sake of appearances, its engine a rusted, inoperable hulk.

But no. Word would get out. Hope had to be kept alive, a dim but persistent spark, in order to wring the maximum amount of cruelty out of it. The ship would be capable of flight.

Not that it matters.

"Not that it matters," Catherine said under her breath, then frowned. *Why did I say that?*

The elevator stopped, the door slid open, and abruptly she knew.

Because they didn't come here to escape. They came here to demonstrate their commitment to the idea of hope . . . and that's exactly what they did, about twenty feet straight in front of me.

The sign in the lobby of the restaurant read:

"Enter to Win a Trip to Outer Space!" A mock-up of a sleek, double-bodied ship hung suspended from the roof with wires, but Catherine recognized it as more than just another prop. It was a model of the *SkyArrow,* a ship now being built by one of the burgeoning space-tourism start-ups; they planned to offer actual rides into orbit for those wealthy enough to shell out a hundred thousand dollars for a few minutes of weightlessness and the most spectacular view they'd ever see. Apparently, one of the ways they were raising the necessary capital was by raffling off a seat on one of their flights.

The model hung over a booth, manned by an attractive young woman wearing a uniform that looked as if a *Star Trek* convention attendee and a stewardess had a mix-up at the dry cleaner's. Catherine walked up and said, "Excuse me. I was wondering if you'd seen this couple in here today?" She handed over a picture.

The woman—her name was either Annika or Veronika; the font on her name tag was so futuristic it was hard to read—glanced at the picture and nodded. "Sure, I remember them. He had one arm in a sling, and he walked with a very pronounced limp—well, actually, it was more like he couldn't bend one of his legs. They bought two draw tickets, one for each of them. I told them that even if they won the draw they'd probably have to pass a physical, but they were very insistent."

"I'll bet. Did they say anything else? In particular, where they were headed after this?"

Annika-or-Veronika frowned. "Well, they did ask me something kind of odd—after they filled out the forms they wanted to know if I was satisfied, or maybe if my boss was satisfied. I told them I was, and so far my boss hasn't had any complaints. They seemed happy with that. As for where they were going next . . . I thought I heard the woman say something about 'following the signs.' "

"Following the signs? You're sure that's what she said?"

The woman thought about it for a moment. "Well, I don't remember the exact way she put it, but I'm pretty sure that was it. Following the signs."

Catherine nodded. "Thank you."

As they descend once more toward the floor of hell, Bannister takes Theria's hand. "You heard what she said. We've done it. You can rest now."

"Yes. At last, I can rest."

"You're sure of the place?"

"I am. It calls to me. Ever since we first laid eyes on it." It was like a gift from Lucifer himself, the sight of it far below beckoning to them as they stared out the window.

Bannister nods. He feels an exhausted sense of accomplishment, but also a deep sadness. Theria will finally be able to rest, but he will not. He will stay here, in hell, and wait. The tickets in his pocket represent the tiniest fragment of hope that they might be able to leave this place, but in order to prove his commitment to that hope, he has to be physically present for whatever farce passes for a draw. He suspects the actual date will be postponed, then postponed again; a brighter tomorrow always just out of reach, in a future constantly receding.

20

Nick and Greg took the casino chip they'd found in the elevator shaft back to the lab. Nick collected the blood and took samples to both Mandy and Hodges, while Greg examined the chip itself.

Casinos used a variety of methods to protect themselves from fake tokens. Chips were made out of metal or compression-molded clay, but other elements—such as sand or chalk—were added to increase their durability. The process used to make them was a closely guarded trade secret, though it was generally acknowledged to be both time-consuming and expensive enough to discourage most would-be counterfeiters.

Greg was examining the chip under a microscope when Nick came back. "Hodges has gone back to thinking this is all part of some elaborate scheme to make him look ridiculous."

Greg looked up from the eyepiece. "Did you tell him he was doing just fine without any help?"

Nick grinned and shook his head. "Seemed a little too easy. I just laughed mysteriously and walked away."

"That's cruel."

"That's Hodges."

"True. Well, I've already found something else interesting about this casino chip. Take a look."

Nick peered into the eyepiece. "What am I looking at?"

"That's the line between the edge spots and the main body of the chip. In a regular chip, the two are made from different colors of clay; the alternating edge sections are actually inserted into the chip afterward."

"Not here, though," said Nick. "At this magnification, we should be able to see that line between the two pieces as clearly as the gutter in a bowling alley. These spots have just been painted on."

"Fake clowns, fake killer bears, and now fake casino chips. I'm starting to wonder exactly what about this case is real."

Nick looked up from the eyepiece. "How about the kind of money you could make from exchanging counterfeit chips for real cash?"

Sara met Brass in the hall outside the interview room. "How'd it go?"

"Oh, it was messy. He broke down in tears, practically begged me to take him into protective custody. I guess I just have a trustworthy face."

"Yeah, that must be it. You think we'll get anything useful from him?"

"Already have." Brass handed her a piece of paper. "He didn't know a whole lot—not high enough on the totem pole. But he did give up a few names."

She scanned the paper, then folded it and stuck it into her pocket. "I'll compare notes with Nick and Greg. Maybe we can find a connection between one of these guys and our case."

"All right. You need me for anything else?"

"No, I've taken up enough of your time."

"No problem."

As she walked away, Brass muttered, "I just hope you know what you've gotten yourself into, Sara."

"Congratulations," said Hodges, handing the print-out of the GC mass-spec results to Greg. "It's a match."

Greg took the sheet and studied it, leaning back against the counter in the trace lab. "This is from the counterfeit chip?"

"Yes. Exactly the same composition as the powder you found in the hotel room—calcium carbonate, silica, sodium, magnesium, and iron. In the same ratio, too."

Greg grinned. "Thanks, Hodges."

"See how helpful I can be when I'm allowed a little me time?"

Greg took the printout to the conference room, where Nick and Sara were already waiting. "Okay," said Greg, taking a seat. "I've got something. I don't know if it'll break the case, but it's starting to crack."

"Give," said Sara.

Greg told them about the powder matching the chip. "I don't know what it means exactly, but it ties that room to an illegal activity."

Nick nodded. "Yeah, and the first reason we've found for anyone to go to all this trouble. Counterfeit chips could mean big money."

"Big money, big motive," said Sara. "But making counterfeit chips isn't easy. You need major resources, insider knowledge, and plenty of lead time."

Greg put his elbows on the table. "In other words, the kind of thing only professional criminals would touch."

"Which brings me to my news," said Sara. "Brass just busted a fake credit-card scam being run out of a storefront on Fremont. Guess who was bankrolling it?"

Greg put up his hand. "Someone who has the extended version of *Dr. Zhivago* on DVD?"

"Exactly. I also ran into a rather large gentleman who does Russian mob tattoos."

"How large?" asked Nick.

"In the same range as our bandage-wrapped two-wheeled suspect. Claims he was working during the party, but I haven't verified that yet."

Nick leaned back and crossed his arms. "Phony cards, phony tokens. Two kinds of surrogate currency, one source?"

"Maybe," said Sara. She handed both of them photocopies of the report Brass had given her. "The guy cranking out the plastic gave up a few names. Any of them look familiar?"

"Actually, yes," said Nick. "Dr. Nikolai Villaruba. Not the most Russian of surnames, but his first name fits. He's the vet for the bears out at the ranch—and someone who doesn't seem to know all that much about bears."

"Well, according to this," said Sara, "he's also one of the sources the operation uses to get credit information. After all, who's more trustworthy than the man who makes little Fido or Fluffy all better?"

"Sounds like we need to have another talk with the good doctor," said Nick.

Dr. Villaruba looked just as unsettled as he had the first time Nick had interviewed him; his gaze kept moving around the interview room, never staying on any one thing for more than a few seconds.

Nick studied him for a moment before speaking. "Well, Dr. Villaruba, I have a few more questions for you."

"About what? I told you all I know about the bear attack, which isn't much—"

"That's true. But then, you don't really know that much about bears, do you?"

Villaruba frowned. "I *am* a trained veterinarian. My hands-on experience may not be that high, but I'm a qualified professional—"

"How's your credit rating, Doctor?"

"I—what?"

"I took a look at your finances. Your little clinic isn't doing too well, is it? You maybe go out on a limb, borrow a little cash from a friend? Maybe somebody you know through a family connection?"

Oddly, Villaruba's reaction was almost exactly the opposite of how most people would respond to pressure; he calmed down. His eyes stopped roaming around the room and settled on Nick. His shoulders went back, ever so slightly, and when he replied, his voice was mild. "I'm afraid I don't know what you're talking about."

"I'm talking about you feeding credit-card receipts to a plastic farm," said Nick. "I'm talking about an organization that wasn't satisfied with that particular repayment of your debt and asked you to do something else as well. Something that had to do with cleaning up a certain bear-related mess."

"That's a serious charge. Am I under arrest?"

"Not yet."

"Then I think I'm done talking to you. Any further questions you have can be directed to my lawyer."

"Well, that was a bust," said Nick. He leaned back in his chair at the conference table and stared first at Greg, then at Sara. Neither of them looked hopeful. "All we have is hearsay, and that's not enough to put any kind of pressure on him. He's not going to buckle the way Brass's guy did—not without any charges hanging over his head, and he lawyered up in a heartbeat. Everybody knows what happens when you cross the Russian mob."

Sara looked thoughtful. "Maybe applying pressure is the wrong way to go."

"So what are we gonna do?" asked Greg. "Have them over for drinks?"

"I was thinking more of an informal conversation—and not with the animal doctor," said Sara. "Every Mafia type I've ever dealt with—Red or not—has a certain amount of inherent arrogance; the higher the position, the bigger the ego. Grigori

Dyalov is at the top of the food chain here in Vegas, and if I talked to him on his own turf, he might let something slip."

Nick shook his head. "I don't know. The few things I've heard about Dyalov make him sound about as friendly as a blizzard, and not nearly as warm."

"So I'll dress for winter," said Sara. "It's not like we have anything to lose."

Nick and Greg looked at each other. Greg shrugged. "I don't have a better idea, do you?"

Nick sighed. "Than poking a grizzly in his own den? Wish I could say yes, but—"

"Hey, it's just another interview," said Sara. "What could go wrong?"

According to Jim Brass, the place Grigori Dyalov could most often be found was the Summerville Country Club, an exclusive gated community that featured eighty luxury homes, two golf courses, a dozen tennis courts, and its own Olympic-sized pool facility. The club itself was the centerpiece, a mansion housing a private library, a fitness center, two restaurants, and a luxury spa.

Sara admired the view as she drove up to the security gates. The ochre cliffs of Red Rock Canyon were visible in the distance, but the property itself was dominated by green: trees, grass, carefully tended shrubs and hedges. All on the other side of the chain-link fence, of course; you could see the lushness, but to experience it fully required getting past the armed security guard on duty twenty-four hours a day. Fortunately, her CSI identification was all she needed to be waved through.

No sign of an economic downturn here; if any of the sprawling mansions she drove by had been fore-closed on, you wouldn't know it from the outside. Of course, living right next to a golf course had its advantages—never any shortage of groundskeep-ers, for one. She wondered about stray golf balls, though. Did windows ever get broken? If so, was it covered by your house insurance? Did you have to return the ball?

Ah, the problems of the rich. She shook her head as she parked beside the clubhouse. How *did* they cope?

The clubhouse featured a pro shop, a dining room, and a bar with no name; Sara supposed that if you found yourself there, there was a pretty good chance you knew where you were. It was decorated in that old-school, stuffy way that decorators the world over seemed to think was synonymous with being rich: everything that wasn't made out of an-cient, highly polished oak was made out of ancient, highly polished brass. Despite this, the place was open and airy, with one entire wall of glass display-ing a panoramic version of the view she'd been ad-miring before.

Grigori Dyalov was a short, broad-shouldered man in his late sixties, almost square in outline; his head had the same contours, with a chin like a block and a brow like an overhanging cliff. A nasty scar started at his cheekbone, curved around to just miss the corner of his right eye, bisected his eye-brow, and faded out of view in the snow-white, bristly field of his crew cut. His face looked as if you hit it with a hammer, the hammer would break.

He was standing at the far end of the room, his suit jacket off and draped over a nearby chair, the sleeves of his white shirt rolled up past the elbow. Tattoos covered his muscular arms. He was playing darts, holding three of them between two fingers of his left hand and aiming carefully with his right.

Two large men, clearly bodyguards, sat hunched over beers at a table a few feet away. They both got to their feet as Sara walked up, though none of the other people in the bar—mostly men in their fifties or older—reacted with anything more than an appraising glance.

Sara stopped a respectful distance away. Dyalov lined up his shot, then threw. The dart thunked into the board. Triple twenty.

"Nice toss," said Sara.

"Thank you." Dyalov turned to look at her, then waved his bodyguards back to their seats. "And you are?"

"Sara Sidle, Las Vegas Crime Lab." She pulled out her ID. "I was hoping to get your perspective on a few recent events."

Dyalov's face gave away nothing. "You want to question me?"

"Nothing like that. You're not a suspect; I'm just gathering information. I was hoping to draw on your experience."

Sara had found that older men usually responded well to that particular approach—some better than others. Dyalov didn't disappoint her.

"I doubt that I could be of much use to you, but

if there's anything a broken-down old warhorse like myself can do to help, I'll do my best. I warn you, though—once you get me telling stories, it's hard to shut me up."

His voice was at odds with his appearance. It was the voice of a cultured man, charming and sincere, with just a tiny amount of amusement. That voice sounded completely at home in this environment, its light Russian accent giving it a touch of the exotic without seeming coarse.

"Please," he said, motioning with one hand to a nearby table. "Let's sit and talk."

She took a seat, but Dyalov remained on his feet. He turned back to the dartboard, lined up another shot. "Now. What concerns you?"

"Well, I'm investigating a case, and the names that keep turning up all have something in common. One of them led me in your direction."

"Ah. Russian names, you mean? I'm no genealogist, but I am fairly well connected to the local . . . families. What name in particular?"

Sara smiled. "The name itself isn't important. I'm more concerned with the fact that it appeared on a fake credit card."

He threw another dart. Another triple twenty. "I don't understand. Fake credit card, fake name, no? I don't see how I could help with that. You want an expert in made-up names, you should talk to a novelist. Not a retired soldier."

"Some soldiers are a little better versed in fake IDs than others."

He turned back toward her and smiled. "I suppose that's true. Especially in the intelligence community, though my own expertise is sadly outdated. Technology makes antiques of us all."

"Maybe." She smiled back. "But old habits die hard. Someone in your profession must still have a lot of contacts."

He chuckled. "In Moscow, yes. Even in Afghanistan, Kazakhstan, Chechnya. But here, I'm just an old bull put out to pasture."

She glanced around the room. "Pretty nice pasture."

"I have no complaints."

"I wasn't aware the *Komitet Gosudarstvennoy Bezopasnosti* had such a generous pension plan."

His smile widened. "Very good. Did you memorize that before coming here?"

"I know a little about Russian history."

"Do you?" He turned back to the dartboard, lifted the third dart but didn't throw it. He held it up, then rolled it back and forth between his index finger and thumb as if admiring a fine cigar. "I'm sorry, I don't mean to sound skeptical. Since the Wall fell and the Internet rose, so much that was hidden is now in plain sight; I'm sure you know things that in my youth would have been considered state secrets. Still, there are some things up here"—he tapped his head with the flights of the dart—"that will never be known by the rest of the world." His emphasis on the word never was light but unmistakable.

"State secrets aren't usually my department—and the ones I'm interested in have less to do with assassinations and more to do with tigers balancing on giant balls."

"Oh, I see. The circus. That's what you wanted to ask me about?"

She studied him carefully, but he seemed genuinely curious, as well as a little surprised. "Yes. The case I'm working on involves a crime that required quite a bit of organization—but the organization involved seems to be one that's fond of tightropes, trained bears, and clowns."

"I see. Not just a circus but a Russian circus. You're sure?"

"That seems to be the direction the investigation is headed."

"Credit-card fraud perpetrated by circus performers. What do they do, apply for accounts in the names of the elephants?"

"It's a little more serious than that. I was hoping that if you knew of any connections between the Russian circus and . . . other organizations, you might let me know."

"Other organizations." He sounded amused. He held the dart up, holding it between two fingers by the point, like a knife thrower preparing to launch possible death at an assistant strapped to a bull's-eye. "You are talking about the *Bratva*, yes? The Brotherhood, the so-called Red Mob?"

"I was speaking hypothetically."

"That's good. Because, in fact, the *vory v zakone* are exactly that, a hypothetical organization."

"I'm not sure I follow."

He turned back to face her, took a step closer. "There are some who say it does not exist."

"I've heard that argument. Usually in court, declared by the lawyers of certain Italian families."

"That's just denial. In the case of the Red Mafiya, no one is saying that certain crimes are not being committed—they're saying there's no central organization, no coordinated group."

"That seems unlikely."

"No. It is simply Russian." He gestured at her with the dart, still holding it by the tip. "It is a direct outgrowth of communism. Under that regime, there were two kinds of criminals: the ones who learned how to manipulate the system and those who lived entirely outside it. For the first type, dishonesty became another facet of survival, something that was part of everyday life. You learned what rules you could break, where you could buy black-market goods, who you had to lie to if you didn't want to be hauled in by the secret police. As in any closed system, there was competition, and those who proved better at it than others. Those who learned how best to break the rules, prospered.

"The second type dwelled entirely outside the law, true rogues. Their existence was even more precarious, the conditions harsher and more unforgiving, the competition ruthless. Over time, the weak were caught and destroyed; only the strongest, the fiercest, survived.

"And then the Wall fell, and those who had spent their entire lives learning to evade authority, to lie and cheat and steal as a matter of everyday life, were suddenly given the opportunity to join other cultures, live in other countries. Countries where the laws were not so Draconian, the punishments not so severe. Places that, in comparison to what they were used to, seemed rife with weaknesses to exploit, loopholes to be explored."

"Not so much a land of opportunity as a sea of

potential victims?" Sara asked. "That seems like a pretty bleak view of humanity."

"Bleak? No. It is simply . . . Russian." Dyalov walked up to the dartboard, pulled out his two darts, then returned and nodded at one of his body-guards. "Boris? A moment, if you please."

Boris rose and was beside Dyalov in one long-legged step. He was tall but gaunt, his eyes dark and sunken, his head shaved. A blurred tattoo of an angel was partially visible on his neck.

"Boris is ex-military as well. They had a very spe-cial way of playing darts in his unit. Boris, if you wouldn't mind demonstrating?"

Boris strode toward the dartboard, where he turned and stood to one side. He put out an ex-tremely large hand, palm down, fingers extended as widely as possible, and placed it over the bull's-eye of the dartboard. The tips of his fingers reached past the edges of the inner ring.

"The rules are very simple," said Dyalov. "Two players take turns placing a hand on the board. Once placed, any movement is a forfeit. Points are scored as usual—except that any dart embedded in flesh counts double whatever space it's over. If it falls out before the player's turn is over the points are disqualified, so the darts are generally thrown a little harder than normal. A bull's-eye is particularly difficult to accomplish."

Sara realized that the dots on the back of Boris's hand weren't freckles. They were scars.

"The hand on the board must be the same one the player throws with," Dyalov continued. "It's a game with more subtlety and strategy than might at first be apparent. A skilled player will try to target the web of skin between the fingers, whereas a novice will rely more on brute force. It is a game of nerves and endurance as much as accuracy."

He threw a dart, putting more effort into it than he had previously. The dart hit the board between two of Boris's fingers with a different sound than before. Boris didn't twitch. A thin line of red began to trace its way down the back of his hand.

"You see," said Dyalov, carefully lining up his next throw, "the fact that Russian names have come up in the course of your investigations does not surprise me. Circus performers, factory workers, blackjack dealers, it doesn't matter. If a group of Russians—any group—have found a way to make some money by breaking the rules, then that is what they will do. And they will not stop, or be intimidated by the authorities."

He threw another dart. *Thwuck,* between the thumb and forefinger. Boris stared at Sara with dead eyes.

"I'm sorry I couldn't be of more help," said Dyalov. He glanced at Sara with a friendly smile, then leaned back and threw the last dart forcefully. It impaled Boris's hand, dead center. The flights on the darts quivered slightly, but the hand itself was utterly still.

Boris smiled.

"Come back and visit anytime," said Dyalov. "Perhaps we can play again."

Andolph Dell stared moodily out the penthouse window at the skyline of Vegas. "You're sure?" he asked.

"Not yet," said Greg. He glanced at Nick before continuing. "We'd like you to pull a representative sample from the casino floor so we can check them."

"Fake chips. In my casino." Dell shook his head. "First the burning blimp and renegade bears, now this. Somebody's got it in for me."

"It's starting to look that way," said Nick. "Any idea who it might be?"

Dell scowled. "No. Maybe. I'm not sure."

"Any information you could give us would help," said Greg.

"I said I'm not sure," Dell snapped. "Give me some time to think about it. I'll talk to the floor bosses, get them to yank some chips. How many you want?"

"Five percent would probably do," said Nick.

Dell groaned. "Fine. But they don't leave the casino. I'll have my own people check them, all right? Or are these supposed fakes so good you need an electron microscope or something to ID them?"

"No, sir," said Nick. "Your own staff should be able to spot them fairly easily. But there is something else we'd like to take a look at."

"What's that?"

"Your alternate set," said Greg. "We'd like to pull some chips from them, make sure they haven't been tampered with either."

"Fine." Dell waved a hand irritably. "Anything else around here you think might be fake? Art, furniture, maybe my dog?"

"No, sir," said Greg.

"We'll get right to work," said Nick.

As they headed for the elevator, Greg whispered to Nick, "Boy, I'm really glad he didn't have a show-girl in there with him when he asked that question."

"Shut up."

"Oh, come on, like you weren't thinking the same thing?"

The Panhandle normally kept about two hundred thousand chips in circulation at any given time. That meant ten thousand had to be taken off the casino floor and checked by staff, a time-consuming process.

Greg and Nick had it easier. They planned to sample only one percent of the alternate chips, a mere two thousand tokens, enough to fill two of the clear Lucite cases the casino used for storage.

They waited outside the basement storage room until the head of security arrived. "I'm under instructions to let you take two cases and no more," said Tanner as he walked up. "And I'll have to personally verify every denomination and have you sign off on the total dollar value."

Nick nodded. "Okay, but this will take a while. We're not just grabbing a single crate; we're going to have to go through all two hundred boxes and take ten from each."

Tanner sighed. "I'll get a chair."

He unlocked the door to the storage room, then followed them in and did the same for the cage the chips were stored in. The clear plastic cases were stacked on twenty large, two-tiered metal units, ten cases per shelf, five deep and two across.

"Let's get started," said Greg.

They worked with two empty cases at a time, Nick transferring stacks of chips from one crate to another, Greg taking a single chip and putting it in his own crate while keeping the various denominations separate. Greg didn't bother with anything worth less than twenty dollars; counterfeiters wouldn't, either.

"I don't see the point of this, to be honest," said Tanner. He pulled an office chair on casters over and sat down. "These tokens are all brand-new. Radio-frequency identification chips in them, which broadcast a very specific signal when they're scanned. I guess you could counterfeit the chips themselves—they're just compression-molded plastic—but there's no way to beat the digital encoding."

"You'd be surprised," said Greg. "Almost anything can be counterfeited, if you're willing to take the time and effort."

"Yeah," said Nick. "You ever hear of superdollars?"

"Don't think so," said Tanner.

"They keep the actual numbers hush-hush," said Nick, "but reliable estimates put the amount of superdollars the Secret Service has taken out of commission since the early nineties at around fifty million dollars. You know why they call them superdollars?"

Tanner shrugged. "They have a little red S on them?"

Nick shook his head. "It's because they're actually *higher* in quality than actual dollars."

Greg dropped a chip into his crate with a tiny *clink*. "Even better than the real thing."

"What do you mean, better?" asked Tanner.

"Well," said Nick, "for starters, they're made out of exactly the same cotton-to-linen ratio that U.S. currency has. They're printed on intaglio presses, which is a very specialized piece of equipment only governments are supposed to own. They even use the same high-tech color-shifting ink we use, and the U.S. government is supposed to have an us-and-only-us contract with the company that makes the stuff."

Tanner leaned forward, his elbows on his knees. "So far, you're saying it's just as good. How's it better?"

"Quality," said Greg. "Under a magnifying glass, some of the details of the artwork are actually sharper than the originals. Talk about taking pride in your work."

"So where's this stuff come from?"

Nick shrugged. "Oh, there are different theories, but most of the evidence points at North Korea. They're known to have the equipment; witnesses have come forward to actually identify where the printing presses are housed. North Korean diplomats have even been arrested carrying the stuff. But it's not like you can just march in and arrest a country, especially not one with the fourth-largest standing army in the world. If you've ever wondered how the guys who run the place can drive around in Mercedeses while the rest of their country starves, though, take a hard look at the next hundred-dollar bill you see. Unless you have access to a forensics lab, you'll probably never be able to tell if it came from Washington or Pyongyang."

"And it's not like this kind of thing hasn't happened before," said Greg. "The Nazis tried to pull the same thing in World War Two. Printed almost nine million British bank notes, with a quality so high they were virtually indistinguishable from the actual currency. The plan was to drop them from aircraft flying over England and destabilize the British economy."

"So what happened? Hitler get greedy and decide to keep it all for himself?"

Greg shrugged. "That part's a little unclear. Some people say the Luftwaffe couldn't spare any planes for the operation, but that's always rung a little false to me. I think the idea of dropping a bunch of money on the heads of their enemy was just too counterintuitive to them. In the end, they wound up dumping a bunch of it into a lake. The rest just disappeared—for a while, at least. Notes kept turning up in Britain for years afterward, enough of them that they finally redesigned their money."

Tanner nodded. "Somebody couldn't resist keeping a little taste for themselves."

Nick finished a case and set it aside. "Well, it was near the end of the war; a lot of high-level Nazis could see the end approaching, and it wasn't one where the Deutschmark became the favored currency. There is part of the story most people don't know, though—my favorite part."

"Do the good guys win?"

Nick grinned. "As a matter of fact, they do. See,

the Nazis were using Jewish concentration-camp prisoners to do all the work—the engraving, the printing, everything. When the project fell apart, the counterfeiters were sent to another camp to be executed, all at once. There was only one truck at the camp they were stationed at, so it took three trips to transport them all. On the third trip, the truck broke down halfway there, and they had to march the rest of the way—but in the meantime, the inmates at the new camp staged a revolt. The soldiers that had been guarding the first two groups of prisoners panicked and ran; when the new group of prisoners showed up, there was enough confusion that they could just melt into the general population of the camp and disappear. Two days later, the Allies liberated the camp."

"That's a pretty good ending."

"If I may?" said Greg, glancing at Nick; he nodded. "That's not the end of the story. A bunch of the money wound up in the hands of the Jewish underground, who then used it to get refugees to Israel. Exactly how they came by the cash isn't clear, but I'm guessing the counterfeiters figured out a way to keep a little of the cash they were cranking out."

Tanner laughed. "Somebody's always skimming, huh? Even when they're printing the money themselves."

"Too true," said Nick. "So if guys in a concentration camp being watched by Nazis with machine guns can figure out a way to cheat the system, a Vegas casino doesn't seem like that big a challenge. No offense."

"None taken. Well, maybe a little—you are

talking about my job." Tanner got to his feet and stretched. "You know, a casino is a lot *like* a little country. I'm not talking about all the touristy stuff that tries to make it seem like you're in some idealized version of Paris or Venice—I mean the fact that each casino has a self-contained economy. Right down to its own currency."

"I guess that makes you a five-star general, then," said Greg.

"Guess so. So far, all I have to worry about is internal security. But what if one of the other casinos took the country idea a little too far?"

Greg stopped counting chips and looked up. "I'm envisioning an army of showgirls and magicians marching down the Strip."

Tanner shook his head. "No, I'm talking about using the same tactics that North Korea and Nazi Germany did. Flooding another country's economy with fake currency in order to destabilize it."

Nick stopped counting, too. He and Greg looked at each other.

"You think?" said Greg.

"It's no crazier than using a human cannonball to crash a party."

"What?" said Tanner.

"Never mind," said Nick. "But thanks, Mr. Tanner—I think you might have given us another avenue of investigation to pursue."

21

WHEN THEY WERE DONE, Greg and Nick took the chips they'd pulled back to the lab. They hauled the cases in and put them on the light table, then slipped into their lab coats.

"Okay," said Greg, rubbing his hands. "Here's where it gets interesting."

Nick was examining the two RFID scanners the casino had given them; they looked a little like a Dustbuster crossed with an electric shaver. "If by interesting you mean boring and repetitive, I'm with you. This is going to be like working a never-ending line at the supermarket, without all the thrills of ringing up purchases."

"That's one way to look at it. I prefer to pretend I'm searching for illegal replicants by scanning their biochips."

"Have you been spending time with Hodges?"

"We had lunch together. But come on, this is

cutting-edge stuff. They're talking about putting RFIDs in everything from passports to people. Cybernetic ID—how cool would that be?"

"Depends. Ever seen *Logan's Run*?"

Greg frowned. "Good point."

Nick handed one of the scanners to Greg. "All right. The chips are programmed with two numbers: one's a serial number, the other's the denomination. The denomination we check visually, the serial number we check against the casino's database. Either one doesn't match up, we know these have been tampered with."

"Right." They got to work.

Working with two scanners, it didn't take long to process two thousand chips—less time than it had taken to pull them.

"So far, so good," said Nick. "Not a single discrepancy."

Greg sighed. "I know. It's disappointing."

"You really thought we were going to find something?"

"I did. I mean, the whole fake bear attack seemed to have been staged to get access to the basement level. I thought for sure it had something to do with the alternate chips."

Nick nodded, tapping one of the chips edge-down on the light table. "Yeah, there is that. Maybe we're not looking hard enough."

"Or maybe we're looking at the wrong thing," said Greg, gesturing with the scanner in his hand. "The GIGO principle of information analysis."

"Your result's only as good as the quality of the

data you collect—Garbage In, Garbage Out. You think the scanners might be what's been tampered with?"

"I don't know—but Archie probably would."

"Then let's get him to take a look at one." Nick held up the chip in his hand and studied it. "I'm going to take apart a few of the chips themselves, take a look at them under the microscope and see if I can spot anything there."

"Reverse engineering and deconstruction. I like it."

"This is a very simple device," said Archie. He had the scanner's components laid out in front of him on a table in the AV lab. "There are three basic kinds of Radio Frequency Identity Chips: active, passive, and semipassive."

"Right," said Greg. "The casino uses passive chips, which don't even have their own energy source. They just take the magnetic field generated by the scanner itself and turn it into enough electricity to broadcast a signal back."

"Exactly. A passive chip is basically just a glorified mirror, but it also breaks down into three subtypes: read only, read/write, and WORM."

"Worm?"

"I'll get to that in a second. A read-only chip is just that: you can read information off it, but you can't ever change it. A read/write chip *can* be altered—that's definitely not the kind you want in a casino token. The kind you do want is the WORM: Write Once, Read Many. You can add something to it once to make it unique—usually a serial number—and then it becomes read-only."

"Let's say you had read/write chips and you wanted to reprogram them. What would you need?"

"A lot more than this scanner. It puts out a magnetic field and reads the radio signal that bounces back—that's it."

"If you had the right equipment, could you reprogram them at a distance?"

Archie frowned. "I don't want to say it's impossible, but it would be really difficult. The range of a system like this depends on two things: the size of the antenna that's part of the chip, and the strength of the radio signal being sent. The antenna in a casino token is so small you normally have to be within inches to read it; you could boost the distance with a really powerful radio transmitter, but I don't know how far you could actually extend the range. Ultra-High Frequency transmitters broadcast at nine hundred fifteen megahertz, and they only operate at a maximum distance of around twenty feet."

"Twenty feet. Or less if there's something like a concrete wall in the way."

"Definitely."

"Thanks, Arch. So there's no way this scanner could be feeding me false data?"

"No. And if it's telling you that the casino chips are WORMs, then that's what they are."

Greg sighed. "I really should be able to work with a straight line like that, but it's been a long day. I'll see you later."

"Well?" asked Nick when Greg returned.

"Scanners check out fine. They—and Archie—say

the chips we pulled can only be altered once, and that's already been done when the serial numbers were assigned. You find anything?"

Nick shook his head. "*Nada*. Near as I can tell, they're authentic."

Nick's cell phone chimed. He answered. "Nick Stokes. Yeah? Is that so? How many? Uh-huh. Okay, we'll be right over." He closed his phone and slipped it back into his pocket. "That was Tanner at the Panhandle. They haven't finished the count yet, but they've found some counterfeit tokens in the sample they pulled off the casino floor—all hundreds."

"So this *is* about the chips. What I don't get is how the alternate set is involved."

"Well, there are two more links in the distribution chain we haven't taken a close look at. The first and the last."

Greg nodded. "The manufacturer and the computer database that keeps track of them. Guess we should have a chat with both."

Nick shrugged out of his lab coat. "Tell you what—you talk to the manufacturer, I'll have a word with whoever's managing the database for the casino. I'm headed down there now to pick up some of the bogus chips, see if they match the one we found in the elevator shaft."

"You got it."

The Panhandle's tokens were produced by a company called Chipsdown Inc., based in Henderson. Greg called to make an appointment, then drove out to their offices.

Chipsdown was outside Henderson itself, in a long white clapboard building that could just as easily have housed a parts dealership or a small electronics firm. There was no sign out front; only the directions he'd been given and the address itself told Greg he was in the right place.

He walked up the wooden steps and opened the front door, an electronic chime announcing his arrival. Inside, the nature of the business was immediately obvious; Greg stepped into a showroom, the walls lined with display cases showing off chips of every design, color, and denomination. Customized chip cases made of aluminum, leather, or clear Lucite stood on columns under spotlights. In the middle of the room, a blackjack table had been converted into a receptionist's desk; a young woman looked up from her computer and smiled at him. "Hello. Can I help you?"

"I'm here to see Mr. Higgins?"

"You're Greg Sanders, right? I'll let him know—he should be out in a minute." She picked up the phone.

Greg took a look around while he waited. Chipsdown apparently manufactured tokens for more than just casinos; it offered chips to the private market as well. The recent surge of public interest in poker probably had a lot to do with that, though much of that was taking place online. Greg doubted there was much of a market for virtual chips, though it wouldn't have surprised him if there was. Money itself, after all, was already more or less a virtual commodity by its very nature.

Higgins came bustling out of a door in the back,

smiling and striding forward with his hand out-stretched. He was a paunchy man in a good suit, with short, slicked-back dark hair and a pair of the narrow, rectangular glasses that were fashionable at the moment.

"Greg Sanders, Vegas Crime Lab," Greg shook his hand. "We spoke on the phone?"

"Yes, yes. Harvey Higgins. I'm the manager here. What can I do to assist Nevada law enforcement today?" Higgins put his hands behind his back and beamed at Greg.

Greg reached into his pocket and pulled out one of the Panhandle's chips. "I was wondering what you could tell me about this."

Higgins took it and held it between thumb and forefinger. "Ah. One of ours, I see. Hundred-dollar denomination, coin-aligned, current. RFID-chipped. Gold hot stamp, red edge insert. No obvious JDLR."

"JDLR?"

Higgins chuckled. "Sorry, that's chip-speak: Just Doesn't Look Right. I meant that if it's a counterfeit, it's not an obvious one."

"Well, that's what I want to talk to you about. I've run about every test I can think of on this chip, and it appears to be genuine."

"But you have reason to believe it isn't?"

"I do. Or if it isn't an outright fake, I think the RFID insert might have been tampered with."

Higgins smile vanished. "Well, we take that sort of thing very seriously. Both the Casino Control Commission and the Division of Game Enforcement examine our facilities on a regular basis; I can as-sure you, we keep very careful track of every chip we make and exactly where it goes. In fact, to even examine this chip, we're going to have to do some paperwork."

Greg sighed. "Well, I'm no stranger to that. If it can help me figure out what the deal is with these chips, bring it on."

Higgins nodded and walked over to the receptionist. "Ms. Parsons? We're going to need the 15-C139, the TX-17, and the standard Privacy and Nondisclosure forms."

Greg did his best not to sigh again.

Nick met Tanner in the security chief's own office, a small, windowless room with a framed picture of dogs playing poker on one wall. Someone had Photoshopped an image of Tanner peering through a window into the background.

Nick examined one of the tokens Tanner had just tossed him. "How many have you found so far?"

"Only five. But we've only gone through about a tenth of what we've pulled."

"So that's what, point five percent of all the chips you have in circulation? Which works out to roughly a hundred thousand dollars' worth of phony clay."

"Yeah. Mr. Dell is pretty upset. He wants us to yank the whole set and replace it, but I told him to hold off until you guys verify the alternates are okay. How's that going?"

Nick shook his head. "Greg's talking to the manufacturer, seeing if they could have been tampered with on that end. I need to talk to whoever handles the database for the alternate chips to make sure that's on the up-and-up. So far, though, every-thing's we've found points to them being the real, unaltered deal."

"Good. The sooner we can swap them, the sooner Dell calms down. If I get out of this with my job in-tact, I'll be amazed."

"So whom do I talk to about the database?"

"That'd be Bernie Ellington. He's the head of our IT department, handles all the tech upgrades and online services. He's just down the hall."

Nick thanked him and followed his directions to another office with "B. ELLINGTON" on the door. A knock produced a loud "Come in!"

Ellington's office was considerably larger than Tanner's. No fewer than five flat-screen monitors crowded the top of Ellington's desk, behind which sat a broad-shouldered black man with a mustache straight out of a 1970s kung fu movie. He wore a pink long-sleeved shirt with suspenders, no tie, his shirt open at the collar. "Yes?"

"Nick Stokes, Vegas Crime Lab. I understand you manage the IT department for the casino?"

"That I do," Ellington said with a smile. "And for the hotel. Everything from online booking to mak-ing sure the security feeds don't crash. You're here about the alternate chips, right?" He motioned for Nick to take a seat.

"You know what's going on?" asked Nick as he sat.

"Information is what I do, Mr. Stokes. Be pretty poor at my job if I didn't pay attention to what was happening around me."

"True enough. What can you tell me about the security—"

Ellington held up a hand. "Hold up. I know where you're going with this—you want to know if someone could have hacked into our system, maybe changed a few digits around, and made it so the alternate chips would be—what? Worth more? Maybe even add nonexistent chips to the system so they could be cashed out without being bought in the first place?"

Nick shrugged. "You tell me."

Ellington leaned back and crossed his arms. "Yes, I *will* tell you. What you're suggesting is as impossible as waltzing into a bank vault and changing all the one-dollar bills into hundreds with a magic marker. I personally supervised the entry of every single chip into our database—all two hundred thousand of them—and I signed off on every single one. I also oversaw the installation of the security protocols into that database, and there is absolutely no way that anyone—not even a fully digitized version of Keanu Reeves himself—could break into it. Now, is that clear enough, or would you like me to go into the technical details?" There was steel behind the man's gentle smile.

Nick shook his head. "I'm sure your security is excellent. But yes, I'm afraid I am going to need the technical details."

"Fine. I hope your programming skills are up to date, because mine certainly are. And you might want to grab some coffee before we start; we're going to be here a while."

Nick forced a smile. "Can't wait to get started . . ."

*   *   *

Greg yawned as he walked into the lab. "Man. If sheer bureaucracy is any indication, then the people who make casino chips are more secure than the employees of Fort Knox."

Nick looked over from where he was sprawled in one of the lab's rolling chairs. "Yeah? Well, try listening to someone speaking in binary for a few hours. I think I caught about a tenth of what he was explaining."

"Which was?"

"Essentially? Computer security good. Chip security good. CSI tech, stupid."

"I know how you feel. The manufacturer insists there was nothing wrong with the chips when they left the factory, and both the CCC and the DGE signed off on them. Any good news on your front?"

"I don't know if it's good or not, but the counterfeits they found on the casino floor match the one we found in the elevator shaft."

Greg groaned. "That makes no sense. What we seem to have discovered is an elaborate plot to introduce counterfeit markers to a casino—chips that anyone could have just walked in the front door and started playing with. You don't need bears and exploding zeppelins and human cannonballs to plant fake tokens."

"No, you don't." Nick straightened up. "Maybe we're thinking about this all wrong. What do all the things you just mentioned have in common?"

Greg thought about it. "They all make the casino look bad?"

"Exactly. Maybe this isn't about making a

profit—maybe it's about making sure somebody else *doesn't*."

"Andolph Dell?"

"I think we need to talk to him again—and this time, let's do it here."

Andolph Dell looked more irritated than intimidated in the interview room. "I don't understand why you had to drag me all the way down here—what, I don't have enough on my plate without jumping through hoops for the police? Just tell me whether or not my alternates are okay so I can put them into use and stop hemorrhaging money."

Jim Brass nodded. Nick and Greg sat on either side of him; they'd asked Brass to join the interview to give it a little more weight. Andolph Dell seemed to believe he could just steamroll over lowly CSI techs, and they thought a police detective might at least slow him down.

"We're still looking into that," said Brass. "The sooner we get this over with, the sooner you can get back to your business. Okay?"

"Whatever. Start asking."

"Who would have the most to gain from the Panhandle losing money?"

"Every other casino on the Strip. Next question."

"I think you can do a little better than that, Mr. Dell."

Dell glowered at him. "You want to know who'd like me brought down? The list is too long to recite. This is a cutthroat business in a cutthroat town, Detective Brass. When I said every other casino on the Strip, I wasn't exaggerating."

"Let's leave business out of it, then. How about something more personal? Somebody who might get their jollies from kicking you where it'll hurt the most?"

Dell's eyes flickered. Up and to the right, an indicator that he was accessing a visual memory. "I've made a few enemies, sure. But nobody—they wouldn't go this far."

Brass caught the qualification. "You obviously have someone in mind. Someone you'd rather not name, which suggests an ongoing relationship you're not sure about. A woman?"

Dell didn't say anything.

"Look," said Nick. "We understand if you're trying to be discreet. But our investigation is going to turn this person up sooner or later, and by that time, we'll have asked a lot of people a lot of very personal questions. If you're trying to minimize this information getting around, it's better to tell us now."

"Besides," said Greg, "if this person does turn out to be responsible, wouldn't you rather *know* than have lingering doubts?"

Dell's glower lost a little of its ferocity. "I suppose," he said grudgingly. "I've been seeing a woman, from a very wealthy family. The relationship has been . . . intense. On again, off again. The last time we broke up, she actually bought the property next to me and told me she was going to put up her own casino and put me out of business. But that all blew over."

"The property next to the Panhandle?" asked Nick. "The one that's under construction right now?"

"It was," said Dell. "Financing fell through after she changed her mind and pulled out. Now it's just a gigantic steel skeleton blocking my view."

"What's this woman's name?" asked Greg.

"Emma Fynell."

22

CATHERINE FOUND RAY in his tiny office off the morgue. "Hey, Professor," she said.

"Catherine," he said, looking up. "I was just going over the case histories of John Bannister and Theria Kostapolis again. Thought I might have missed something the first time."

"Any luck?"

"Possibly. I have an idea, but it's somewhat—experimental. How about you?"

She pulled up a chair and sat down. "I was doing pretty well for a while. Tracked them from the Orpheus to the Lincoln to the Silver Spire. That's where the trail went cold." She sighed. "The only clue I have to where Theria ultimately wound up is something they said to a clerk at a booth selling raffle tickets. Something about 'following the signs.' In their state, that could mean anything."

"True. I've tried talking to Bannister, but he refuses to cooperate. I can counteract the effects of the

BZ with drugs, but his CBDS is too advanced; even without the coterminous hallucinations, he remains convinced he's in hell."

"So what do we do?" She shook her head. "You know what really gets me? Everything Bannister's done has been out of compassion. He's literally braved the horrors of the underworld to try to bring this woman some peace, and if we don't find her soon, his actions could wind up being what kills her."

"The irony isn't lost on me. But I may have a way to accomplish the reverse and turn a negative into a positive."

"How? Slap on a pair of wings and convince him this is actually heaven?"

Ray smiled. "No. I was thinking about turning one of the symptoms of his condition to our advantage. How much do you know about anarchic hand syndrome?"

"Just what you told me—one of his hands will act of its own volition, as if it has a mind of its own."

Ray nodded. "That's not strictly true, though early studies of the condition were cited as proof that more than a single consciousness could inhabit one mind. But even though the hand of a patient with AHS will demonstrate what seems to be a separate, intelligent agenda—performing complex tasks, for example—what it's actually doing is quite different."

"So what *is* it doing?"

"Essentially, it's performing what's known as environmentally stimulated actions. These are things the limb is used to doing—a prerehearsed routine, if you will—that are triggered by a stimulus in the environment, usually by something visual. For instance, let's say the patient has a cup of coffee every morning. He's performed the action of lifting the mug to his lips many thousands of times. A patient with AHS will, upon simply seeing the mug, grab it and lift it to his lips without making the decision to do so."

"An automatic reflex taken to the nth degree."

"Yes. In certain cases, the hand can even become hostile—attempting to hit or throttle its owner—but even aggressive behavior can be reflexive."

"Absolutely. Martial-arts training relies on repetition."

"Exactly. Now, John Bannister was in the Army, which means many of his reflexive actions could be related to his military training—but I was hoping to tap into something a little deeper. Something he's been doing all his life, in fact."

Ray pulled a sheet of paper out of the folder in front of him and held it out.

Catherine took it and studied it. It was a pencil sketch of Theria Kostapolis, looking out a barred window with a sad expression on her face. "The art therapy they were both doing?"

"For Bannister, it goes beyond that—he's been an amateur artist all his life. The amazing thing is, this was done after he'd already lost control of the limb. Drawing is a complex skill, but it's one Bannister's been using for a long time—long enough that it's apparently become second nature to him."

"Okay, but how does this help us?"

Ray picked up a pen and gestured with it. "Bannister's conscious mind might not be willing to help us. But another part of his brain might."

Catherine and Ray stood at the foot of Bannister's hospital bed. The back of the bed was elevated so that Bannister was sitting upright; he was immobilized at his chest, his waist, his wrists, and his ankles by thick leather straps. His right hand twitched and strained against the restraints, clenching and unclenching.

He stared at the CSIs with nothing but weariness on his face. "You're wasting your time. I'm not going to tell you where she is."

"Don't worry about that, John," said Ray. "We'd just like to perform some function tests on your hand. Nothing invasive or painful."

Ray pulled over a rolling food table and positioned it so the tray was over Bannister's upper thighs. A yellow sketchpad and a ballpoint pen lay on the tray. Ray picked up the pen and held it up with his left hand; with his right, he unbuckled the strap on Bannister's twitching arm.

The hand made an immediate grab for the pen. Ray felt something as the hand clutched his own, some deep internal tremor generated by Bannister's twitching muscles, almost like touching a wild animal; then it snatched the pen from his grasp.

Catherine turned off the lights. Then she switched on the overhead projector they'd brought with them, aimed at the blank whiteness of the far wall.

A picture of Theria Kostapolis appeared, but it

only filled half the screen. The other half was taken up by a photo of a skull.

John Bannister stared at the screen, the look on his face now one of grief. He made no sound, but tears began to spill down his cheeks.

Ray joined Catherine by the projector. "I don't know about this," Catherine whispered. "It seems . . . morbid. Bordering on crazy."

"Bordering on crazy is exactly where we are," Ray whispered back. "But he's on one side, and we're on the other. Any chance Theria Kostapolis has depends on us getting a message across that border . . ."

The hand began to scribble.

Ray had explained his proposed method to Catherine beforehand: "Simply showing him a picture of Theria won't be enough; that might only get us mimicry. We need him to generate an image that he associates with the last location he saw her in—what he thinks will be her final resting place. The simplest, most basic of concepts should produce the best results—and a skull is the universal symbol for death in all human cultures."

Theria plus skull equals . . . what? Catherine thought. *Will this work, or are we just going to get a drawing of a woman in a pirate outfit?*

Bannister abruptly became aware of what they were trying to do. "No!" he shouted. He squeezed his eyes shut, then tried to disrupt what his hand was doing by violently shifting his body back and forth. The straps didn't give him much leeway, but he didn't stop trying; muscles in his neck stood out as he whipped his head back and forth. "No! You can't! *Stop* it, damn you! *I'll rip you off with my own goddamn teeth!*"

His hand continued to sketch. It drew with broad, bold strokes, without hesitation. *Almost as if it had been waiting for its chance,* thought Catherine. *Almost as if it knew there wasn't any time to waste.*

Bannister's thrashing became even more severe, his face a mottled red. Ray signaled for Catherine to turn the projector off and stepped forward. "That's enough. John, calm down. I'm taking the pen and paper away. It's over, John. It's over."

Bannister stopped thrashing and lay with his head to one side, breathing heavily. His hand, deprived of its instrument, scuttled around the surface of the table like a crab trying to escape.

"You bastards," Bannister groaned. "You *bastards.*"

"We're leaving now, John." Ray grabbed the arm and rebuckled it into the restraint. "Try to rest."

Outside in the corridor, Ray showed Catherine what John Bannister's hand had drawn: a rough sketch of the "Welcome to Las Vegas" sign.

"Not 'follow the signs,' " said Catherine. "Just follow the *sign.*"

23

THE LAST TIME NICK STOKES had talked to Emma Fynell, he'd asked her to send him the pictures she'd taken of the flaming dirigible. Her nails were still the same glossy black with inset rhinestones, but she was dressed much more conservatively now in a dark blue business suit, black pumps, and a matching handbag. She smiled at Nick from the other side of the interview table in the crime lab and said, "Nice to see you, Mr. Stokes. You need to borrow my phone again?"

Nick smiled back. "No, I need to talk to you about Andolph Dell."

"What would you like to know?"

"I understand you and he are involved."

"If you're trying to ask me out, that's the wrong way to do it."

"I'm flattered, but I'm not trying to ask you out. I'm trying to figure out the nature of your relationship."

She leaned back in her chair. "Well, if you reach any kind of understanding, let me know. I've been trying to do the same thing myself for the last six months."

"Things not going smoothly?"

"What docs this have to do with anything?"

"Someone seems to be targeting Mr. Dell's casino. You made a threat along those lines not too long ago."

"I make all kinds of threats. Sometimes I even follow through—other times, I forgive and forget."

"And this time?"

She shrugged. "We're back together, at the moment."

"So you've canceled your plans for a rival casino?"

"Call it a gesture of reconciliation."

Nick frowned. "That seems . . . kind of out of proportion, don't you think? I mean, you're talking about a project worth tens of millions of dollars."

She studied him for a second before replying. "Do you know who played at my sixteenth birthday party? The Rolling Stones. I'm not sure how many cars I own, but it's more than a dozen. I once lost a necklace worth more than most people's houses in the cushions of my couch—one of my couches, in one of my living rooms, in one of my houses. And I didn't care. So, out of proportion? I no longer have any idea what that word even means."

Nick blinked. "Okay, then. Thank you for coming in."

"My pleasure. *That*, at least, is a principle I thoroughly understand."

*   *   *

"Well, so much for that," said Greg. He and Nick were commiserating in the break room. "Emma Fynell's story checks out. She divested herself completely from the project a few months ago—it's been stalled ever since."

"Plus it makes no sense for her to be involved, anyway," said Nick, stirring his coffee. "She was at the party, remember? No need for a human cannonball—she could have just told the doorman to let the nurse and her boyfriend in herself."

"Yeah, I guess so. So what's that leave us?"

Nick took a sip of his coffee. "Still waiting on DNA results for the strongman. I guess we could pull in the veterinarian for a reinterview, but I doubt if it'll do any good."

"Hey, guys," said Sara, walking up. "Anything new?"

"Only the imminent failure of our careers," said Greg gloomily.

"Never mind him," said Nick. "How about you? How was your visit with the Red Godfather?"

She pulled up a chair and sat down. "Pointed," she said.

She related her conversation with Dyalov, including the game of darts. "Scary guy. I had no doubt he would have been just as willing to have those darts thrown at his hand as vice versa."

"Did he let anything slip?" asked Greg.

Sara frowned. "You know, he seemed a little too flippant when I brought up the circus. Then he shifted gears and tried to make me believe that Russians in general were just naturally predisposed to crime because of living under the repression of communism. He saved the dart game for his big finish."

"Trying to throw you off the trail?" asked Nick.

"Could be." She shrugged. "Not a lot to go on, I know. Oh, and you know that oversize tattoo artist I mentioned? I finally ran down his alibi—it checks out. No way he could be the guy in the wheelchair."

Greg sighed. "Great. Another dead end."

"C'mon, guys," said Nick. "Cheer up. Something'll break."

"It better," said Greg.

Despite their misgivings, Nick, Sara, and Greg had no choice; in the absence of any evidence to the contrary, they had to give the Panhandle's alternate chips a clean bill of health. Andolph Dell instituted an immediate swap, shutting down the casino for two hours while every chip on the casino floor was replaced. Customers holding chips were told they would have to exchange them before they could continue to play, though the casino would still cash any old chips left in circulation—after an inspection.

For the first few hours after the swap, everything went well.

Jim Brass stuck his head in the lab door. "Hey, Nick, Sara—you're not gonna believe this."

Sara looked up from the report she'd been reading. "What's up?"

Nick swiveled on his lab chair, away from his workstation. "Hodges ask you for an 'honest appraisal' of a first draft of his memoirs? If so, now's a good time to develop a spontaneous case of dyslexia."

"He did," said Brass, "but I turned him down on the grounds that I hate seeing a grown man cry. No, this is more in the realm of the implausible than the unfathomable. A guy just walked into the Panhandle and tried to cash ten thousand dollars' worth of chips."

"Which set?" asked Sara.

"The new ones. But get this—when they try to scan the chips, there's no signal. *Nada,* nothing, zip. They look authentic, but the RFID chip is completely inoperative in each and every one. Security called us, and we have him in custody. Three guesses what his favorite James Bond movie is—and it ain't *Moonraker.*"

"*From Russia with Love*?" said Nick.

"*Da,* comrade. But apparently *without* any sense."

"Can we talk to him?" asked Sara.

"Sure. But I get the feeling you'll be the ones doing all the talking."

Ilya Khavin didn't look much like a Russian gangster. He was short, with curly black hair, a prominent nose, and a perpetually mild expression on his face. He was dressed like a tourist—Hard Rock Casino T-shirt, baggy orange shorts, tennis shoes without socks.

Nick and Sara stared at him from the other side of the interview table. He gazed back, unperturbed.

"Mr. Khavin," Sara said. "We understand you tried to pass some bad chips today."

Khavin shook his head and looked mildly apologetic. "This is all just a misunderstanding. Those chips are perfectly good."

"No, they're not," said Nick. "They're fakes."

"No, no, they're just new. Those—what are they called, radio chips?—inside must not be working right."

Nick smiled. "You seem pretty knowledgeable about the subject."

Khavin shrugged. "I guess. It's not exactly a secret."

"Not exactly," said Sara. "Tell me, Mr. Khavin, where did you get those chips?"

"At the casino, of course."

"Uh-huh," said Nick. "They don't have any record of you making such a purchase. The thing about RFID chips is, you know who has what at any given time. You never bought any chips from the casino."

"Like I said, they must be malfunctioning. This is all just some kind of computer glitch."

"I see," said Sara. "A programming error, some sort of fault in the hotel's database."

Nick nodded. "Maybe even a flaw in the chips themselves. Could be they're broadcasting on the wrong frequency or something."

Khavin nodded back. "Sure. Technology breaks down all the time. Especially when it's new."

"Right," said Sara. "Lucky for you, we're pretty good at diagnosing problems like that. Aren't we, Nick?"

"Practically experts. In fact, we took a very, very close look at those casino tokens of yours, Mr. Khavin, and you're absolutely right; there's something wrong with the RFID chips. It's kind of technical—I don't know how well versed you are in electronic engineering—but we'll do our best to explain it to you. Sara?"

"They're not there," said Sara.

Khavin blinked. Mildly.

"I'm sorry," said Nick. "Are we going too fast for you? *Not there* is a technical term meaning missing. Absent. The opposite of *there*."

"I've always liked existence-challenged," said Sara.

"Too politically correct for me," said Nick.

"Somebody must have sold me some bogus chips," said Khavin.

"Possibly," said Sara. "Or maybe you made them yourself. Either way, trying to pass them off as the real thing is definitely illegal."

"How was I supposed to know they weren't the real thing?" said Khavin. "It's not like you can tell just by looking."

"True," admitted Nick.

"Which is what puzzles us," said Sara. "How can someone with a bunch of counterfeit chips be so confident that he tries to pass ten thousand dollars' worth at one go, but be so clueless he doesn't know the most important component is missing?"

"Yeah, it's really bugging us," said Nick. "I mean, I've met some pretty dumb criminals in my day, but man, this is *epic*. Like trying-to-rob-a-bank-with-a-banana kind of epic."

"I think," said Khavin, "I would like to talk to my lawyer now."

"In your position?" said Sara. "Yeah, so would I."

*   *   *

Wendy Simms, DNA tech for the CSI lab, was not having a good day.

She'd started her shift by being late, because the battery in her car had just enough juice to generate a few loud clicks from the starter before expiring. Then she'd spilled coffee all over her lab coat. Finally, Hodges kept badgering her for her review of the autobiography he'd been working on—*Hodges, the Early Years*—and she'd been trying to avoid him ever since she'd finished the first two chapters.

But they worked in the same lab, so that was pretty much impossible. And Hodges was nothing if not persistent.

"So," he said, materializing behind her so abruptly she jumped, "what did you think of the earthworm story?"

"I . . ."

"You must have gotten that far. You've had the manuscript for two weeks, and it's in the first chapter."

"Yes, I've gotten that far." She smiled at him, then looked away. "It was . . . unusual."

"Well, of course it was unusual. That's why I included it. What I want to know is, was it entertaining? Did it hold your attention?"

"Entertaining? I . . . guess you could describe it that way."

Hodges frowned. "Look, I asked for your feedback because I value your honest opinion. I'm not thin-skinned; feel free to be as brutal in your appraisal as necessary. I won't be offended."

"Really?"

"Really."

"Okay. Well, the earthworm story was . . . kind of disgusting."

"I see." Hodges crossed his arms.

"Especially your description of the smell."

"I was trying to be evocative."

"You succeeded. I could practically smell them rotting in the sun."

He nodded. "The stench *was* quite remarkable. I could never play in that sandbox again, you know."

"I can understand why." She paused. "Did you *really* collect that many? It seems a little obsessive."

Hodges smiled. "It had just rained, and there were earthworms everywhere. I'd read about earthworm farms—though I was a little unclear on the details—so I thought I'd start my own. My sandbox seemed like a logical location."

"Except they were *earth*worms, not *sand*worms."

"Well, it's easy to say that *now,* from the heights of experience. In any case, that was one of my early forays into science; I thought including it would give readers some insight into how I became the man I am today."

"Hodges, you killed more than a thousand worms. Throw in some anecdotes of bed wetting and fire setting, and you'll have your readers convinced you were a serial killer in training, not a scientist."

Hodges tapped his chin with a forefinger. "Ah. You haven't gotten to chapter four, then?"

"What?"

"Never mind. It's all there in the text—I really should be careful with spoilers."

Greg walked in. "Hey, guys."

Wendy turned quickly. "Greg! Glad you're here."

"Oh? Any reason in particular, or just general Greg-gladness?"

"I just finished running the DNA samples you got me from Bronislav Alexandrei and compared them against the epithelials you found on the bandages from the penthouse."

"And?"

"No match. But when I ran the samples through CODIS, I got something strange from the epithelials." She picked up a printout and handed it to him.

Greg scanned it and frowned. "The identity of the donor is classified?"

"By the CIA, no less."

Hodges cleared his throat. "So your suspect is— what? A government agent?"

"Looks like," said Greg. "But which government?"

"See?" Jeff Holloway said to his wife. "The perfect temperature."

Nancy Holloway yawned. "Perfect, sure. You know what was the perfect temperature? The inside of our sleeping bag."

Jeff raised his hand, shading his eyes from the rising sun. "Oh, come on. This is gorgeous." He and Nancy were hiking down a gravel road, part of the Lake Mead Historic Railroad Trail. Jeff had insisted they get up early, not only because dawn in the desert was spectacular but because he insisted that it was the most comfortable time of the day; not too hot, not too cold.

Nancy defined the most comfortable time of the day as the interval immediately following her second cup of coffee, and she preferred for it to occur closer to noon. But she had to admit Jeff had a point; the early-morning view was spectacular, the air fresh and invigorating. Of course, the fact that they were on their honeymoon might have been coloring her perceptions somewhat.

She studied her new husband in the rosy glow of the rising sun. Okay, so his hair was thinning. He wore glasses that were badly out of style. He had the tendency to burn and peel rather than tan, and his body was more paunchy than muscular. But he was smart and kind and funny, and she loved him so much it hurt.

He turned and caught her looking at him. "Right back atcha," he said. He was also pretty good at being able to tell what she was thinking.

Jeff scratched his upper arm absently as they walked. "Damn spider bites."

"Excuse me?"

"Spider bites, a whole bunch of 'em. Got me while I was sleeping—itch like hell, too."

Nancy sighed. "Honey, you know how we talked about the fact that everybody has their little rants about things that bug them?"

"I wasn't ranting, was I?"

"No. But I'm about to."

"Ah. Fire when ready."

"Did you see the alleged spider?"

"Well, no. I was asleep."

She nodded. "And have you ever, in fact, seen a spider bite you? Or anyone?"

He thought about it. "Well, no. But spiders *do* bite people."

"They do, but very rarely and almost always in self-defense. In fact, the jaws of most spiders aren't strong enough to penetrate human skin. And spiders do not—I repeat, do *not*—feed on human beings. Ever."

"But—they inject poison into their prey, right? And then suck the juices out."

"That's what they do to small insects but not to larger creatures. There are lots of bugs that do feed on animals through parasitism—mosquitoes, bedbugs, ticks, fleas—but not spiders. Bugs that feed on larger animals inject an anticoagulant to keep the blood flowing, which is what makes the bite itch. Spiders don't do that."

"But—"

She stopped, turned, and grabbed him by the shoulders. "Spiders. Don't. Do. That. This is not my opinion, this is not a theory, this is not open to debate. It is an easily verifiable biological fact, and it drives me crazy when people say, 'Ooh, I got all these spider bites when I was camping.' It's a *myth*."

He gazed into her eyes. "I've never loved you more than I do at this moment."

She stuck her tongue out at him. He retaliated.

When the kiss ended, he said, "That was quite a rant. Passionate, well researched, utterly committed. The spider lobby can sleep well tonight."

"I'll pass that along the next time we meet."

They kept walking. Craggy mounds of rough ochre rock lay jumbled on either side of the road. The air smelled of sage and dust.

"You know, I think I know how the whole spider-bite thing got started," said Jeff. "It's a survival reflex. The more prejudiced you are against spiders, the more you avoid them. Statistically, over time, these people become more numerous."

"Why?"

"Everyone else is dead. Of spider bites."

She punched him on the shoulder. He ignored it bravely and kept talking.

"Blaming spiders—whether they're guilty or not—reinforces our fear of them, which is ultimately a good survival tactic. When the evil Spider Overlords from Arachnia land in their webships, being all friendly and "Hey, *Charlotte's Web* is *my* favorite book, too!" people like you will line up to shake their mandibles and invite them to go camping."

"Where, in an ironic twist of fate, we'll be devoured in our own sleeping bags?"

"Undoubtedly. Don't worry, though—I'll avenge you."

"That will come as a great relief to my desiccated, web-wrapped corpse."

She reached out and took his hand. He squeezed it.

"Hey, look!" said Jeff. "I can see the first one!"

Another craggy, jumbled mound of rocks lay ahead, but this one sat directly in the middle of the road. At its base, an archway had been cut into the stone, running all the way through to the other side. During the construction of the Hoover Dam, this tunnel and others like it had held railroad tracks, used for ferrying supplies and manpower to the dam site. The tracks had long since been removed, but the tunnels had been turned into part of a hiking trail.

"Good," said Nancy. "It looks nice and shady—you didn't tell me that 'perfect temperature' you were talking about had a duration of around five minutes."

"Not only will it be cool and shady," said Jeff with a grin, "but at this time of day it'll be completely, absolutely deserted."

She grinned back. "If it wasn't already too hot, I'd offer to race you."

"I'd conserve my strength if I were you."

"Oh, really?"

"Really."

But when Jeff and Nancy Holloway reached the dark, cool mouth of the tunnel, they found that somebody else was already there.

"Hell of a thing to find on your honeymoon," said Jim Brass. He stood just inside the mouth of the tunnel, out of the punishing glare of the sun.

Dr. Albert Robbins stood on the other side of the body. "Hell of a thing to find anytime," he said. "At least this way they've got a good story."

"I know this guy," said Brass. "Russian mob. Never figured he'd end up like this, though."

Robbins nodded. "I'd say the COD was asphyxiation, though I won't be able to confirm that until after the autopsy."

One of the Denalis used by the CSI lab pulled up, and Sara got out. "Just got the call," she said. "We have an ID on the vic yet?"

"You tell me," said Brass, and stood aside.

Sara looked down and frowned. "That's Grigori Dyalov."

"Yeah," said Brass. "Looks like he was on the receiving end of his own personal coup. Body was found by a couple out hiking."

Sara knelt and examined the body. "Ligature marks on the wrists and ankles. Throat is distended. There's bruising and cuts on the lips and chin, and it looks like something's been inserted in the mouth."

She reached down and pried the partly open jaws apart gently with two gloved fingers. A round object slid out between the bruised lips and clinked softly on the hard ground.

Sara picked it up. It was a casino chip—one of the new ones from the Panhandle. "His mouth is full of them," she said. "I think his esophagus might be, too."

"Well, no matter what you might say about Grigori Dyalov," said Brass, "he was always a guy you could count on when the chips were down."

Sara and Doc Robbins both stared at him.

"What?" said Brass. "I thought you two might be missing Grissom."

"Actually, I was," said Sara. "Right until a second ago . . ."

She continued with her examination of the body, getting Brass to help her turn it over. On the underside of the DB's upper right arm, she found three tiny brown dots on his sleeve. "I've got what looks like a bloodstain," said Sara. She pulled out her bottle of Luminol and a cotton swab. "A very distinctive one, too. Doesn't look like spatter—I think it's transfer."

"Three little dots?" said Brass. "From what?"

"Someone trying to make a point," said Sara. "Or, more accurately, points—but I don't think this is what he had in mind."

24

Boris Svenko was an atheist.

This was not the result of any rigorous intellectual analysis on his part. He was an atheist because his parents had been atheists, and they had been atheists because the state had told them that God did not exist. Boris had been raised to think that anyone who prayed to some mythical invisible figure who controlled his destiny was a fool and, worse, an enemy of communism. Only the weak-minded, superstitious morons of the capitalist West believed such nonsense.

But like all children, Boris did not necessarily believe *everything* his parents told him. That, after all, was one of the lessons of atheism: if you could not see it, hold it, *know* it, it was suspect. And while communism was definitely real, Boris soon learned that it was not something he wished to worship, regardless of how his mother and father felt.

His time in the Special Forces had only reinforced these opinions. Communism was a vast, dumb beast, controlled not by any central intelligence but by a swarm of parasites that passed themselves off as faithful Party members while growing fat and bloated on the jugular of their country. To be a loyal Soviet citizen, Boris realized, was to be a minute part of a much larger organism; and as such, you were about as important or necessary as a single skin cell—with about as much chance of advancement.

But sometimes, even a tiny creature could have a major impact. Bacteria could invade and kill even an ox—and was it not better to be a victorious virus than a forgotten scrap of fingernail?

And so, having rejected both God and country, Boris chose the *vory v zakone*.

It was, he thought, a good choice. The army had given him a set of skills that had proven quite transferable to his new career, and the career had provided him with money, women, and an opportunity to travel. All in all, he was more than satisfied with his life. Of course, his current job had its pitfalls as well, but that was true of any given occupation, at any given time. All employees were sometimes forced to do things that they would rather not—but the appetite comes during the meal, as his father used to say; and no matter how unpleasant the task, Boris had found that once he started, enthusiasm usually followed.

"Any fish is good if it's on the hook," Boris muttered in Russian, getting a blank-eyed stare from his escort, a pretty brunette from Sarajevo. They were sitting in a booth at Abrahami, the Japanese restaurant on top of the Lincoln Hotel. Boris had developed a taste for raw fish while stationed at Yuzhno-Sakhalinsk, and it was something he often craved after a particularily grueling assignment. Abrahami was one of the few places in Vegas where you could get caviar nigiri, and that was exactly what Boris needed a big helping of right now.

The brunette—he hadn't bothered to learn her name—was studying her menu as if she had a choice. Boris glanced around for a waiter; America or Russia, there was never one around when you were hungry. They had all vanished into the kitchen or behind the ferns or wherever waiters went when they weren't bringing you food.

Ah, there was one. She was dressed in full geisha regalia, elaborate kimono and hair piled up on top of her head, shuffling forward with a tray in her hands. There was a small covered dish on the tray, which she put down on the table in front of them. She smiled and nodded, then turned and shuffled away before he could open his mouth.

His escort reached out and lifted the cover. There was a cell phone underneath.

Boris frowned. He was not unused to such things, but it did not make him happy. It meant that a superior wished to speak with him and had arranged this method out of a need for secrecy. It was a shame—he might have to forgo his Beluga sushi for work.

The phone began to play music—a ringtone, he surmised. He recognized the tune as some sort of discoteque song from the '70s: "Rasputin," he believed it was called. Apparently his bosses had a sense of humor.

He picked it up and answered. *"Da?"*

"Hey there, Boris," an unfamiliar voice said. "My name's Jim Brass. You don't know me, but we're about to get very well acquainted. I understand you've ordered the red dot special?"

"I don't understand."

"Look down."

Boris glanced downward. Nothing on the table in front of him . . . and then he saw it. A tiny circle of red light, hovering directly over his heart.

"See that?" said Brass. "I can tell by the look on your face that you do. Now, let's talk about what *I* want to see—which is your hands. On the table and empty."

Boris did as he was told.

"Good," said Brass. "Now, don't move. Our friendly staff will be by in a moment to take your order—and just *wait* until you hear our specials . . ."

Sara studied Boris Svenko, handcuffed to the interview table. Boris stared back with heavy-lidded eyes.

"Sorry about all the theatrics," said Sara. "I would have been just as happy pulling you in with a radio car, but hey, what do you expect? You go to all the trouble of making the world think you're a dangerous guy, you have to expect a somewhat overblown response."

Boris said nothing.

Sara smiled. "Not much of a talker, huh? Well, you didn't say much the last time we met, either. By the way, who wound up winning that game of darts you and your boss were having? It sort of looked like he had the upper hand when I left."

Boris smiled back. It wasn't much of a smile. "It didn't last."

"No, I guess not. Kind of an occupational hazard in your line of work, isn't it? Nobody stays on top forever. And if you stop being on top, you wind up underground."

"As does everyone."

"True. But everyone doesn't wind up in a tunnel with a throat full of counterfeit casino chips."

"I wouldn't think so."

Sara reached out and took one of his hands. She turned it over, revealing three small scabs on the palm. "Not everyone has this wound pattern, either. You should have been more careful when moving the body, Boris. Your boss might have lost the game, but those marks he gave you mean he's still going to have the last laugh."

Sara pushed a sheet of paper toward him across the surface of the table. "This is a court order authorizing me to take a sample of your blood. I could have just gone with a buccal swab to get your DNA, but a blood-to-blood comparison is more accurate."

She unzipped the small black leather case in front of her on the table, revealing a slim hypodermic, two empty vials, a short length of surgical tubing and some antiseptic swabs in sealed plastic packages.

"Besides," Sara said as she took out the hypo, "I already know you're not afraid of a little jab."

"I'm not the one who should be afraid," said Boris as Sara got up and approached his side of the table.

Sara stopped, the needle in one hand, a swab and the tubing in the other. "Is that a threat?"

"The animal most associated with Russia is the bear," said Boris casually. "I've always thought that was wrong. You know what animal I think it should be? The boar. My father used to take me hunting when I was young, and he would tell me many fascinating facts about them. Did you know there are some that can grow to weigh eight hundred pounds? They will eat almost anything. They are found all over the world, including America—not because they evolved there but because colonists from Europe brought them over, and they escaped. They are true immigrants, not only adapting to their new country but making it their own. They breed quickly, have bristles that are closer to armor than fur, and most of all, they are social creatures. The males hunt in packs, never fewer than three. Their tusks can disembowel an opponent as easily as a grizzly's claws."

He paused. "But most important of all—from a hunter's perspective—is how a large group of them will react when they sense a predator nearby. The entire herd will fan out in a long line, the ends of which will then begin to bend like a bow. Slowly but surely, they form a circle *around* the predator, fencing it into a corral of tusks. The hunter becomes the hunted. There is no other animal in nature that does this."

Boris met Sara's eyes. "Except the *vory v zakone*," he said softly. "Take your sample. Prison holds no terrors for me; I have many brothers there. It is my enemies who should live in fear."

*   *   *

Sara held up one of the chips that had been found in Grigori Dyalov's mouth—and throat, and stomach—and asked Nick, "Okay. When is a chip *not* a chip?"

Nick picked one up from the light table and studied it. "When it's a fake?"

"When it's not there. As in an RFID chip that *should* be present but isn't."

Nick nodded. "Same as the ones Ilya Khavin was trying to pass at the Panhandle. They look good—almost flawless, in fact—but there's nothing inside."

"Unlike Grigori Dyalov."

"Yeah. I think the message being sent there is pretty clear, don't you?"

"If that message is 'You screwed up and now you're dead,' then yes. But I'd expect a man like Dyalov to be sending that message, not receiving it."

Nick shrugged. "There's always a bigger shark. Whoever Dyalov answered to, he obviously didn't tolerate failure. And that's what those chips have to represent: complete, epic failure."

Sara tossed the chip she held onto the table. "The ten thousand dollars' worth of chips Khavin was trying to pass must have been just the tip of the iceberg."

"Yeah. And Dyalov was the *Titanic*."

"Okay," said Greg. He stood at the front of the AV lab with a wireless keyboard in his hands. Nick and Sara sat in two lab chairs behind a table. "I think I've—sort of—figured it out. It doesn't all quite make sense, but I've at least put together a sequence of events. I was really hoping to do an actual re-creation, but I couldn't convince Catherine that we needed to build an operating air cannon that could fire a ballistic dummy a hundred and fifty feet."

"You did your best, buddy," said Nick.

"Thanks. Anyway, we'll have to settle for a computer simulation." He tapped on the keyboard; the large flat-screen on the wall switched from the lab's logo to a wire-frame graphic of two skyscrapers, one on either end of the screen.

"What finally brought things together for me was the fire hose," said Greg. "I'll get to that in a minute. We start with the dirigible." He hit a key and an object shaped like a short, fat cigar appeared over one of the buildings. "It was inflated on the roof of this building, next to the Panhandle. Someone in a third building—probably across the street and between the first two—controlled it remotely via radio. It crossed the distance between the two buildings without being noticed, probably at a greater height."

The dirigible moved across the screen. "Once it got there, it came back down and started circling within sight of the north end of the penthouse. The sound system started to play prerecorded music, to make sure people noticed it.

"Back at the launch point, Fyodor Brish is preparing for his own launch. He gets inside the air cannon he's set up, wearing only a pair of swimming trunks and holding the activator in one hand.

"Meanwhile, the dirigible—apparently piloted by a clown, who's actually just an inflatable dummy—has gotten the attention of just about everyone at the party. To make absolutely sure everyone's eyes are on it, the person controlling it activates an ignition device, which causes it to burst into flames." The wire-frame dirigible was now outlined in glowing red and orange. "It contains a mix of hydrogen and helium, which makes it burn slower. It takes at least three full minutes to slowly spiral down and crash in the parking lot of the Panhandle."

"And somewhere in those three minutes," said Nick, "Mr. Brish blasts off."

"Right," said Greg. He hit a key. A small human figure arced from the top of one building to another. "Landing in the rooftop pool. This isn't as improbable as it sounds; it's well within the range of what human cannonballs do, and that includes water landings."

Sara nodded. "So he makes splashdown, and loses the remote on impact. We find it later, at the bottom of the pool."

"He doesn't have time to look for it," says Greg. "This whole thing is on a very tight schedule. At that very second, Alisa Golovina and her oversized, bandage-wrapped friend are pushing the intercom button for the private elevator that leads to the penthouse. Brish has to leap out of the pool and get to the doorman in time to vouch for his two accomplices."

"And they have to get upstairs before the elevator shuts down," said Nick.

"Exactly," said Greg. "Because the second the dirigible hits the pavement, someone frees the trained bear. It charges into the casino, with two of its friends in tow. Now the pandemonium really starts. The fake security guard trips the fire alarm, sending the elevators into lockdown on the ground floor. The bear ignores the kitchen and heads straight for the elevator, where our fake security guard is waiting for it. The bear traps him—sorry, her—against the elevator door and pretends to menace her."

"Security overrides the door, hoping to give the guard a place to escape to," said Sara. "Door opens, guard jumps inside. Bear charges and wrestles with guard."

"Who creates a very bloody, very effective illusion of being mauled," said Greg. "Enough gore splashes around that it obscures the camera in the elevator—fake gore that's been carefully mixed to do exactly that. The elevator door shuts."

Nick tapped a pencil on the table. "Once that happens, the guard hits the down button. Elevator goes to the basement level, bear gets out and makes a circuit of the whole floor, making sure every single person stampedes outside via the fire exit. Phony guard gets up and adds a little more gore to the camera lens just to be sure."

"Meanwhile, things are happening upstairs," said Greg. "Brish, Golovina, and the wheelchair mummy ignore all of the people outside staring down at the burning wreckage and head straight for one of the back bedrooms. Once inside, they open the window and pull a bunch of equipment from a compartment under the seat of the wheelchair: pulleys mounted on clamps and a bunch of rope. They run the rope out the window, and Ms. Golovina kicks off her shoes and goes for a little stroll down the side of the building.

"When she reaches a particular hotel window—one that's been tinkered with from the inside, letting it open—she goes in. Then she has to get from the hotel room to the part of the roof where the elevator machine room is, so they can break in—but that's only two stories, straight up. I think a professional acrobat could handle that pretty easily with nothing more than a grappling hook and twenty feet of clothesline."

"So far I'm with you," said Nick. "Is this where the fire hose comes in?"

"It is. But if an object's function defines its label, then it wasn't a fire hose at all."

Sara arched an eyebrow. "Are you saying a fire hose should more appropriately be called a water hose because of what it does? That seems like splitting hairs."

"Not fire or water, actually. It was hooked up to an air compressor."

A look of comprehension spread across Nick's face. "The indents we found in the carpet."

"Exactly. The hose was hooked up to that at one end, while the other was run back up to the roof."

"For what purpose?" asked Sara.

"Because it was the easiest way to move these." Greg held up one of the Panhandle's casino chips. "Pneumatically. They literally piped them up to the roof from the hotel room. And all those chips clinking together in transit would have produced a tiny amount of wear and tear on each chip."

"The fine powder we found in the hotel room," said Sara. "Residue from all those chips knocking together."

"That's what I figure." Greg hit a few more keys, and the simulation changed to show the top of the Panhandle, with the elevator machine room in the background. "So here's where the pulleys come in. They attach them here to the pipe, here to the edge of the roof, and here to the top of the elevator shaft."

"To lower the chips all the way down to the top of the elevator car parked in the basement?" said Nick. "Why not use the hose method again?"

"Two reasons," said Greg. "First, possible damage to the chips—twenty stories is a long way to fall, even inside a cloth tube. Second, because twenty stories is also too far to push chips up."

"Wait," said Sara. "You're saying this was all about a switch—that they stole real chips and replaced them with fakes?"

"Please," said Greg, holding up one hand. "Refrain from making any conclusions until the end of the presentation." He turned back to the screen. "Here's where it gets interesting. The number of chips we're talking about is the entire alternate set for the Panhandle, around two hundred thousand clay-composite disks, each one weighing eight point five grams. That works out to roughly thirty-eight thousand pounds' worth of casino currency—and that's where our friend the strongman comes in."

"He's a strongman, not a superman," said Nick.

"True, but let's not forget the pulleys. If they were rigged at a three-to-one ratio, that drops the weight to around twelve hundred fifty. Or to put it another way, he has to haul a little more than three hundred pounds up twenty stories, four times. Believe it or not, that's doable."

"Wow," said Sara. "Really?"

Greg shrugged. "I did some research on strong-man competitions. There's no event that correlates exactly, but there is something called the loading race, where competitors have to haul weights of up to three hundred sixty pounds over a distance of fifty feet, five times in a row. That works out to moving eighteen hundred pounds a distance of two hundred and fifty feet. Anyone who can do that could probably move twelve-fifty a distance of two hundred feet."

"Except one's vertical and the other's horizontal," Sara pointed out.

"True," Greg admitted. "But you have to admit it's in the realm of possibility."

"Let's say it is," said Nick. "They lower the fake chips down and haul the real chips up, using the strongman in the penthouse bedroom as their engine. Then what?"

"Then they transfer the real chips to the hotel room by simply reversing the air flow. The pulleys and rope are moved to the hotel room and removed later, but not the wheelchair—it gets left in the penthouse bedroom. Once she's finished transferring the chips, the ersatz security guard scales the maintenance ladder in the elevator shaft, changes her clothes, and climbs down through the hotel-room window."

"I think I know who that guard might be," said Nick. "Nadya Karnova has the right height, build, and expertise, and whoever was pretending to be mauled by that bear had to be an expert. Not a lot of female bear experts on our suspect list."

"How about the remote pilot for the dirigible drone?" asked Sara. "You run into any possibilities?"

"Maybe," said Nick. "The pyro guy who showed me around was helpful after I applied a little pressure, but I got the feeling he wasn't telling me the whole truth. And from what I saw, building and flying a craft that like that are well within his capabilities. Too bad we can't prove it."

"I guess all of it's possible," admitted Sara. "But there's only one way to know for sure."

"I was hoping you'd say that," said Greg.

25

"Okay," said Greg. He, Nick, and Sara stood on top of the simulated rooftop in the parking lot that they'd used earlier. "We've got an electric winch standing in for Mr. Muscles, a cargo net full of sandbags that weigh approximately a quarter of what the entire alternate chip set does, and a set of pulleys rigged at a three-to-one ratio. Instead of lifting the whole load up twenty stories, we're going to lift it two. Multiply our results by ten, and we should get accurate data."

"I'll work the winch," said Sara. "We'll have to run it in short, slow bursts, to simulate someone hauling on a rope by hand."

"I'm on the stopwatch," said Nick.

Greg nodded. "Then I guess the only thing left for me to do," he said, "is say . . . go!"

*   *   *

"Well," said Sara, taking a long drink from her water bottle before sinking into a seat at the conference table, "now we know."

Nick, already seated, put his hands behind his head. "Yeah. Too bad it's not the answer we were hoping for."

Greg tore open the granola bar he'd just bought from the vending machine. "Technically, the test was a success. We proved that it was possible to haul that much mass up that distance using that particular configuration of equipment."

Sara sighed. "That was never in question, Greg. We were using mechanical horsepower, so it was simple physics. Whether or not a human being could do the same thing is still up for debate—but one thing isn't."

"How long it would take them to do it," said Nick. "Using a three-to-one ratio on the pulley system triples lifting power, but it also triples the time it takes to do the job. Even if our strongman could haul that much weight up twenty stories, there's no way he could do it in the time frame we've established. It's just not possible."

Greg nodded. "Yeah, yeah, okay. Agreed. It doesn't work."

"It's not the only thing that doesn't work," said Sara. "We also tested the alternate set every way we could think of. They weren't fakes."

"True," Greg admitted. "I don't know how to explain that one, either."

Nick crossed his arms. "And what about the DNA on the bandages? If we believe that, then the guy wrapped up wasn't the strongman at all—and without him, the whole thing falls apart."

"I realize that," said Greg. "For a while I thought maybe they used their own electric winch in the hotel room, but there were no tool marks on the window frame where they would have had to attach a clamp and pulley. I also don't know exactly what happened to the strongman afterward, unless he climbed down the rope and left through the hotel room—I mean, nobody saw him leave the party at all. And if that was the case, why arrive wrapped up like a mummy? Why not just climb up the rope from the hotel window once Golovina put things in place?"

"Maybe he didn't fit," said Sara. "He's an awfully big guy."

"In that case," said Nick, "what happened to him? He didn't just evaporate."

"Maybe he did," said Greg. "After all, isn't that what spooks do?"

Greg told them about the hit he'd gotten on the government database. "So just to make things even more confusing, our circus strongman might be some kind of secret agent," said Greg. "Or maybe just a government informer. I haven't been able to find out anything else."

Sara groaned. "This is like trying to hike through quicksand. Every step we take just gets us in deeper. I say we break for lunch."

"Seconded," said Nick. "Let's regroup afterward—maybe some protein will recharge our brains as well as our stomachs."

*   *   *

Greg was about to bite into his cheeseburger when the man in the dark green suit took a seat opposite him in the diner's booth.

Greg paused. "Uh, hello?"

The man was in his fifties, powerfully built, with a shelf of white hair around a wide, flattened head. "Mr. Sanders," he said. He pulled a wallet out of his breast pocket and flipped it open. "Your government would like a word with you."

Greg put down his burger.

The man grinned. "Oh, don't look so worried. I'm not even an active agent anymore—I'm retired, live in Henderson. Name's Chet Caldwell. I'm here as a favor."

Greg swallowed. "To whom?"

"The local office. They couldn't be bothered to actually assign someone to check this out, so I volunteered. Seeing how I was in the neighborhood and all."

"I thought you were retired."

Caldwell chuckled. "I like to keep my finger on the pulse of things. You know how it is."

Greg had no idea how it was, but he didn't think asking would be a good idea. "How can I help you, Mr. Caldwell?"

"Chet, please. You can tell me about the DNA sample you ran that turned up a hit on a classified database."

"Oh, that."

"Yeah. That."

Greg hesitated. "How about a little quid pro quo?"

"What did you have in mind?"

"Anything that would help me make sense of this case. Look, I know you're not able to divulge anything classified, and I'm not asking you to. Tell you what; I'll tell you everything I know about my investigation, and you can think it over and decide if there's anything—a hint, a direction—that you can share with me. How's that?"

"Keep talking."

Greg did. He told Caldwell about the flaming dirigible, the bear attack, the involvement of the Red Star Circus and the Red Mafiya. Lastly, he told him about the bandages that had apparently swathed a Russian strongman—only the skin cells left behind had instead pointed at a mysterious individual in a government database.

Caldwell listened carefully, interrupting only to ask Greg to clarify a point or provide more information. A waitress came by halfway through, and Caldwell ordered an iced tea. Greg's burger grew cold on his plate.

When Greg was finished, Caldwell took a long sip of his iced tea and stared out the window. "Huh," he said.

"So . . . can you tell me anything? Anything at all?"

Caldwell scratched his chin. "I think I can. Hell, it's all ancient history at this point—part of why I'm the one talking to you instead of two guys with earpieces and matching sunglasses. I'm pretty much ancient history myself."

Caldwell leaned back in his seat and put one arm over the back of the booth. "How much do you know about the Cold War?"

"About as much as most people, I guess. Imminent threat of nuclear destruction, the Berlin Wall, James Bond movies."

Caldwell snorted. "James Bond. Forget all that crap. The Cold War wasn't about cars that drove underwater, beautiful women with kinky names, or wristwatches that shot heat-seeking missiles. It was mostly a game of hide-and-seek. The better you were at hiding, the more you could seek. And what you were seeking was the cold, hard currency of the Cold War: information. Which, just like any currency—cash, gold, gems—grew in value as it grew in rarity.

"Some places generated secrets the way a mint generates money. Washington, Langley, Quantico . . . and here."

"Vegas?"

"Nevada. Atomic testing, Air Force bases developing experimental aircraft, even the Hoover Dam—all of them had files with "Top Secret" stamped all over them. Secrets the Soviets wanted and did their best to get."

"Wow. I mean, that all makes sense—I just never thought of Vegas as being a hotbed of international espionage."

"That's exactly what it was." Caldwell picked up his glass and gestured with it. "A hotbed. Especially in the sixties—Vegas was already a party town, but once you added in free love, plenty of drugs, and radical politics? This place was *ripe*."

Greg frowned. "Ripe for *what*, exactly? Were the Russians planning on starting the revolution here? 'Cause no matter how many hippies rolled through town, this place has *always* been about capitalism."

Caldwell grinned. "That it has. No, that wasn't it. See, there was one element of all those cheesy spy movies that was actually accurate: the seduction. Yes, there are actually agents of foreign powers who use sex to get close to people and learn things they shouldn't. But sex is just the start—the real lever in cases like that is blackmail. Get someone loaded or naked or fervent, get them to shoot their mouth off, and get it on tape. Or maybe offer a nice big chunk of cash to someone who likes the craps table a little too much. Then, once you've got your hooks into someone—maybe a clerk at Nellis Air Force Base, maybe an engineer at the Hoover—you start to ask them for favors. Believe me, that scenario was played out more than once in this town."

"Wait a minute. Are you saying that our suspect—"

Caldwell interrupted, talking as if Greg hadn't said a thing. "Of course, we were aware of the situation. We had our own people in play, our own strategies to counter theirs. It was more like a poker game than chess, though—plenty of bluffing, lots of raising the stakes. And then, eventually, one side folded. The wall came down, and the Soviet Union fell with it."

Caldwell paused again, staring out the diner's window. Greg waited.

Caldwell turned back to Greg and smiled. "It was quite something to be in the field in those days. Suddenly, any number of spies wanted to come in from the cold. Not so much defection as desertion, as the great communist ship of state capsized. Suddenly, we had more potential assets than we knew what to do with, all of them willing to trade what they knew for whatever they could get. Needless to say, quite a few of those assets were residents of Nevada."

Greg nodded. "That makes sense."

"But like I said—ancient history. Even spies retire." He chuckled. "These days, all those ex-Soviets probably spend their days in trailer parks outside Reno, or playing the slots in Caesars."

"Or maybe Circus Circus?"

Caldwell met Greg's eyes. "Sure," he said softly. "But these guys, they're all old now. In their seventies, the ones who are still alive. Even getting out of bed in the morning is probably a circus act for most of them."

"I guess so. The idea that one of these 'assets' could be posing as a strongman is ridiculous."

"Ridiculous," Caldwell agreed. "I don't know how the DNA you found wound up where you found it, but it clearly couldn't be what it appears to be."

"Yeah," said Greg glumly. "That seems to be a pretty good description of this entire case."

Caldwell got to his feet, pulled out a five, and tossed it on the table. "Sorry I couldn't be of more help. If it's any consolation, remember one thing: in this business, almost *nothing* is what it appears to be."

After Caldwell left, Greg stared down at his cold burger. "Almost nothing," he said. "*Almost* nothing . . ."

*　　*　　*

Catherine and Ray stood beneath the famous "Welcome to Fabulous Las Vegas" sign at 5100 Las Vegas Boulevard South. A small parking lot was off to one side, with enough spots for a dozen cars and two buses. A limousine currently occupied one of the bus spots, loud music pulsing from behind its tinted windows.

"Well, she's not here," said Ray. "There's no place to hide." They'd even checked inside the sign itself, to no avail.

"Maybe we're at the wrong sign," said Catherine. "This is the original, but there are two others: the 'Welcome to Fabulous Downtown Las Vegas' is technically more accurate—it's also on Las Vegas Boulevard but at the actual city limits."

"Oh?" said Ray. "You mean we're not in Vegas right now?"

"Nope. Vegas is largely a state of mind, Professor; the only reason this sign is here is to mark the southern edge of the Strip, which is a completely artificial zone with no official boundaries. Believe it or not, most of Vegas isn't in Vegas."

"Then where is it?"

Catherine gave him a wry smile. "Paradise."

"I don't think I follow."

"That's the name of the unincorporated township the Strip is located in. Paradise."

"I wonder if our two runaways knew that."

"Does it matter?" Catherine shook her head. "Like I said—paradise or hell, Vegas is largely a state of mind."

"You mentioned a third sign?"

"Yeah, there's also one on the Boulder Highway,

near Harmon. It's not at any official boundary, either—it's just there to direct tourists off the road. About as historic as an off-ramp sign."

"Think we'll have any luck?"

"I doubt it. If she isn't at the original, I think we made a wrong turn somehow. But maybe I'm wrong."

"Let's hope so."

They walked back to their Denali and got in. The sunroof of the limo slid open and a woman wearing sunglasses and a black push-up bra popped up, a bottle of champagne in one hand. "I love Las Vegas!" she yelled.

"And she loves you," muttered Catherine as she started the car. "Just don't expect roses the next day . . ."

Catherine and Ray had no luck at either the downtown Vegas sign or the one on the Boulder Highway.

Catherine leaned back in the driver's seat of the Denali and tapped her fingers on the steering wheel in frustration. "Another dead end. At this rate, she really will be a corpse by the time we find her."

Ray, sitting beside her, studied the sketch John Bannister—or part of him, anyway—had made. "Perhaps we're being too literal," he said. "Or not literal enough. What was it that clerk told you? That John and Theria were going to 'follow the signs'?"

"That's what she said. But we've been to all three signs without any luck."

"Yes, but we didn't actually 'follow' them. That implies some sort of direction being given—the Las Vegas signs are simply a greeting."

"I'd be happy to follow any and all directions at this point. Too bad we don't have any."

Ray squinted at the drawing. "Catherine, I need your opinion. The longer I stare at this drawing, the more my evaluation of it changes. At first I thought it was somewhat crude, probably the result of loss of fine motor control—but now I see the simple elegance of Chinese brushstrokes, almost like calligraphy. I don't think the roughness of the style is an accident. See where these lines don't quite match up? I think this is supposed to be a rendering of a sign in decay, one that's falling apart. Not unlike John Bannister himself."

Catherine took the picture from him and studied it herself. "But the Vegas signs aren't decaying—the original was recently declared a national landmark. The chamber of commerce makes sure it stays in perfect condition." She paused. "Well, except for the time the company that actually *owns* the sign forgot to pay their bill and the electric company shut it off for a month."

Ray frowned. "Truly?"

"For sure. If there's one thing Vegas can't stand, it's a deadbeat."

Ray paused. "It could be that the drawing of the sign is a symbol, that it isn't supposed to represent the sign itself. What might be literally true, though, is the remark overheard by that clerk—because there's another, quite different way to follow a sign."

Catherine nodded. "When that sign is moving."

"Exactly. Perhaps we need to look for some sort of marker on a vehicle—"

Catherine leaned down and started the Denali. "No. You were on the right track with the metaphor angle, Professor, but you didn't take it far enough." She pulled into traffic with a squeal of protesting tires; Ray fumbled for his seatbelt.

"We're all on a journey," said Catherine as she accelerated. "From cradle to grave, right? In the eyes of John Bannister and Theria Kostapolis, they're almost at the end of the road—a road that leads everyone and everything to the same place."

"Oblivion?"

"For people, yes. For something more physical—like a large neon sign—it's more like obsolescence."

"Where are we headed, Catherine?"

"We're following the signs, Professor," said Catherine as she snapped across two lanes. "All the way to the graveyard."

26

GREG FOUND NICK AND SARA in the break room and told them about his visit from Caldwell. "He didn't tell me who his 'asset' was," said Greg, "but if the guy is Russian and in his seventies, that pretty much narrows the field."

"Nazar Masterkov," said Nick. "The owner of the Bruin Rescue Ranch."

"You know," said Sara, staring first at Nick and then at Greg, "I think I get it. If Nazar Masterkov is an ex-Soviet spy, then there's a clear link between him and our vic. Grigori Dyalov was ex-KGB."

"And now he's just ex," said Greg. "From what Caldwell told me, a lot of people spying for the Russians during the Cold War were pressured to do so, often through blackmail. Maybe Masterkov was one of those guys."

"If so," said Nick, "he must have had a handler. Someone he passed information to, someone who kept him in line."

"Somebody in the KGB?" said Sara.

"Sure," said Greg. "Until the Wall came down and suddenly everyone was a free agent. Dyalov used his skills and contacts to sign up with the Red Mafiya, while Masterkov traded whatever he knew to the U.S. government."

"Sounds like Dyalov got a better deal," said Sara. "Country-club memberships don't come cheap."

"I don't know," said Nick. "Masterkov obviously has contacts and experience, too—in an entirely different world. His family's been involved with the Russian circus for generations."

"And from what I understand," said Greg, "if there's one thing a Russian family knows how to do, it's hold a grudge."

"This whole elaborate scheme?" said Sara. "It was never about the money. It was about revenge."

Nick looked at Sara, then at Greg. "There was no heist."

"There was no heist," said Sara. "Just a command performance by the Red Star Circus, cleverly staged to make certain people *think* there was a heist."

"Including us," said Nick. "They must have planted some of the forensic evidence—like the chip powder and the tool marks from the pulleys."

"Don't forget the bent pipe," said Greg. "Not that it would have been hard to fake—given the right leverage, you could do it with a car jack."

"But some of it was real," said Sara. "They really did launch and burn a dirigible and fire someone a hundred and fifty feet into a pool."

"Sure," said Nick. "It had to be convincing. Dyalov must have been keeping a pretty close eye on the whole operation."

"The veterinarian, Villaruba," said Greg. "Dyalov must have insisted the ranch hire him so he had a man on the inside."

Nick nodded. "And they made sure he saw exactly what he was supposed to see. But for people in their line of work, every unbelievable stunt they had to pull off was just another day at the office. And their job on this particular day was to get Grigori Dyalov to go out on a limb."

Greg shook his head. "Yeah, so Masterkov could chop it off. How badly does someone like Dyalov have to screw up to wind up in a desert tunnel with a gullet full of poker chips?"

"I don't know," said Nick, getting up from the table. "But I know someone who does."

"She's got to be here," said Catherine as the Denali slammed to a halt. She jumped out and looked around, Ray right behind her.

They were at the entrance to a junkyard. Not just any junkyard, though; this was where old neon came to die, an elephant's graveyard of rusting and discarded signs from old Vegas. The shattered plastic remains of two-dimensional cowboys and showgirls leaned against the skeletal framework of a giant roulette wheel; burned-out bulbs lay scattered on the ground like the dead eggs of blown-glass birds.

"Follow the signs," said Ray. "This is where they ultimately end up?"

"Some of them," said Catherine. "The ones too

broken to be fixed up and resold, anyway. I'm going to go this way, you go the other."

"All right."

This has to be it, Catherine thought. *A final resting place, a place where there aren't any more words, any more messages. A place where the lights can go down. A permanent sunset.*

And then she heard it. A scraping noise, somewhere off to the left.

She broke into a trot. "Theria?" she called out. "Theria, can you hear me?"

No response. She stopped, looked around. A sign shaped like a fanned hand of cards was right in front of her, a 3-D royal flush. The last card was the ace of spades.

She got closer, peered around the edge of the sign. An old piece of plywood had been propped against it, but when she moved it out of the way, she could see a jagged hole behind it that led into the body of the sign itself.

"Over here!" she yelled. "Ray, she's over here!"

Theria Kostapolis lay on an improvised bed of flattened cardboard boxes, her head pillowed by a folded piece of clothing. Her eyes were closed. Catherine couldn't tell if she was breathing or not.

Ray's voice called out, "Catherine? Where are you?"

"I'm in here, Ray! The card sign!"

He appeared a second later and ducked inside. Catherine moved aside to let him work. "Is she alive?"

"Barely. I've got a pulse, but it's weak. She's badly dehydrated and probably suffering from heatstroke."

Catherine was already on the walkie, giving directions to the dispatcher. "Paramedics will be here in a few minutes," she said.

"You're going to be all right, Theria," Ray said. "Your nightmare is over."

If Theria Kostapolis could hear him, she gave no response.

The last time Nick had been at the Bruin Rescue Ranch, he'd only gotten as far as the front porch of the house Nazar Masterkov lived in. This time, he came bearing an invitation. Nadya Karnova opened the door when he rang the doorbell. She wore jeans and a plaid shirt tied in a knot in front. "Hello, Mr. Stokes," she said. The twang of her Texas accent held a thin layer of frost. "I understand you want to speak to Mr. Masterkov."

"I phoned ahead," said Nick. "He said it was—"

"Come with me." She turned and headed back into the house without waiting to see if he was following.

Nick wasn't sure what to expect of the interior—communist flags and busts of Lenin? kitschy Americana?—but what he saw was many, many mementos of the circus. Signed and framed photos covered the walls, along with brightly colored posters in different languages: English, French, Cyrillic.

She led him down a long hall lined with pictures of bears riding motorcycles, bears on seesaws, bears wearing dresses and flowered hats. It ended at a sprawling living room, Navajo rugs on a hardwood floor, low-slung, comfortable couches and chairs upholstered in a pattern of cacti and blazing suns. Nazar Masterkov was in one of them, reading a book, dressed casually in lightweight summer clothes and sandals. He looked up and smiled as Nick entered.

"Ah, Mr. Stokes. Please, have a seat." He motioned with his book before putting it down on the coffee table in front of him.

Nick picked a couch and sat. Nadya Karnova remained on her feet, unsmiling, until a nod from Masterkov told her she could go. She didn't say good-bye.

"Thanks for agreeing to talk to me," said Nick.

Masterkov leaned back in his chair. "And why wouldn't I?" His tone was light, but there was the barest hint of a challenge in it.

"Well, sir, that's a good question. The best answer I can give you is that you might not want to."

"Ah. Well, Mr. Stokes, in my experience it's best to answer questions, even uncomfortable ones. Silence can lead to others making mistaken assumptions."

"Even if you don't answer honestly?"

"Honesty is not always an option. Nonetheless, that doesn't mean information can't still be exchanged."

"Just that it can't necessarily be trusted."

"Exactly. But that's the nature of your job, is it not? To verify what *can* be trusted?"

"Pretty much," Nick admitted. "And I think I'm good at what I do. But every now and then, I run into someone who's almost as good at deception as I am at uncovering it."

"Really? I have a hard time imagining such a creature. If I could, what would I be looking at?"

"Well, they'd have a great deal of experience in concealing their true identity and motives. Like me, they'd be very good at collecting information, though they'd also be adept at falsifying data. They'd have to have a certain amount of show business in their blood, because they'd have to play their role convincingly."

"All performers have a bit of liar and a bit of thief in them, it's true," Masterkov said with a chuckle.

"Overall, I'd say they'd have to be highly intelligent, extremely motivated, and very, very patient." Nick paused. "Not to mention more than a little ruthless."

Masterkov's smile was gentle, but his eyes were cold. "What some people call ruthlessness others simply call expediency."

"Not in this particular case. A man was systematically manipulated, with the end result being his death. I don't call that expediency; I call it an execution."

Masterkov nodded. "Perhaps so. But systematic manipulation resulting in death—that's an accurate description of many processes, wouldn't you say? War. Slavery. Politics."

"Most politicians don't wind up dead at the hands of their constituents."

"You miss my meaning. It's not the ones in control who die; it's the ones being manipulated. The soldiers, the slaves, the citizens. And then there are the ones who are all three."

"You're talking about spies."

"I'm talking about people who had no choice. People who were blackmailed with the welfare of their families, threatened with death or worse, hammered with an ideology that said to steal secrets for the good of their country was their sacred duty."

Nick shook his head. "I can't imagine what that would have been like."

"But you must, Mr. Stokes. Imagination is the only tool available to us at this moment, and so we must use it as best we can." He nodded. "Allow me to assist. As an old performer, I'm something of a storyteller—or so my associates tell me—and I rarely get the chance to indulge anymore. Forgive me if I wander a bit afield in the narrative; I am, after all, an entertainer and not a scientist. Do you mind?"

"Go ahead, Mr. Masterkov. I'm interested in hearing what you have to say."

Masterkov leaned back and stared into space for a moment before starting. His eyes grew distant, and then he began to speak.

"Let us imagine a young man who idolizes the circus. He wants nothing more than to stand in the center of one of those rings, to hear the roar of the crowd and know that all eyes are upon him. Perhaps he is an acrobat, perhaps a clown; perhaps he works with animals. The details are not important. He studies, he trains, he works hard and diligently to master his craft—and he succeeds.

"One day, a man comes to see him. A man who smiles, and compliments him on his craft, and then tells the young performer that he has an opportunity to travel to a far land. And in this land, he will stage his greatest act of all—in fact, his whole life will become a performance."

Masterkov fell silent. When he continued, his voice was soft. "And if the young performer refuses, then everyone he knows and loves will suffer. They will be sent to gulags, or tortured, or put to death. The performer comes from a large family—something he always thought of as a blessing. But now that blessing is turned against him. The number of people he loves—who love him—means simply that the state has a surplus of hostages. They can afford to destroy one or two, just to convince him that they are serious. There are always more."

Nick opened his mouth to speak, then closed it. He wasn't sure what he should say.

"But family, in the end, is always a strength. The young performer came from a long line of performers, you see, men and women who had been taught their skills by their parents and grandparents. The circus is more than a family, more than a way of life; it is, in some ways, like belonging to another species entirely. And a species can outlast many things—even political ideology.

"It took many decades, but things changed. The United Soviet Socialist Republic fell. The performer—not so young anymore—made a deal with certain people. An agreement was reached, and his family was able to join him in the new land, hostages no more." Masterkov shrugged. "Perhaps that is where the story ends."

"I don't think so, Mr. Masterkov. In fact, from my point of view, that's where the story starts." Nick leaned forward. "It goes something like this. A retired spy, living in Vegas, runs into his old KGB handler. There's no love lost between the two—in fact, I think it's pretty fair to say the ex-spy hates the ex-KGB man with a passion. But the handler—let's call him Mr. D—is now a big wheel with the Red Mafiya. He's just as dangerous and untouchable as he ever was. But the situation *has* changed, because the ex-spy is no longer alone.

"He's got his family with him now, a family with a whole host of very specialized talents. So he decides to put on one more show—a real barn burner—for the benefit of Mr. D.

"It takes a lot of preparation. It has to convince someone whose entire life has been based around deception, and do so in a way that will persuade him to stick his own neck out. The reward has to be as substantial as the risk. But if there's any town in the world where those two things go together, it's Vegas."

Masterkov raised his eyebrows. "And what, do you think, that reward would have been?"

"A casino. The ability to manipulate the value, input, and output of every single chip that passed through its doors. A prize like that would be incalculable, and not just for the sheer monetary worth; a criminal enterprise like the Red Mafiya could use it to launder hundreds of millions in illegal income. There's no way Mr. D could pass up something like that—not when someone else was willing to take all the risks. Well, almost all of them; the chips themselves would have to be manufactured, and they aren't cheap. Throw in overhead, profit sharing for all the people involved, plus the price tag for whatever advanced tech was supposed to let him control the RFID chips, and I'm thinking our ex-spy talked Mr. D into one heck of a layout of cash. Enough that when it didn't pay off, Mr. D paid the ultimate price."

"I think I like your story. How about we give a name to that number, just for fun? I'm thinking somewhere in the neighborhood of, oh . . . say ten million dollars."

It was Nick's turn to raise his eyebrows. "Ten million?"

"Why not? It's just a story, after all."

Nick grinned and shook his head. "Fair enough. It's a pretty good one, too—but there are still a few plot points that bother me."

Masterkov spread his hands to either side. "Well, we seem to be doing a fine job of collaborating so far. Tell me your concerns—perhaps I can suggest a few details."

"From a forensics point of view, all of the facts lined up—all except for one. DNA found in some bandages should have belonged to the strongman who supposedly hauled the chips up the elevator shaft—but it wasn't a match. In fact, it belonged to the ex-spy."

Masterkov gave Nick a slow smile. "Yes, that is curious. I can think of two reasons for it, one practical, one personal. First, it provides a rather elegant alibi, does it not? This retired intelligence operative, I take it he is somewhat advanced in years? Not so advanced that he couldn't wrap something around his body to make it appear larger—a fire hose, perhaps—then add a layer of bandages over that . . . but certainly too frail to be performing superhuman feats of strength."

"I guess not."

"And second—it sends a message, does it not? A way, perhaps, of claiming responsibility after the fact."

"Or of reclaiming something else?" said Nick.

Masterkov nodded. "Yes. Something he thought he lost a long time ago, something he can't really give a name to anymore. Pride? Honor? Courage? A little of all of those things, I suspect. After lying and hiding for all those years, I think our ex-spy wanted to finally stand up and receive his due. A small bit of truth in a mirage of deception."

"Sounds to me like he earned it," said Nick. He got to his feet. "Well, I don't think our ex-spy has anything to worry about. The only crime he could even be prosecuted for is the arson, and all of the evidence in that part of the case is speculative. The Russian mob isn't going to complain about being defrauded—though they might decide they want their money back."

Masterkov chuckled. "Only if they know who to ask for it. I have the feeling that our Mr. D might have been keeping this enterprise entirely to himself. That way, all of the profit would have been his."

"And all of the blame when it didn't work out." Nick paused. "Nice and neat, every puzzle piece in place. The thing is, a lot of those pieces were only ever seen by a very limited number of eyes—eyes belonging to CSIs or people who work in the lab. If the target was Mr. D, why all the attention to forensic detail? The only person who actually had to believe it was a real heist was the one financing it."

Masterkov smiled. "I take it you know something of the history of Nevada and the intelligence community? That it was rife with recruiters and turncoats in the first years of the Cold War?"

"I've heard that, yes."

"Well, what do you think happened to them all? Some have moved away or died, to be sure . . . but not all. If our ex-spy is still alive and well, then others certainly are, too. Some of them would have worked their way into positions of influence, even though they no longer report to their masters. A former KGB operative would be able to exert a considerable deal of pressure on these people; in fact, for them, the Cold War might as well have never ended."

Nick frowned. "You're telling me Mr. D still had spies feeding him information? Spies inside the lab or the police?"

Masterkov shrugged. "I'm not telling you anything, Mr. Stokes. I'm merely an old man, spinning a story to pass the time. But all stories are true, in one way or another, and the truth to this story is this: people are always watching. No matter who or where you are, no matter what you do, someone is taking notice. And if that someone has secrets, too, they may give away yours in order to protect their own."

Nick shook his head. "That's a very paranoid way to live, Mr. Masterkov."

Masterkov sighed. "Yes, it is . . . but I have lived that way for a very long time. And there is one question that you have failed to consider, Mr. Stokes."

"What's that?"

"In order for this hypothetical plan to succeed, the former spy would have to have produced a very convincing counterfeit casino chip ahead of time, in order to sell the idea—an imitation of a chip not in circulation yet, one kept under lock and key. How do you think he did that?"

Nick gave him a slow nod and a smile. "I guess maybe Mr. D wasn't the only guy in town with a few contacts left. *Spaseba,* Mr. Masterkov."

"You're very welcome, Mr. Stokes."

"She'll live," Ray said.

Catherine looked down at the hospital bed in the ICU unit. Theria Kostapolis's eyes were closed, but her chest rose and fell in a slow, steady rhythm.

"We got to her in time," said Ray. "She's in rough shape, but she'll recover. Exposure to BZ isn't lethal, and neither is Cotard's syndrome. I can't speak to her mental condition, but people with Cotard's have recovered."

"I hope so. She's suffered so much, Ray. She's literally been to hell and back."

"I suppose she has. I wish I had better news for her when she wakes up." John Bannister had slipped into a coma a little more than an hour after Theria was rescued. "Corticobasal degeneration *is* fatal; life expectancy postdiagnosis is six to eight years. Exposure to the BZ might have worsened his condition—he may never recover from the coma."

"There's no treatment?"

"Not for the disease itself, no. The best we can do is treat some of the symptoms and try to make him comfortable. It's not a pleasant way to go—gradually increasing dementia, loss of muscular control and even the ability to speak."

"So maybe not waking up isn't so bad in his case." Catherine shook her head. "Poor guy deserves some peace, though. He fought pretty hard to give Theria her chance at it. His mind might have been somewhere else, but his heart was in the right place."

" 'The mind is its own place, and in itself can make Heaven of Hell, and a Hell of Heaven.' "

Catherine glanced at him and smiled. "A Milton quote? How very Grissom of you, Professor."

Ray smiled back. "I'll take that as a compliment."

"You should."

Catherine looked back at Theria, and her smile faded. "I've got a quote for you myself—I think John Bannister would appreciate it. Something Winston Churchill said."

"What's that?"

"If you find yourself going through hell? *Keep going.*"

ABOUT THE AUTHOR

DONN CORTEZ is the pseudonym for Don DeBrandt, who has authored several novels. He lives in Vancouver, Canada.